KENDRICK

TOREY HOPE: THE LATER YEARS

A.D. ELLIS

KENDRICK

TOREY HOPE:
THE LATER YEARS

A.D. ELLIS
WWW.FACEBOOK.COM/ADELLISAUTHOR

COVER UPDATED 2019
BY A.D. ELLIS

QUOTES OF INSPIRATION

"Reputation is what folks think you are. Personality is what
you seem to be. Character is what you really are."
~ *Alfred Armand Montapert*

"When everything seems like an uphill struggle, just think of
the view from the top."
~*Author Unknown*

"Maybe you have to know the darkness before you can
appreciate the light."
~*Madeleine L'Engle*

To those who have struggled or who are still struggling. May you find peace.

INTRODUCTION

Kendrick's story was always planned for the last book. Why? I'm not sure, but I think I sort of felt like it was a little like *save the best for last*. Not because I don't love my other books, I do. But Kendrick has been special to me from the very beginning. All of my characters have a bit of my personality, but Kendrick was the most fun to write. He says things I *think* and *want to say*.

I want to address what Kendrick goes through (without giving too much away). The events of his past and the events that take place in this story are ones *many* people have had experience with. Kendrick deals with things in his own ways. That's not to say he's right or wrong, but he and his family make decisions based on what they feel are best for them.

The negative/painful things that happen to Kendrick as this book progresses are based on very real-life experiences of a handful of readers, one in particular, who allowed me to ask them questions so I could make the situations as real as possible.

I am very well aware that many people who suffer through what Kendrick does, do not have the same kind of support available to them. Many who are in the same situation as Kendrick don't make it through as quickly, or as easily, or at all. Kendrick's situation and the way he travels through the painful journey are his and his alone. Many are in much darker and more desperate places in their journey, and Kendrick's story is in no way meant to make light of the struggles those people face.

I want to acknowledge that there is no certain person who is more likely to face the struggles Kendrick faces. Every person could be faced with these trials, tribulations, and painful moments. Rich or poor, male or female, great family or no family at all...no one is immune from the struggles life brings.

A Note from the Author

For those who like a little narrative along with a family tree. Here are the families of Torey Hope. Meet the Morgans, the Jordans, the Deckers, and the Martins. If the family tree image is hard for you to see on your device, you can click here to find it on my website.

John and Cindy Morgan have twin boys Nate and Nicky Morgan.

Nicky Morgan married Carly Malone and had children Zachary Malone Morgan and Alyson Elizabeth Morgan.

Nate Morgan married Libby Decker and had children Abigail Emerson Morgan and twins Decker Nathaniel and Sawyer Nicholas Morgan.

Libby Decker is sister to **Audrey Decker**, both are daughters of **Captain Robert Decker** and the late **Lois Decker**. Robert later married **Janie**.

Audrey Decker married **Jeremiah Jordan**. Jeremiah had a son, **Beckett**, from a previous marriage. Jeremiah and Audrey had **Megan Elise Jordan** and **Kendrick Robert Jordan**. Beckett got married in the first book of this series to a girl named Kenja.

Jeremiah is the son of **Jack and Judy Jordan**.

Captain Robert Decker had an estranged brother,

Richard, who was married to Corrine, and they had a daughter named **Josie**. Josie married Jeremiah Jordan's best friend, **Kyle Martin,** and they had children **Zoey Belle Martin** and **Asher Jeremiah Jordan**.

REGARDING THE CENTER+

This is a local community center in Torey Hope. In the first Torey Hope series, Nicky Morgan (Zach and Aly's dad) attended what was then known as The Center. This place runs educational programs, especially for students struggling in public schools, along with various programs revolving around the arts, sports, and fitness. When Zach, Decker, Sawyer, and Kendrick returned to Torey Hope from college, they took over the business, which many members of the family are involved with in some way and renamed it The Center+.

Decker is the manager, his girlfriend, Katie, is the assistant manager. Sawyer is in charge of the art programs, including painting, pottery, dance, etc. He also works closely with his boyfriend, Luke, in the martial arts programs. Kendrick is in charge of the sports programs. Zach is the advertising executive. Many of the parents are also involved with programs at The Center+.

1

"So, we're heading to my place for a very special night of fun." The blonde little sprite trailed her finger down his arm. "I thought you might like to join us."

Us? Please let it be another girl just as hot as this one. The tiny thing standing in front of him was nothing like the curvy, voluptuous women he usually went for, but she definitely held his interest. Damn, those brown eyes were like pools of chocolate. *If her friend is as cute as this one, I'll be in heaven all night long.* But when she gestured toward the door where an attractive man waited with hungry eyes, Kendrick Jordan had to shake his head in an attempt to understand the invitation.

He blinked once, twice, in hopes of focusing his eyes. He knew he shouldn't have ordered that last drink; he'd gone from really buzzed to pretty much drunk in the last fifteen minutes. The little imp standing beside him continued to trace her finger up and down his arm and looked up at him with a challenging, sexy smile.

She didn't have the look of trashy bar-fly, but she also didn't come across as a fake-ass bimbo. Truly, she spoke like a girl just looking to have a good time. But, of course, that could be his vodka-ized brain talking.

"Come on, sexy. You look like you've had enough. Tony and I were watching you, we think you'd be a great addition to our plans for tonight. No rules, no pressure, no strings, just a good time had by all. Whatdya say?" She batted her lashes and bit her lip while waiting on him to answer.

Well, hell. Not long ago he'd mentioned to his cousins that he may be bi-curious or some shit like that. Guess he was about to find out if he was still interested in sex with a man.

Throwing some money on the bar, he stood, perhaps a bit too quickly because he had to close his eyes to steady himself before walking toward the door. The cell phone he held in his hand buzzed as he walked. Glancing down at it, he saw his cousin, Decker, was calling. Again. He let it go to voicemail. So far, he had twenty-seven texts from various family members, and thirteen voicemails.

He knew he eventually had to go back home, had to face what had haunted him for several years and finally sent him into a downward spiral. He also knew he had the most supportive family in Torey Hope and surrounding areas, there was no way they'd expect him to go through any of this by himself. But, he had a sick feeling that things were going to get much worse before they got better, and the thought of that scared the ever-loving shit out of him.

So, for the time being, he'd see where the tiny little blonde wanted to take him. He'd keep blocking out the bad, laughing it off, fucking it away, and pretending that his heart wasn't broken and hidden behind a complete and total façade. Whatever she had planned *had* to be better than the exhaustion, the nightmares, the blanket of darkness he felt had started to suffocate him recently.

When they reached the door, Tony gave a subtle nod of his head before reaching out a hand. "Tony."

Kendrick took his hand, "Kendrick."

"Okay, so my two sexy men for the evening have met. I'm Jay. Let's go have some fun, boys."

He'd never left a bar with both a man and a woman. *What the hell are you doing, man?*

I have absofuckinglutely no clue.

But if it keeps my mind off other things for the night, it's got to be worth it.

Right?

2
_____

His body came awake slowly, but it was quicker than his brain. He immediately noticed the heat surrounding him, but that was secondary to the pounding in his head. Without opening his eyes, knowing the light would make his head explode, he used his other senses to evaluate the situation.

He was naked, that much was obvious. He was plastered to a tiny body on his front side, and a freaking furnace on his backside. Tony if he had to guess.

Based on several years of experiencing *the morning after*, he knew from the way his body felt he'd had sex. Clenching his ass he was relieved to find it wasn't sore, so at least he knew he hadn't gotten fucked by a guy while he was too drunk to experience it the right way.

Question was, who had he fucked? Jay? Tony? Both?

Holy hell, Jordan. What the fuck have you gotten yourself into?

Slowly, not wanting to wake the other two bodies, he cracked an eye. The girl, Jay, had her back to him, but she was pressed up against him. The hair he'd thought was mostly blonde in the dark bar was actually a mixture of platinum blonde and jet black.

His hand rested on her chest lightly cupping a small but firm breast. Without thinking, he flicked the tiny pebbled nipple. She shifted, moaning as she awakened. Her backside rubbed against him, causing his dick to wake up and say good morning.

Behind him, the furnace he assumed was Tony, rocked his own morning glory against Kendrick's ass. As much as he'd been telling the truth about wondering what it would be like to be with a guy, in all of his musings it had always been him doing the topping, not the other way around. Shifting his body slightly so his ass was safe from Tony's insistent rocking, Kendrick took note of his hangover.

He'd always had a fairly high tolerance for alcohol, but he knew he'd pushed it too far last night. He didn't regret what they'd done, at least he didn't remember doing anything he should regret, but the fact that he didn't remember much of what went on proved to him that he'd been too far gone.

He hated it. Hated that he was so fucked up inside about

something that happened so long ago. Wasn't it supposed to get easier? But instead, it was eating him alive year after year. His family was right, he probably should talk to someone about it, but putting words to his pain was frightening and not something he was chomping at the bit to do.

Wondering if he should try to get out of bed to attempt the long walk of shame back to the bar to get his car, he glanced at the clock on the bedside table. Next to it were three condom wrappers. Way to play it safe. Three is an odd number between two men and a woman. Wonder how that all worked out. Damn it all to hell for being so drunk you don't know how your first male, male, female experience went.

What the hell? The clock read four o'clock. It was much too bright outside to be 4:00 a.m., but there was no way in hell they'd slept until 4:00 p.m. Surely her clock was just set wrong.

Easing up on his arm, he slowly groped the table for a phone, any phone. 4:01 fucking p.m. No fucking way. He sighed heavily and laid himself back down, taking a bit of comfort in the heated bodies wrapped around him.

Minutes, maybe hours later, he woke to the bed dipping as Jay got up. He watched her tiny frame, tight ass, perky little breasts as she threw on a t-shirt and headed to the bathroom. When the water began to run, he closed his eyes again.

"She's a great girl." Tony's sleepy voice rumbled from behind him.

"Yeah? Seems nice enough." Kendrick wasn't sure if there was a warning in Tony's words or not.

"Don't get too attached." Tony shifted.

"Don't want to share her, huh? Maybe should have thought of that before letting her invite me into your bed." Kendrick's words held no heat, just an observation. He got out of bed.

"Man, *I'm* the one who wanted you in her bed. I'm bi. Sleeping with Jay is a perfect setup. She gets the no-strings-attached fun she's looking for, and I get the best of both worlds. It's a win-win."

When Kendrick whipped his head to the side to squint at Tony, the other man laughed.

"So, did we, uh..." Kendrick's question trailed off.

"Have sex? Yeah, we did. It was awesome by the way." Tony waggled his eyebrows.

Kendrick studied him. He was a very attractive man. Would Kendrick ever be able to be in the type of relationship which required him to divide his time between both a man and a woman? His hungover brain had no desire to think about it at that moment.

"So, who did what? I mean, um...," Kendrick felt like an idiot. He'd never been one to mince words.

"You fucked her. Then I fucked her while you did me. Hotter than hell, man." Tony pulled a pair of boxers up. "That's what's so great about Jay. She wants nothing to do with sweet whispers, or dates, or hearts and roses. As long as we keep it light and fun, she's up for anything. And getting another guy in our bed is always easier when she's doing the inviting."

"So, you guys are 'together'?" Kendrick questioned.

"Oh, hell no. She's not one to settle down. We are friends with fabulous benefits, but if she weren't willing to bring other guys in, I wouldn't be sticking around. I definitely want it both ways."

"I feel sort of bad that I don't remember anything from last night." Kendrick chuckled. "My first time with a guy, and I can't recall a single moment. I'm glad it was good for you." He was trying to keep it light, but it did bother him he'd been so out of it. If one of his cousins or siblings had behaved in the unsafe way he had last night, he'd be stringing them up by their toes for a week at a time in punishment.

"No worries, man. I'm pretty sure Jay has plans on round two taking place tonight. Maybe we'll order in and watch a movie, avoid the overabundance so everyone can be clear-headed." Tony winked and walked toward Kendrick.

Stopping in front of him, Tony flattened a palm against Kendrick's groin. Leaning in, he lightly kissed Kendrick's mouth. He stepped back, smirking at him.

"You're so very not gay, but I like that you're up for experimenting. We'll have fun tonight, and for however long she wants this to last. Then we'll move on. Just don't fall for her, man, because it's not ever going to happen. I've known her for over a year. She never gets attached. Doesn't talk about her past, doesn't talk about why she never falls, doesn't really let anyone in at all. She's friendly and fun, spends time with friends from work and some of the mutual friends we have, but it's like she's always on the outside of everything, never allowing herself to be on the inside of life."

Tony's words saddened Kendrick, but also made him aware he'd fallen right into the perfect situation. He could experiment as much as he wanted, have fun, forget the bad shit, and keep on keeping on. Before he could pull himself from his musings, he realized Tony had dropped to his knees and taken him in his mouth.

"Fuck, man. A little warning would be nice." Kendrick's arms reached for something to grasp, hoping to steady himself. When he found nothing, he settled for resting his hands on Tony's head.

"I'm going to suck you off now. Warning enough?" Tony smiled before returning to his mission.

In the distance, Kendrick recognized the sound of water shutting off and a door opening. Jay walked from the bathroom, appearing dressed for an evening in, like Tony had predicted.

"Damn boys, that's freaking hot." Walking to Kendrick's side, she pulled his head down for a searing kiss. "Ever had your cock sucked by another guy?"

Knowing he was close to exploding, the kiss making the ending even more assured. Kendrick grunted a no before focusing completely on kissing Jay and pumping into Tony's mouth.

Several seconds later as he came down from the most extreme high he'd ever known, Kendrick heard the voices of various family members echoing in his head, asking him what the *hell* he was doing.

Pushing them to the back of his mind, he answered quickly, *just having fun. I'll deal with the real shit later.*

3

"That's probably the pizza, I'll get it." Tony walked to the door.

"I've got water, wine, soda, beer, juice, and milk. What would you like?" Jay checked the fridge and offered Kendrick a beverage.

"Since I drank enough last night to drown a fish and incapacitate my liver, I better stick with milk." Kendrick grabbed a large glass from the cabinet, feeling comfortable enough with Jay and Tony to do so. They'd spent the late afternoon watching a movie after individual showers and toast and tea for 'breakfast'. He'd felt a little funny eating his toast and tea, but Jay had insisted it would help them all recover from their hangovers. And damn if she wasn't right. She'd gotten a funny look on her face when he'd told her she reminded him of his Aunt Libby always pushing her tea, but it had passed quickly enough, so he'd let it go.

Now he was faced with another strange look from her. She wrinkled her nose, "You want a glass of milk that size? You really like milk, huh?"

Smiling at her, Kendrick winked, "What can I say? I'm a growing boy. I need my vitamin D and calcium." He poured the glass full, chugged half of it, and filled it again.

"Milk, it sure does do a body good." Tony growled in his ear when he walked into the kitchen with the pizza.

Kendrick laughed. He felt very little toward the man. He wasn't put off or offended by the sexual come-ons, but he also didn't feel overly attracted to him. Tony was a good-looking guy, and his cock-sucking skills deserved a trophy, but Kendrick didn't see anything between them going further than a few good times.

He turned to look at Jay. She was beautiful. But not really his type at all. He didn't discriminate, but he usually found himself drawn to taller, curvy, big-breasted women. More to hold onto, and he didn't feel like he'd break them in two.

Jay was short, very short. He dwarfed her with his 6'2" frame; he guessed her to be about 5'1" and he was being generous with that extra inch. And she was curvy, but it was like mini curves. He'd never really looked at a girl unless she was well-endowed, but Jay's chest enticed him. He found himself wanting to touch, and lick, and make her whimper, to hell with his usual handful or more rule.

The conversation was easy as they ate their pizza. Jay had been born in California, moved to Indiana when she was eight, and moved to Illinois when she was sixteen. She'd recently moved to Torey Hope from a couple towns over. At twenty-one, she was content to be waiting tables at the Torey Hope Café. She had no plans of going to college, although she had thought about looking into becoming a hairstylist. However, she'd have to get a second job to save up for that.

Tony had lived in Chicago his entire life, but he moved to help his uncle. He had a degree in interior design but didn't use it much. At age twenty-eight, he wasn't thrilled to be living with his aunt and uncle, but he knew his uncle needed help refinishing the house now that his aunt's arthritis had gotten so bad. He didn't plan on staying long, just until he got the house completed for his aunt and uncle. He was hoping a month at the most.

Kendrick realized quickly that he had the advantage in the 'where I came from' stories. Growing up with the perfect family, working at The Center+, going off to college with his best friends/cousins, and coming back home to settle down while taking his rightful place at The Center+ as the athletic director, Kendrick had a pretty blessed life.

Sure, he had some bad shit that had never let him go, but he had a great family who meant the world to him. He didn't pry, but he got the feeling Tony's parents weren't in his life, and his uncle seemed to only want him around to finish the work on his house. Jay didn't mention any family. Not a single word.

He wanted to ask, especially, about Jay's family. But he knew the score in this game, no strings. The less he knew about her the better. But, he couldn't help but wonder about what made her huge chocolate eyes look sad while she tried to pretend she was just out to have fun.

"WHATDYA SAY, boys? Ready to take this little party to the bedroom?" Jay stood and stretched. Walking toward her bedroom, she threw a look over her shoulder. "Am I going to have to start without you?"

Tony and Kendrick looked at each other. Tony wagged his brows at Kendrick with a wolfish grin. Kendrick had to laugh and just shook his head. Who was he to turn down a night of good ol' fashioned sex? *Although, the fact that you're likely going to take Tony up the ass again sort of negates the 'ol' fashioned' part. Oh well, still not planning on turning it down.*

The men followed Jay to her room.

"So, I'm feeling a little bossy tonight. I want you guys to do some things for me, then you can have me. Take your clothes off." She gestured at the two men, indicating they should strip.

When his brain registered the implication, his dick immediately took notice. Shrugging his shoulders, Kendrick stripped down. He had a feeling Jay was getting ready to orchestrate a scene straight from one of the gay porn videos he knew his cousin, Sawyer, watched with his boyfriend, Luke. Tossing his pants on the floor, he noticed a missed call on his phone. Pushing the real-world troubles to the back of his mind, he turned toward Jay.

Stark naked, visibly aroused, Kendrick held his arms out from his sides.

"Like what you see, Pixie?" He chuckled as she bit her lip, it felt good to know she was affected by his body.

"Don't call me Pixie. And, yes, I like what I see very much. What about you, Tony? Do you like what you see?" Jay reclined on the bed, looking very much like she was preparing for her own personal show.

"I definitely like what I see." Tony's arms wrapped around Kendrick's waist, his arousal pressing firmly against Kendrick's ass.

Accepting the challenge Jay and Tony were wordlessly issuing, Kendrick held her gaze. "You look like a pixie. Tiny, cute, blonde, even have the right haircut. It fits." He felt his face heat, his lips drawing into a smirk, when she blushed and rolled her eyes.

"Whatever." Jay sat up, removing her sweater and pants. "Okay, boys, you are tonight's preshow entertainment. Just don't finish each other off, I want in on that part. Kendrick, kiss Tony."

Feeling like he was playing a game of high stakes poker, Kendrick met her fiery gaze before grabbing the back of Tony's neck and pulling the man into a hard kiss. He had to admit, kissing a man was hot. Mainly because it was familiar, but at the same time it was so very different. *Pretty sure I'd rather have my mouth on Jay right now.* But, this was her show, so he took her orders.

"Tony, show him why you were voted Blowjob Queen of the Windy City three years in a row." Jay's eyes sparkled, her smile lighting up her whole face.

Kendrick found himself mesmerized by that face. Until the heat of Tony's mouth engulfed him and he could think of nothing more.

"Okay, enough of just you two getting to play. I want to join the fun." Stripping the rest of her clothes, Jay knelt in the middle of the bed. Crooking a finger, she motioned for both men to join her.

After several moments of heated kissing, she broke from them. Panting slightly, she whispered loudly to Kendrick, knowing Tony could hear her.

"I'm pretty sure Tony is a whole lot more gay than he is bi, but I also know he'll sacrifice and have sex with me if it means he gets you up his ass."

Kendrick laughed when Tony pretended to huff in protest.

"Yeah, it's a major sacrifice to fuck your perfect little body, but I'll take one for the team." Tony winked at her.

Kendrick felt a pang. He had no ill-fated notions the three of them would last more than a few more nights, but he found himself feeling jealous of Tony. *He* wanted to be the one burying himself in Jay's perfect little body. So why in the hell was he getting ready to fuck a guy he barely knew? All because some damn little waif of a woman found it sexy? Yeah, he was more fucked up than he realized.

"Wrap it before you tap it, boys." Jay tossed condoms at their chests.

"Hey, that's my signature line, Pixie."

"Stop calling me that!"

Tony stopped the argument before it had time to go any further when he swooped in to kiss Jay, toppling her to her back on the bed.

Gritting his teeth hard enough he was sure his jaw would pop, Kendrick's heart pounded as he watched Tony nudged Jay's legs apart with his knee. The whimper that sounded from her perfect pink mouth sent heat straight to his cock. He knew the moment Tony had entered her completely.

"Kendrick, get behind him. I want to feel you fuck him." Jay's voice was breathless.

Dribbling a generous amount of lube on himself, Kendrick took his place behind Tony. Knowing this was the second time he'd been inside this man was somewhat comforting, but also disconcerting seeing as how he didn't remember the first time. *Hell, I said I was curious about being with a man. Time to put up or shut up.*

With his eyes focused on Jay, Kendrick pressed forward, letting Tony's body engulf him. The heat and squeeze was intense. Thinking only of Jay, Kendrick rocked himself into Tony's ass, knowing it would press the other man deeper into Jay's body.

"Shit, shit, shit. I'm not going to make it. Damn..." Tony stilled, his body clenching around Kendrick.

"Tap out, Tony. Let Kendrick take over." Jay giggled.

Tony stood to dispose of the condom. "I'm going to shower while you two finish up. Damn, Kendrick, you take the prize for getting me off quicker than ever before."

Barely hearing the man's words, Kendrick immediately discarded the condom and reached for another.

Bringing himself face-to-face with Jay, he rocked his hard length against her core.

"Hi."

"Hi." She blushed, rolling her hips in an attempt to take him in.

"I think your show is over. It's the Kendrick show now, Pixie." Capturing her mouth in a searing hot kiss, he let her body adjust to his full length.

"Oh, God." She whimpered.

"No, just me." He surged forward. "Just me, no one else." For some reason, he felt the need to possess her, make her forget the feel of another man inside her. A thin sheen of sweat broke on his skin, his body pumping, his breath becoming choppy.

"Fuck me, Kendrick. Hard." Jay's voice caught.

Kendrick wondered if she used detached sex to cover up a bad past the same way he used jokes and sex to hide from his own.

THE NEXT MORNING, Kendrick was happy to see a note from Tony. The man stated he had gotten a call from a friend in Chicago, and he needed to go back home. He'd be back at some point to finish as much of his uncle's house as possible, but the friend in Chicago needed him.

"I'm sad to see him go. Tony was good people. And he was totally fine with no-strings-attached. I'll miss having him around." Jay sat at the kitchen table, sipping hot tea. Her hair was a mess, but he was drawn to her like a moth to a flame.

Now probably wouldn't be a smart time to ask her if she'd be interested in a date. Reel it in, Jordan. She's talking about no-strings-attached sex the morning after you fucked her and another guy. Not the best time to start looking needy.

And, damn, what was up with feeling needy about this girl? Sex was sex. She wasn't interested in more, and he should have been grateful. But a tiny little buzz in his head, like an annoying little fairy, pointed out over and over that he would be happy to spend many more nights in her bed.

"So, I've got to work at the café today. I better get cleaned up." Jay put her cup in the sink. "Let's be sure to meet up again sometime. You're a lot of fun, Kendrick."

When she turned and walked toward the bathroom, he realized he'd been dismissed. Gathering up his things, he left her place.

What the hell?

Heading home on the walk of shame, head spinning at how quickly he'd been kicked out, and wondering why he felt so empty after a night of outstanding sex was too much for him. He needed coffee, maybe with a little whiskey, and a nice quiet day to regroup his thoughts.

Knowing he'd have to forgo the whiskey, he stopped at the tiny coffee shop on his way home. Walking through the door, being blasted by the fragrant air, he stopped short at the vision before him.

What the hell? No way it's her, it can't be. Has to just be someone who looks a lot like her.

The barista was a spitting image of his first real girlfriend. Sarah.

The hair, the dimple, the shy smile. If he didn't know there was *no way* it could be her, he would bet money it was her.

"Sir, can I help you?" Even her soft voice was Sarah's as it finally registered in his head.

With little recollection of the act, he ordered his coffee and headed out the door.

Memories bombarded him as he walked.

Kissing Sarah for the first time under the tree at the park. Thinking there was no one he'd rather kiss.

Her laughing at him when he cut his hand attempting to carve their initials in the old oak tree. Believing their love was the real deal, forever.

The way his heart thumped against his chest as he worked up the nerve to hold her hand in the hallway at school.

How it took him over half the movie to finally get his arm around her on their first 'date'.

"Someday, after college, we'll have our own little house here in Torey Hope with a white picket fence, two gorgeous kids, and a dog named Fido. The boy will look just like you, and the girl will have your eyes, but my hair." Sarah had teased him one day as they lazed in the afternoon sun. At fifteen, they were completely wrapped up in the relationship. As the years went by, and he matured, he realized it was much more infatuation than love. At the time, though, it was so very real.

Then there was the mess of desire and confusion clouding his mind when they took that next step. He'd known they were likely too young, but there was no telling his burgeoning hormones no when Sarah was convinced it would make things perfect between them.

The sting of tears, the lump in his throat, and the ache in his heart when she was no longer by his side stayed with him all these years later. She was a friend, a sweet girl, someone he enjoyed spending time with, someone who held his heart, even if for a short time. To have her no longer in his life, the way things went down, was extremely hard at that young age.

Damn. He really hadn't wanted to travel down memory lane, especially that particular pathway. What he wanted, no *needed,* was a nice long, hot shower and a nap. Followed by some greasy food and a couple beers.

What he didn't need was a family intervention. But that's exactly what he got.

Fuck.

4

*K*endrick had agreed to housesit for a colleague at The Center+. It gave him a place to stay while he escaped the suffocating reality of his life for a while.

His dad, Jeremiah, had figured out where he was staying, but he'd promised to give him a bit longer before unleashing the rest of the family on him. It appeared his time was up.

As Kendrick sat in the driveway of his colleague's house, he stared forlornly at his three cousins and their significant others. They stared back at him with sad, pensive eyes.

Decker, the controlled, serious one of the group walked with purpose to Kendrick's driver-side door.

"Get out of the car, fucker." Turning on his heel, Decker walked away. Just like Decker to assume his orders would be followed.

He could back up and drive away from them. He could. But he wouldn't. These people were his life, they were just there to help the same way he'd be there for them.

"What the hell? Here goes nothing." Kendrick sighed as he climbed from his gray Ford Mustang.

Walking toward his three best friends, Kendrick stopped in front of them. "Who called in the cavalry?"

"You're lucky it's just us, next time we'll bring the whole fam-dam-ly." Zach crossed his arms across his chest.

"Well, I guess we may as well get this over with. Come on in." Kendrick gestured toward the door. When they'd all filed inside, he directed them to the living room. "I'd offer you drinks, but I don't really have anything here."

He sat on the recliner and took in the six others spread out around the room.

Decker and his girlfriend, soon-to-be fiancé if Kendrick had to guess, Katie, sat together on the loveseat. Decker's twin, Sawyer, sat on the couch with his partner, Luke, seated on the floor in front of him. Zach and his loved-since-the-beginning-of-time girlfriend, Zoey, took up the rest of the couch.

"So, is this like an intervention?" Kendrick tried to laugh it off.

"Stop trying to joke your way out of this. We're here because we love you, and you've been gone too long." Sawyer's words were serious.

"Kendrick, you made a deal with me. If I'd go to therapy,

take the medicine, and get myself on the road to healing, you'd do the same. I've held up my part of the deal, it's your turn now." Zoey's bright green eyes glistened with tears. He knew she had been through hell and back after a stalker attacked her recently. She was right, he *had* made that deal with her, but he wasn't ready to hold up his end yet.

"Not too long ago, you took me away from a dangerous situation. You were my lifeline when Decker couldn't be. I'm not going to sit around and watch you sink deeper into whatever this is. You mean the world to us, Kendrick. We need you to get through this, and be back with us." Katie leaned forward on her knees, pleading with him.

"Listen, man. Whatever you're dealing with, we want you to know we understand it's real and it's painful and it's killing you, but we also need you to know we're here for you. Not just when times are light and fun, we're family, we're friends, that's for life. You hurt, we hurt. We want to help in any way we can, but we can't help you until you open up to us. Or at least open up to someone." Sawyer's eyes never left Kendrick's, but he reached down and took Luke's hand as it caressed his knee.

"We obviously would like for you to talk to us now, but we realize that may be pushing it. So, we're sort of here to issue an ultimatum. Keep in mind, we do all of this out of love. We also do it out of the knowledge that you'd be doing the exact same thing to help one of us." Decker's eyes had a hard glint. "You've got two more weeks. Get the drinking, sex, partying out of your system, because then you're coming home and facing this shit head-on."

"Or what?" Kendrick challenged, although his voice held a lot less force than he meant for it to.

"Or we come back with reinforcements. And we don't leave. Plus, I know the guy who owns this house will be back in just over two weeks, so it's perfect timing." Decker smirked knowing he had the upper hand.

"So, I can spend the next two weeks having sex, drinking, and partying. Then I have to submit myself to the six of you or face the entire Morgan-Jordan-Martin family? Gee, when you put it like that I guess I have no choice. Although, it could be fun to have the grandmas over here. I could tell them about my recent sexcapades with a guy." He knew exactly what he was doing. If he could get them distracted enough, maybe they'd stop pushing at him.

Unfortunately for him, the whole group also knew what he was doing.

"Nice try, fucker. You can't use the shock and awe in hopes of distracting us." Zach shook his head.

"While we won't take the bait of distraction, we will take a momentary break from the serious to ask for details of the guy-on-guy action." Luke winked at him, and Kendrick was grateful to the man for offering a brief reprieve.

"Not a whole lot to tell. I'm not sold on kissing a guy. It's not unpleasant, but I think I prefer the softness of a girl. I was too drunk to remember the first time, but the second time was pretty enjoyable. He's bi, so he's into her, but I think he's a lot more into taking cock if you want to know the truth." Kendrick hesitated in a rare moment of uncertainty. "Truth be told, if I'm being honest, I was really glad he got off first, because then I could focus more on her."

"Yeah, you're definitely not gay." Sawyer and Luke laughed.

"And, while we're taking this break before diving back into the whole 'get Kendrick over this and back home' plan, let's hear about this girl." Katie wagged her brows.

"Not a whole lot to tell. Her name is Jay. Totally not my type, body-wise or personality-wise. Tiny little thing, no huge anything on this girl. Not a complete bimbo or flake either. Completely detached. She's a waitress at The Café. I'm guessing she may keep me around for another couple weeks before she moves on. Tony says that's her usual M.O." Kendrick let his mind wander to Jay. Was she alone? Getting ready for work? Planning another night of fun? Would it include him?

"Be careful. You don't need the added drama of a girl while you're trying to get through this shit. Speaking of this shit, you plan on telling us about it?" Decker challenged.

Kendrick leaned forward, taking his head into his hands. It would be so easy to just open up, tell them all about it. But opening those flood gates meant pain and anger and fear. He just wasn't ready.

"I'm just not ready. It hurts, and I don't especially feel

like ripping that particular band-aid off right now." Kendrick stood, effectively shutting down the conversation.

The rest of the group stood as well.

"Well, prepare yourself to rip that band-aid off, because we'll expect you home in two weeks. Home for good, or we're coming back with the rest of the group." Decker squeezed his shoulder.

"And we know it hurts, Kendrick. Bad stuff always hurts. But it will never stop hurting if you don't open it up so it can drain and heal. Look at us. Between the seven people standing here, four of us aside from you have gone through some hard shit, but we're healing. Why? Because we let others in; we told our story; we let it hurt for a while. And we let our family and friends hold us while we cried." Sawyer hugged him close.

"This will happen, Kendrick. It will be hard. It will hurt. And it likely will get worse before it gets better. But, you've got this, you'll survive and thrive. You just have to make that first step and be willing to make yourself vulnerable." Zoey let him hug her tightly.

It will likely get worse before it gets better.

Yeah, that was the shit he was most afraid of.

Two weeks later, after several late night booty calls and hookups with Jay, Kendrick found himself sitting at what had quickly become his favorite table at the Torey Hope Café. The place had charm, as did so many establishments in his beloved little hometown, and the food was great. But what made him keep coming in for lunch each day wasn't the ambiance or the menu. It was Jay. He knew the little fling they had going would end soon. He knew she wasn't looking to settle down. And he knew he had way too much on his plate to seriously contemplate a real relationship. But none of that stopped him from coming in for a meal each day since he'd met her. She'd obviously noticed his sudden love of café food, and his perfect timing to always show up right when the rush was over and she had more time to devote to serving his food and talking to him.

Today was no different.

"I'm going to sit with Kendrick and take my break." Jay called to her boss when the last of Torey Hope's lunch munchers had bustled out the door.

"Hey there, sexy guy. What brings you by? Just can't get enough of the turkey on rye and some tasty apple pie?" She delivered her rhymes with barely a smirk.

"Aww, my little Pixie is a poet who doesn't know it." He reached out to tweak her nose.

"Don't call me Pixie."

"Sorry, can't help it. It just fits." Kendrick finished his sandwich and took a swig of milk.

"I can't believe you drink so much milk." She wrinkled her nose.

"What? It's good and healthy. Better than soda, right?"

"I guess."

"Speaking of names, what's your full name?" Kendrick had been wondering, assuming Jay was a nickname.

"I don't think we were really speaking of names, but it's just Jay. I don't tell people my whole first name. Too personal." She shifted in her seat looking unnerved.

"Hmmm, maybe I'll play Rumpelstiltskin and try to guess it. If I ever guess will you tell me?"

"Fine. But you'll never guess. I don't mind telling my middle name. It's Marie. Speaking of names, I am embarrassed to admit this, but I don't know your last name." She cocked her head, looking at him curiously.

"Kendrick Robert Jordan. Middle name after my grandfather. And since I've slept with you several times, Miss Jay Marie, may I know your last name?" He teased, but felt a bit slutty to know they were just getting to the name business after so many intimate encounters.

"Keller is my last name." She blushed as if she were feeling the same as him.

"Well, now Jay Marie 'Pixie' Keller...I'm not giving up on the first name...Julie? Jane? Jamie?" He tried to think of as many J names as he could.

"Nope, nope, and nope. Listen, my break is up. You want

to come over tonight? No worries if you've got plans." She stood and straightened her apron.

He did his best not to run admiring eyes up and down her tiny little body, but he failed miserably. "Yeah, I'm pretty sure I'm free tonight. I'll be over around 6:00."

ROLLING TO HIS SIDE, pulling her close to him even though he knew she didn't like to cuddle, he tried to catch his breath.

Jay sighed heavily, sounding very satisfied. "Damn, sexy boy, you're pretty good at that." He heard the smile in her voice.

"Why, thank you, ma'am. You're not half bad yourself." He chuckled.

When she didn't roll away from him, Kendrick decided to press his luck a bit. "Jazmine? Jessie? Jezabel?"

"No, no, and no." She laughed against his chest. After a few moments she spoke again. "You know I'll have to end this pretty soon, right?"

"I wouldn't be upset if it didn't end right away." Kendrick kept his voice steady.

"I think I've let it go on a bit too long already. I've never kept a guy around this long. I mean, I kept Tony around, but he was more like bait."

Kendrick laughed, "That's flattering."

A few more moments of silence passed. Kendrick tried to think of ways to persuade her to keep their pseudo relationship going a bit longer, Jay cuddled into his chest.

"I've got a ton of crap in my past. It's caught up with me. I sort of ran away from it, but my family is waiting on me to come back and face it. I'm moving back to the house I share with my cousins this weekend." He paused.

"And you're telling me all of this because?" Jay leaned back to look up at him.

"Just to say that I'm going to have a ton of shit going on, but having a friend to spend time with would be really nice. I would be happy if it were you I was hanging out with when things are rough." He tried to sound nonchalant, not too needy, but damn he wanted this girl to stay in his life.

"What about your cousins?"

"Well, they all got the good looks of the family, but I'm really not interested in having sex with them. Incest and all that you know..." He ducked quickly away from the hand that swatted at his head.

"I didn't mean it that way, you dork."

He leaned in to kiss her, "I know, Pixie, I know. Just joking around."

"Okay, we can keep this going. But I need a couple parameters." She paused to look at him, waiting to see if he would agree.

"Parameters would probably be good. Lay'em on me."

"First, I can call it quits at any moment if I feel like either of us is getting too attached. Second, I am the only one who invites in a third. If you find someone you'd like to invite, just let me know. Guys only. Third, we keep it light, fun, and detached. If you can handle those, I'm in. At least for now."

Too late, Pixie, I'm already attached. But, if you need to believe it's detached, so be it. For now.

"Sure, sounds good. We can hang out at my place or yours. No 'meet the family' relationship stuff, but I think you'll really like my cousins. Actually, you'll like my whole family." He noticed the extreme panic in her eyes. "I mean, if you were to ever meet them. Like randomly, not like me introducing you to the whole clan or anything like that."

Her eyes calmed and she sagged in relief.

Not now, but someday. Count on it, Pixie.

5

"*H*oney! I'm home!" Kendrick sing-songed as he walked through the front door of the house he shared with his cousins.

Coming home on a Sunday afternoon guaranteed most of them would be home. He'd known that, but he decided it was time to stop hiding, stop pussyfooting around, grab this thing by the balls and face it head on.

When Zach and Zoey came from the bedroom, hair mussed, cheeks red, Kendrick felt a little bad for interrupting them. But when Decker and Katie came to the living room looking the same, and Sawyer and Luke ambled in with that one-and-only glow, he just shook his head.

"Well, I'll be damned, I go away and come home to a fucking brothel." He tried to sound disgusted, but he really just wanted to laugh.

"What the hell are you talking about? We were all together when you left, it's not like you didn't know we were having sex at that point." Decker rolled his eyes.

"You're right. I was just momentarily stunned by the glaring 'I just got fucked' glow which radiated from the six of you. Damn, who ever thought *you'd* be getting more action than *me*?"

The group laughed, and Kendrick instantly felt his heart swell at being back home where he belonged.

"Can we go to the kitchen?" Maybe a drink would sooth his parched throat and help him get through what he was going to say.

When everyone was seated, Kendrick looked around.

"Thank you all for getting my ass in gear. I'm sure I would have stayed away for a lot longer if you'd left me alone. And while I still want to bury my head in the sand, I'm also feeling anxious to get past this shit." He drained the water. "I want to talk to the whole family. We still having family dinner at someone's house tonight?"

The Morgan, Jordan, Martin families, along with Captain Decker and Janie, had been getting together for weekly dinners since Kendrick's older brother, Beckett, was a little boy. As the families grew, the family dinners continued. These dinners were often where big news was shared. Several pregnancies had been announced over the years. Drama sometimes ensued when things were brought up. They were a very large family. When lots of people are mixed together, you can expect differences of opinions. But, Kendrick knew he owed it to his parents, grandparents, cousins, and the rest of the family to tell them what had been haunting him. Might as well do it when most of the group was together. He'd have to share with Beckett and his wife, Kenja, and his older sister, Megan, when they were home. Or he could call them. But he knew the family grapevine would likely reach them first.

"Yeah, we're at John and Cindy's tonight. I think we're doing stir-fry. The grandmas plan on having a huge pot of rice, along with three woks for different meats and veggies." Zoey offered.

"Okay, well, can you guys wait until dinner then? I'd rather tell everyone at once if that's okay."

"Sure, man. No pressure. You don't even have to tell us. We just know if you talk about it you can start healing from it." Sawyer clapped him on the back.

"No way I'm telling a stranger about this shit before I even tell my family. He may have a license, but my family has been with me my whole life. You guys deserve first dibs on my fucked-up-ness." Kendrick joked, but his tension was evident.

KENDRICK KNEW his family had all heard he was back home. He'd gone to see his mom and dad before he'd gone to his own place. He struggled against the overwhelming anticipation and nervous anxiety that rippled through him as he climbed the steps to John and Cindy's home. The elder Morgans were blood related to Zach, Decker, and Sawyer, but he'd grown up with them as his *grandparents* his whole life, it didn't matter there was no actual blood relation.

Entering the house, he was immediately greeted with warmth. Warm smiles, warm hugs, and an overall warm feeling of being loved and welcomed. He'd enjoyed his four years at college, but the feeling he got when he came back to Torey Hope, the feeling he got when he spent time with those most important to him, those feelings were what grounded him and kept him rooted where he'd grown up.

"Kendrick. It's good to see you, son." John Morgan, and Kendrick's paternal grandfather, Jack Jordan, clapped him on the back and hugged him.

"'Bout time you dragged your ass back home. It's time to face this shit head on." Captain Robert Decker, his maternal grandfather, had a bark worse than his bite, but Kendrick appreciated the man keeping it real.

He didn't mind being fawned over by his three grand-mothers, in fact, if he stopped to examine it long enough, the fawning made him feel loved, cared for, needed.

"There's my baby boy." Audrey gathered him in a hug.

Kendrick knew his announcement tonight would be hard on everyone involved. He'd tried to warn his mom and dad earlier in the day that he'd be talking about some things regarding information they already knew, but also some new information.

After a delicious meal of stir-fry, the dishes and kitchen were cleaned up quickly. With both the men and women helping, the job was done in no time.

"So, since you all know I wanted to talk to you about some things, I guess we can head to the living room." Kendrick cleared his throat.

In the living room, Sawyer immediately pulled the ottoman front and center, and indicated Kendrick should sit on it.

One-by-one, the parents and grandparents took seats on comfy sofas around the room. Kendrick would have expected his cousins to do the same, but they didn't. With his heart in his throat, he waited as all six of his cousins/friends gathered around him. Decker and Katie at his back. Zach and Zoey to his right. Sawyer and Luke to his left. They built a shield, a wall, to protect him. Not that they needed to protect him from his family, but the cousins stood in solidarity to show their unending support for whatever was to come.

Grasping the hand Katie laid on his shoulder, Kendrick began.

"So, I'm guessing most of you remember Sarah at least a little bit. I dated her when I was about fifteen. She was a sweet girl, but she was having a lot of issues at school and home. Her parents were worried about her, thought maybe our dating was causing some of the trouble. They felt we were too serious. Looking back, we probably were way too involved for that age." He paused and looked at his youngest cousin, Asher, pointedly. Some chuckles traveled around the room. Asher hadn't yet shown interest in dating anyone, but they all knew it would be coming soon.

"Anyway, Sarah was having a lot more bad days than good days. We tried to see each other as often as we could, but her parents had started making it harder and harder for us to get together. Sarah wanted to have sex, said it would make us closer and help her know that I loved her." He winced as he spoke, knowing no mother or grandmother ever really wants to hear about one of their boys having sex, especially at the age of fifteen. "I was worried about how up and down Sarah's behaviors were, but I was also a horny kid, and I loved her as much as a teenaged kid can love another, maybe infatuated is a better word. We worked out a way for us to get together a few times when her parents were away. She lied to them and told them we had completely broken up."

He stopped and rubbed his forehead.

"At some point, Sarah started skipping school. I couldn't go over and check on her because we had supposedly broken up. But I was worried. When I'd catch a few moments with her here and there she'd lost weight, looked terrible, and was just sad and quiet. I couldn't tell anyone about what was going on because she needed her parents to think we'd broken up."

Another pause sounded as he gathered his thoughts.

"When she didn't show up to school for a whole week, I couldn't stand it any longer. I went to her house. Her parents met me at the door, red-eyed. They told me Sarah had killed herself three days earlier. They made me come in and sit down, and they called my mom and dad. I got the feeling they wanted me to suffer, and hoped that my parents would shame me."

Kendrick's eyes filled with tears as he looked to Audrey and Jeremiah.

"Sarah's parents didn't want her to be remembered as the girl who committed suicide, so they were staging it to look like they were just moving out of town. They begged us to just go along with the moving story; they were always so damn concerned about what others in town would think of them. So, instead of grieving my girlfriend's suicide, and getting answers as to what caused her to take her own life, I had to go about pretending that she'd just abruptly moved away. I wish I'd been older, more sure of myself, I would have told them to go fuck themselves. I have always felt like her parents caused a lot of her problems."

The family was quiet as they absorbed the information. But he wasn't finished.

"Mom and Dad left, but I asked to stay for a bit. I know now that Sarah probably wasn't my one-and-only, but at the time I was pretty sure I was in love with the girl. I was sad; it hurt to know she was gone. And I was confused to say the least. Once Mom and Dad had left, making me promise to come home soon so we could talk about it, her parents dropped an even bigger bomb shell. Sarah was pregnant. They watched me with these looks on their faces that I can't even describe. Anger, disgust, sadness, their faces were more than just parents who had lost a child. They had no reason to believe Sarah had been with anyone but me, even though the pregnancy had come as quite a shock when the autopsy was completed. I think they told me that information, especially out of earshot of Mom and Dad, to punish me. Make me feel bad, like maybe the pregnancy was something that pushed her over the edge. I don't know if Sarah even knew she was pregnant before she died."

Audrey's hand had flown to cover her mouth, trying to stifle the sobs threatening to erupt. Zoey climbed onto the ottoman and wrapped her arms around him.

"They begged me to let Sarah's name stay untainted. Begged me to not talk about the suicide, and definitely not about the pregnancy. I remember thinking they seemed almost more upset about the pregnancy at age fifteen than they did about their daughter taking her own life."

Dropping his head into his hands, Kendrick took a deep breath, trying to soldier on.

"So, Mom and Dad knew she'd killed herself, but I didn't tell them about the pregnancy. We all just pretended I was upset because my girlfriend had moved away. I started dating other girls. Life went on."

Kendrick's red-rimmed eyes looked up.

"Until it didn't. Every year, around the time I think the baby would have been born, I think about him; the older I get, the harder the loss of my child hits me. What would he look like? Would he have blonde hair? What would he like about starting Kindergarten? For some reason, this year, when I knew the baby would be ten, it hit me harder than ever. He would be going to school, doing homework, playing sports, making friends. It kills me to wonder about that baby. Would I be a good daddy? What would have happened to me if Sarah and the baby had lived? I didn't want to be a teen dad, I didn't want to give up my dreams. I don't know that Sarah and I would have stayed together, but I would have loved that baby." He stopped, tears streaming down his face.

There wasn't a dry eye in the room as the family took in the information. Losing a family member, a baby, a child they didn't even know existed...it tore at their hearts.

Jeremiah and Audrey pulled Kendrick into a hug.

"Thank you for sharing with us. I wish you'd been able to tell us so many years ago. But you'll get through this. You would have been a terrific dad, and you still will be a great dad someday. I think our thoughts and feelings are mighty jumbled right now, so maybe we should save other discussions for later, huh?" Audrey held her youngest tightly.

Kyle Martin knew the pain of losing an unborn child, and that pain was etched on his face when he approached Kendrick.

"We can talk later. Anytime. I mean it, Kendrick,

anytime. I know about the wondering and what ifs, I get it, man." Kyle's voice broke, and he pulled his wife, Josie, close to his side for comfort.

Kendrick knew Kyle would be a good person to talk to in the coming months as he worked through his feelings. He had grown up hearing the story about Kyle's first wife and child, the loss which had spurred him to move to Torey Hope, the hurdles he and Josie had to overcome.

Each member of the family took a moment to comfort him and share their love for him. In the end, the cousins all headed back to the guys' house. It was time for a little drinking, talking, and laughing.

"Before we drink, first I want to thank you all for forcing me to talk about it. It hurts, but saying it out loud really helps. It's like a weight was lifted from my shoulders." Kendrick spoke to them all.

"*Forced* sounds so negative. I'd like to think we persuaded you to talk to us." Zach joked.

"Also, *before we drink,* I'd like to put a two shot limit on everyone in this room. Need I remind you what took place the last time certain members of this group were drinking together?" Decker looked sternly at Kendrick and Zach; Zoey blushed.

"You mean when I started my downward spiral and got Zach and Zoey shitfaced, and then they got busy doing the nasty for their first time? Yeah, that was some messed up shit." Kendrick just smirked and shook his head.

"Jesus, man. I'm glad you're feeling better, but I'm not 100% sure I like the crude and crass side of you coming back." Zach punched his arm.

"I disagree, crude and crass is Kendrick. I want him just the way he is." Zoey hugged him close.

"Let's drink, fuckers." Kendrick laid out the shot glasses.

Several moments later, when each person had taken their allotted two shots, and the alcohol was safely stored away, they ambled to the living room.

"I think it's time for story time." Kendrick was feeling the heat of the alcohol traveling through his system.

6

"*D*o you remember that time we accidentally beaned the Captain with a snowball to the face?" Zach's eyes bugged as he smiled at the memory.

"Oh man, I *do* remember that. I was only like five, but I thought the Captain was going to skin you guys alive." Zach's younger sister, and Zoey's best friend, Aly, had joined the group.

"Yeah, he was so mad his face melted the snow. I thought for sure he'd have us doing push-ups until midnight or something." Decker shook his head.

"That's the great thing about him meeting Janie. He probably *would have* tanned our hides before Janie, but she softened him up a lot. So, instead of punishing us, he told us our *energy* would be better used elsewhere, and helped us to shovel every single driveway and sidewalk on his street." Sawyer's smile was bright.

"My damn arms hurt for days after that." Kendrick rubbed his shoulder. "What about the time our sweet Zoey Belle brought us along on breaking and entering her dad's little home studio? She promised he had lots of 'pretty paint' we could use to paint our model cars. Little did we know she had us using his tattoo ink."

"Ohhhh, I remember that. Dad is pretty laid back, but I'm pretty sure he wanted to hang me by my toes for ruining all that ink." Zoey giggled a little, the shots obvious in her eyes.

"Do you remember the year we got the flu before we were able to get the flu shot? The four of us were quarantined to Grandma Cindy's basement at the first sign of symptoms in hopes we wouldn't contaminate everyone else. The grandmas took turns caring for us so our moms wouldn't take germs back to the younger ones." Zach shook his head in amazement. "I didn't think about it at the time because I was sure I was going to die, but it's pretty crazy the grandmas didn't get sick at all. Grandma Cindy once told me it was because they had all been through it so many times with their own kids they were immune to the bugs."

"Man, we were *sick*. I remember telling Mom to make my appointment right then for the flu shot the following year so I could avoid it the next time. The only good thing about it was after the fever and headache went away, we had the rest of the week to play video games and be waited on hand-and-foot." Sawyer laughed.

"Yeah, we were sort of like little celebrities when we returned to school the following week. Rumors had started flying that we'd died from the flu." Decker shook his head. "When they found out we'd just been lying around drinking juice and playing games they were envious. No need to tell them we'd been miserable for four days."

Decker agreed to one more shot for everyone since it was evident no one was getting sloshed. Glasses held high in the air, the group toasted to family and friends.

"I've got to ask. When that boy stood me up for the dance, and Zach took me instead, he told me Kendrick took care of the boys involved. But I never heard the whole story. It had to be good, because those boys were like whipped puppies the next week at school; getting flowers every day from them was a treat, but I never knew with certainty how that all went down. Kendrick, what exactly did you do?" Zoey's curiosity glowed from her face.

"Ahhh, yeah, that was a fun night." Kendrick laughed, clearly enjoying the memory. "So, Zach had an upset Zoey Belle on his hands, and planned to take her to the dance in place of the douche bag who stood her up. He called me to take care of the little prick."

Kendrick launched into a retelling of that night.

"Hey there, I see you're playing some ball. Care if I join?"

I bestowed my signature grin on the middle school boys playing basketball at the local park.

The four boys looked a little baffled why a teenage boy like me would want to play ball with them, but they readily agreed.

As the game continued, I made chit-chat.

"What's going on over at the middle school? Looked crowded." I kept my face completely blank.

"Some stupid dance." One of the boys stated, and the rest of them broke into a fit of laughter.

Fighting to keep my composure, I continued to play it cool.

"Oh yeah, why aren't you guys there? Fine young men like yourselves probably have to fight the ladies off." I drained a three-pointer and waited on the kids to hang themselves.

"Yeah, we fight the ladies off, but we had a little bet going about tonight." The kid who spoke seemed to be the leader of the group.

"A bet? Like you bet each other you wouldn't go to the dance? Sounds pretty lame if you ask me." I was beginning to understand what had happened, but I waited for the boys to say it out loud.

"Nah, man. We each asked a girl to the dance, then dumped her. We assigned points for their reactions. Skipping the dance, getting angry, going by herself, every possible reaction earned certain points. The one of us who earned the most points gets his lunch bought for him all week at school." The boys smirked and nodded their heads as if they thought their game was awesome.

Taking a couple minutes to gather my thoughts, I dribbled and shot the ball over their heads a few times. Feeling ready to deliver my smack down, I held the ball and turned to face them.

"Wow, that's...cool?" I shook my head and made sure the boys realized I thought their bet was stupid.

"So, you let a girl buy a dress, jewelry, new shoes, do her make-up, get excited about the dance, and then stand her up... all so you have the chance of having a cafeteria lunch bought for you?" I stopped and watched the boys' faces to see if realization was setting in. It wasn't.

"Must have a lot better lunches at the middle school these days. Five years ago they pretty much sucked. Or at least they were bad enough I wouldn't have given up the chance to hold a girl in my arms and maybe kiss her just for a couple of free lunches."

The boys just shrugged and looked like they wished I'd leave.

No such luck.

"So, what are the points for a beautiful girl getting stood up, but her very attractive, older cousin drives her to the dance and spends the evening making sure she has the time of her life?"

"Um, well, we didn't plan for that one. Probably 5 points." The leader began to shuffle his feet, and the asswipe who'd stood Zoey up was starting to look extremely pale.

"What about the points for the girl who has a cousin who

hates little shit-ass punks like you, and comes to the ball courts to teach you a lesson?"

When the boys realized they'd been caught, they started to back away like they planned to leave.

"Not so fast, gentlemen."

I moved behind them and stretched my long arms to gather them all close.

"I'd say I'm worth at least 10 points. Dontcha think?" I grinned evilly and winked.

"What are you going to do to us?" The one who had stood Zoey up had trouble keeping the abject fear from his voice.

"Oh, I'm not going to hurt you, although I'd really like to hurt you the same way you hurt those three girls tonight."

"It was actually six girls..."

"Dude! Shut up, don't tell him that!"

"Ah, so not only did you each stand one girl up, you stood up multiple girls who all thought they had dates to the dance? Bravo, bravo." I shook my head in disgust.

"So, here's what you're going to do, and don't think you can skip out of it. I have two cousins, an uncle, and several friends at your school, so I'll know if you try to get out of your punishment."

I sat the boys down on the bleachers and listed my requirements.

"One, you will take each girl you stood up a flower every day this coming week. Deliver it to her at her locker. If you get punched or slapped, take it like a man because you deserve it.

Two, buy a lunch and give it to a kid who looks hungry or sad or alone. Three, you won't need to buy another lunch because you'll be brown-baggin-it with bologna or PBJ from home for the entire week."

Just when I thought I was done, inspiration struck.

"Oh, and you have to sit together at a lone table, and put up a sign that says, 'We can't eat with the rest of the school because we suck for what we did.' And of course you won't breathe a word of this to anyone unless you want more punishment. I'm betting your parents had no clue you made the bet and planned to hurt those girls.'"

By the time the boys scrambled from the bleachers and ran from the park, I was laughing and truly wished I'd be able to watch the lunch room that week. I'd have to make sure Uncle Nate knew what was going on. I also knew Zoey and Aly would keep me apprised of the boys' progress in their week-long punishment.

I headed home while I texted Zach, "It's all taken care of, dude."

"Oh my gosh, Kendrick, that was perfect. Every girl those assholes stood up loved watching them suffer the next week at school. I always knew you had something to do with it, but I never knew the whole story. Thanks for that." Zoey kissed him on the cheek.

A comfortable silence settled over the group for several minutes.

Then Sawyer chuckled.

"Anyone else here feel like we've likely seen *way too much* of our parents and grandparents making out or having sex? I swear, Decker and I probably walked in on Mom and Dad at least ten times growing up. And we caught John and Cindy making out like teenagers in the bathroom one time when we were spending the night." Sawyer pretended to shiver.

"Don't get me started on the times I've caught my mom and dad." Aly shook her head in exaggerated disgust. "Dad is a total horn dog."

"Aly, stop! Please, say no more. I can't stand the images you're bringing to my mind." Zach covered his ears and everyone laughed.

"Catching the grandparents kissing doesn't gross me out nearly as much as walking in and seeing my dad's bare ass in the air." Kendrick winced. "Of course, in hindsight, we all probably should have learned more quickly that a closed door is a sign to *keep out, dangerous sights ahead.*"

"*Or,* maybe we all should remember that *closing a door* when choosing to make out with someone is a good idea. Because leaving the door open means your girlfriend may just see you making out with a guy on your bed." Katie giggled and looked pointedly at Sawyer.

Red-faced, Sawyer laughed, "You're never going to let me live that one down, are you Katie-girl?"

"Nope." She popped the *p* loudly, smiling widely.

"How about the awkwardness of having your girlfriend's

grandma talk about your ass and indicate you better keep your junk in your pants around her granddaughter? Yeah, that's all sorts of fun." Decker teased Katie.

"Oh, Katie, your grandma is a hoot. Remember when she saw me with my friend Adam and thought I was Decker? She went ballistic on me, thinking Decker was cheating on you with a guy. When you brought her to apologize, she looked like she'd swallowed a lemon having to admit she was wrong." Sawyer laughed, rubbing Luke's shoulders. "Damn, that woman was pissed. I was glad she didn't have a cane when she saw me in the coffee shop with Adam. I'm pretty sure she would have walloped me with it."

"Dude, do you still have that book we found in Grandma Judy's attic? *The Joys of Satisfying Sex After the Age of Forty.* It was a full color book, complete with demonstrative illustrations. It was all fun and games and laughter when we found that book. Until we realized that Grandma Judy and Grandpa Jack were older than forty and they'd probably been reading that book at some point. When she called us down to lunch, Kendrick stuck it in his waistband." Zach looked to Kendrick.

"Man, that book had some good pointers. Really helped my sexual prowess grow and develop, and now I have no fear of middle-aged sex being boring or bad." Kendrick smirked and winked. "Yeah, I have it in my sock drawer I think. We should present it to our parents sometime. Gather everyone around, tell them about our discovery so many years ago, and let them know they can borrow the book on a rotating basis."

Silence and fatigue settled upon the room again.

"So, I better be getting home. Zach, are you taking Zoey home?" Aly stood and stretched.

"I think Zoey was going to spend the night here." Zach spoke cautiously, knowing not long ago this announcement would have sent his sister into a tailspin.

"No worries, I walked over so I can walk home. I didn't know how much we'd be drinking so I didn't want to drive." Aly shrugged and gathered her belongings.

"Nah, we've gotcha, Aly. I'm staying at Luke's tonight, so we can drop you off." Sawyer stood behind Luke, wrapping his arms around his waist.

"Thanks for making my coming home so easy, guys. I'm calling the therapist tomorrow to set up appointments. I'll be back at work as usual as well." Kendrick hugged each and every one of them.

"We're all really glad to have you back home, this group isn't the same without you." Katie kissed his cheek.

"Call on any of us, at any time. I mean it, man." Sawyer slapped him on the shoulder.

When those who were leaving were gone, Kendrick faced Zach and Zoey in the overly-bright kitchen. Taking a deep breath, he ran a hand over his face.

"What's up, man?" Zach's concern was genuine.

With pained eyes, Kendrick looked at them, "I'm scared. I

don't want to go talk to someone. I'm afraid talking about it will make it worse. But I also know I've got to do *something* to clear my head and get myself back on track."

Zoey gathered him in her arms. "It will hurt, and it will be uncomfortable. You'll hate it, you'll feel exhausted, but once you start talking and moving past it, you'll start to feel lighter. You'll feel like you can breathe again. Seriously, talk to us, and talk to my dad. He knows a lot about what you're going through."

"Yeah, I hate that he does, but it sounds like he knows the pain all too well." Kendrick kissed Zoey on the cheek and slapped Zach on the back. "I'm heading to bed. See you guys at The Center+ tomorrow."

Once in bed, he pulled up Jay's number.

Kendrick: Hey.

Jay: Hey.

Kendrick: So, I'll be back at work full time this week. And I'm starting appointments with a therapist. Just wanted you to know what was going on if I'm not as available as I've been, or if you don't see me at lunch. I'd like to make plans with you though. Maybe for Friday or Saturday night?

Jay: Let's play it by ear and see how you're feeling by the end of the week. Text me. I'll miss my favorite new end-of-lunch-rush customer.

He smiled.

Kendrick: And I'll miss my Pixie.

Jay: Stop calling me that.

Kendrick: How about I call you Jayden?

Jay: Nope

Kendrick: Jordan?

Jay: No

Kendrick: Jemimah?

Jay: No!

Kendrick: Okay, then I'll just stick with Pixie for now. Unless you want to tell me your real name?

Jay: You're infuriating, you know that?

Kendrick: So I've been told. But don't forget charming, charismatic, and sexy as hell.

Jay: Cocky much?

Kendrick: You want to talk about cock? Miss Jay Marie, I do believe you've got me blushing.

Jay: This conversation just went from bad to worse. Good night, Kendrick "Cocky-As-They-Come" Jordan.

Kendrick: Now you want to talk about come? Dang, kinky little Pixie.

Jay: Ugh, you make me want to throw my phone. GOOD NIGHT!!

Kendrick couldn't help but laugh. He knew she was all worked up; she was easy to tease. He really hoped the week didn't come crashing down around him, because he really wanted to spend time with her on Friday or Saturday. Hell, he'd take the whole weekend if it were offered. And that was how he knew she was different. Kendrick Jordan had never longed to spend a whole weekend with a girl.

7

"Hello, Kendrick. I'm Dr. Parks. It's nice to meet you. Please, have a seat." The man was very professional, but Kendrick immediately felt at ease in his warm, cozy office.

"Yeah, nice to meet you too, Doc. My cousins Sawyer and Zoey speak very highly of you." Kendrick took a seat on an overstuffed chair which threatened to suck him into its inner depths. "Damn, Doc, is this chair a secret weapon to make sure no one leaves your office until you pry them out of it limb-by-limb?"

Dr. Parks smiled at Kendrick.

"I'm glad your cousins felt they could recommend my services to you. I'm actually going to be volunteering my services at The Center+ over the next month or so to help get the therapy program set up for Zoey. I've been in town a couple years, and I've got to tell you I'm very impressed with your family business. It was great before, but I'm really liking what you and your cousins are doing with the place." The doctor settled himself in a worn desk chair across from Kendrick.

Kendrick appreciated the unassuming nature of the office. It didn't scream, "Tell me your secrets, give me your money, help me buy another Porsche." Kendrick knew it was crazy, maybe wishful thinking, but his surroundings, the doctor's soft demeanor, they whispered to him, "Share your secrets, let someone else help with the burden."

"So, how does this work? Do you ask questions? Or do I just start spilling my guts?" Kendrick found he was anxious to get started.

"Well, first I need you to know that I'm a licensed therapist, but I specialize in lesbian, gay, bisexual, and transgendered youth. This doesn't mean I can't help you, but if at any time you feel that our professional relationship isn't working for you, you have every right to ask for another recommendation."

"Yeah, I got no problem with that, Doc."

"Okay, sounds good. Now, I'd like you to just start telling me the reasons you're here. Start wherever you're comfortable. I'll write my questions down as I think of them, but I will try not to interrupt. At the end of our session, we'll set up our next appointment and maybe some goals." Dr. Parks pulled out his notebook.

Thirty minutes later, Kendrick shook his head from what felt like an emotional and verbal upchuck. Blinking his eyes, realizing he'd just poured out his whole past to the man sitting in front of him, he took a deep breath.

"Yeah, so there it is. Teen girlfriend committed suicide, but only after our teen sex led to an unplanned pregnancy which I knew nothing about until both of them were dead." Exhaustion tinged his voice.

"That's a lot for a young man to take on." Dr. Parks scanned his notes. "I'd like to break this into two separate issues. Sarah's suicide, and the death of your unborn baby. Is that alright with you?"

"You're the expert, Doc."

"How do you feel when you think about Sarah's suicide?"

"Confused. Sad. Guilty." Kendrick struggled with the next word, "Angry."

"Tell me about each of those feelings."

"Confused. I don't get it. We were young, happy, in love, we had our whole lives. She was super smart, pretty, I just don't get what could have been so bad that she had to take her own life. Why wasn't my love enough for her?"

"Was Sarah bullied? Abused at home?" Dr. Parks asked.

"No, I spent a lot of time with her at school, and she wasn't super popular, but she had a couple quiet friends and no one ever bothered her. Even if they waited until I wasn't around, I would have heard about it through cousins or friends."

"Okay, so we're going to assume there was likely an underlying mental condition going on. Do you know if she was being treated for anything?" Dr. Parks scribbled on his notepad.

"Her mom always ragged her about making sure she took her vitamins and supplements, but she didn't take anything prescription." Kendrick stopped momentarily. "You know, looking back on it, I don't know if her parents would have accepted a diagnosis of a mental illness. They seemed pretty insistent on putting on a good front and making sure everyone viewed them as completely normal, so I doubt they took her to the doctor if she even told them about the way she was feeling."

Dr. Parks wrote more notes before speaking again. "Okay, continue telling me about those feelings."

"Sad. It just seems like such a damn sad loss. Sarah could have been something. She had plans for college. It just makes me sad to think she was struggling with something like suicidal thoughts. I guess sad too because I can't even imagine feeling that way."

"Tell me about that."

"Well, even when things are at their most shit-tastic, I've never thought of ending it all."

"You left your family for quite a while."

"Yeah, left to get some time away, not end my whole life. I love them too much to put them through that. I mean, it's not like I think I'm all that special, but I know without a doubt my family would be devastated by my death."

"Okay, go on." Dr. Parks kept writing. What the hell was he scribbling?

"Guilty and angry sort of go hand-in-hand. I feel guilty because I didn't realize she was so sad, so sick, so on edge. Then I feel angry because she took her life, took our baby's life, turned my life upside down. Then I go back to feeling guilty. I shouldn't be angry. It was her life, her pain, who am I to blame her? The anger and guilt are on a continuous loop in my head."

Dr. Parks abruptly stood. Walking to his phone, he picked it up. "Do I have time after this appointment? Okay, block it out."

Walking back to his seat, the doctor spoke, "I rarely do sessions longer than an hour, but I feel like we need to get this all out, then we can work through more of it at subsequent appointments."

Waiting for Kendrick to take a drink from his bottle of water, Dr. Parks watched him thoughtfully.

"Do you think you could have stopped her from killing herself?

"What? I don't know. I mean, I guess I think I probably

could have stopped it at the moment she was actually doing it, but if she was sick and her parents wouldn't get her the help she needed, I probably couldn't have stopped it in the long run."

"You're right. You and Sarah were victims in this situation. In a way, so were her parents. Mental illness doesn't discriminate. It doesn't care if you've got a reputation to uphold. It doesn't care if you're rich or poor. It doesn't matter if you've got a supportive family or you're alone. If her parents knew she was sick and refused to get her help, some blame can be placed on them. But, they may not have realized she was sick. They may have thought it was usual hormonal, teenage angst type stuff. Did they have other children?"

"No, Sarah was an only child."

"So they had nothing to compare her behavior to."

The men were quiet for several moments.

Dr. Parks wrote something else on his notepad. "I want you to write down all of your reasons and thoughts of guilt and anger. Next time we will talk about them at length, and I have an exercise to help with letting them go."

He turned to a new page in his notebook. "Now, let's talk about the baby. What's the first thing that comes to your mind?"

Kendrick held his face in his hands.

"What if. And relief. Then the guilt and anger comes back."

"Tell me about those things."

"What if. What if the baby had lived? Would I have dropped out of school? Would my mom or grandmas have taken care of the baby so I could go on dates and play sports? Was it a little boy? In my thoughts it's always a boy. What would I have done about college? And that's when the relief hits. Relief that my complete and total screw up didn't affect my life. Relief I was able to keep dating, playing, being with my cousins, going to college."

A deep breath ended with a whispered sob.

"And then I feel so damn guilty. I got a girl pregnant, but it never stopped me from screwing around. I mean, yeah, I was more careful with condoms, but even my baby dying didn't make me stop recreational sex. Not even now. And a poor innocent baby who didn't ask to be brought into the world, didn't ask to have his life cut short in an instant, doesn't get to live because of me."

The doctor looked like he wanted to resist, but he interrupted anyway. "How is the baby's death your fault?"

"If I hadn't been thinking with my dick, we wouldn't have had a baby in the first place."

"So, take some of the blame for the pregnancy, but did you kill Sarah or the baby?"

"No, Doc, you know I didn't."

"And you should know you didn't either." Dr. Parks waved him on after making his point.

"That doesn't change the fact that I got to keep living my

life because my girlfriend killed herself and our baby. Parties, sex, drinking, school, friends, I got it all. How can I want so badly to know my child, but be so relieved that I never had to change? I feel like the lowest lifeform on the planet. And then the anger comes back. Anger at myself, anger at Sarah, anger at the whole situation, even anger at her parents for asking me to hide it, and anger at my parents for letting it stay hidden instead of taking me to get help for it."

Kendrick looked up, surprised at his words.

"I don't think I've ever admitted to being angry with my own parents in all of this. I struggled so much, for so long. Not being able to tell my cousins, or anyone. The pretending, the hiding, it was all too much. I think I wanted my parents to demand I talk about it, but they believed my charade of being *fine*. I laughed, I joked, I moved on. So, I hid my anger and confusion and sadness, but then I would get angrier that my parents didn't see it. Then I feel guilty again for blaming them for not catching on. Damn, Doc, I feel so fucked up."

"It's okay. Everything you're feeling is okay, and normal, and expected." Dr. Parks looked at the clock. "Well, even with the added time, we'll have to call it quits for today. I want to see you back in the next day or two. Don't forget your assignment."

Kendrick left the appointment and headed to work. He really hoped a cousin or two was available for some basketball, he needed to sweat before he settled in to do some work.

BY THE END of the week, he felt like he'd been run over by a steamroller. He'd had a lot to catch up on at work. The two sessions he'd had with Dr. Parks had been mentally and emotionally exhausting. Wanting to let go of the anger and guilt was one thing, actually letting go of them was a completely different thing.

But he knew without a doubt that he wanted to see Jay. He'd made it to the café once that week, but she'd seemed distracted.

Calling her, he thought about movies he knew were playing, she was probably more a comedy or action girl, she didn't seem the romance type. But maybe that's what she needed. Hell, he could be romantic. And dinner? Somewhere off the beaten path, not same old same old. She was the type of girl who appreciated the irregular.

"Hey there, Pixie. How's Italian and a romantic suspense movie sound?" He couldn't help but smile as he spoke.

Silence greeted him on the other end of the phone.

"Jay? You there? Whatdya think? Date night?" Attempting not to sound desperate, he was pretty sure he failed miserably.

"Tonight's just not going to work, Kendrick. Some things have come up. Maybe tomorrow, okay?" He swore he heard tears in her voice.

"You okay, Pixie?"

"Damn it, don't call me that," she said with very little force.

"Sorry, it just fits. But I could always call you Jackie."

"No."

"Jayde?"

"No."

"This one is it, I can feel it. Jaycie."

"No. Listen, Kendrick, I really need to go."

He frowned at the quick retreat, knowing for sure he heard a sob before the call disconnected.

What the hell?

He hadn't planned on spending his Friday evening having a heart-to-heart with his parents, but he figured if he couldn't be with Jay, he might as well complete his weekend home-work assignment from Dr. Parks.

"Beckett! Man, I didn't know you'd be here. Hey, Kenja. How the hell are you guys?" Kendrick's enthusiasm was genuine when he found his older brother and sister-in-law at the table in his parents' kitchen.

"Kendrick. It's so nice to see you." Kenja smiled warmly. The beautiful, petite, Asian woman had been a very quiet, but solid, support at Beckett's side ever since they first met in college.

"I still think it's unfair my 'little' brother is taller than me." Beckett pushed his glasses up his nose.

Kendrick had never thought of his brother as different, but he knew Beckett had overcome a lot including a premature birth and a few other physical challenges. To see Beckett and Kenja, successfully graduated from college and medical school, no one would ever guess the struggles they'd both dealt with in their early years.

When his older sister, Megan, showed up, Kendrick knew it was fate giving him a chance to talk to his whole family at once. He wished she had brought her baby, but her husband had the baby at his own parents' house for the evening.

"Can I talk to you all while we wait on the pizza to get here?" Kendrick rubbed his sweaty hands on his jeans.

Audrey cocked her head to the side, immediately recognizing her son had something important to say.

They all sat in the living room. Kendrick quickly replayed the story of Sarah and the baby for Megan, Beckett, and Kenja. When they'd offered their sincere apologies and support, Kendrick took a deep breath.

"Please know that this isn't meant to hurt anyone. Dr. Parks says I just need to say it if I'm going to let it go."

"I'm pretty sure what you've got to say to us is the same thing we've been dealing with for the past ten years, but go ahead." Audrey's eyes glittered with tears.

"Okay, I'm dealing with a lot of things regarding Sarah and the baby. Guilt and anger are the top contenders. And the anger is pointed in several directions, including at myself, but if I'm being honest, I'm also angry at you guys for letting Sarah's suicide be hidden. Well, not so much that you went along with hiding it, but I'm angry you didn't get me help to deal with it." He took a deep breath, feeling more guilt for making his mom cry. "I guess I just wonder if I could have avoided this fucked up stuff now if I'd gotten through some of it back when it first happened."

Audrey and Jeremiah held hands and stood from the couch to pull Kendrick up into a group hug.

"Baby boy, it's one of our biggest regrets as parents. We are so proud of the three of you, but we know we've messed up on occasion. This is one of those huge parenting screw-ups. We are so very sorry. There's no excuse, we should have automatically gotten you into therapy, but you seemed to handle it so well we assumed you were doing okay. It's not been until the last two or three years when we started putting two and two together and realizing you maybe hadn't dealt with it so well. I wish we'd made a better judgement call. If we'd known about the baby, would we have handled it differently? I don't know." They hugged him again. "Please just know how very sorry we are."

There was nothing they could go back and fix, but just admitting he was angry helped to lift a lot of that anger. He hated seeing his mom and dad blaming themselves, but it felt like the whole discussion allowed everyone to clear some of their guilt and anger.

Later, sitting around the kitchen eating pizza with his family, Kendrick felt a slight bit of peace settle over him for the first time in several months.

"Sorry, Kendrick. I'm not going to be able to get away tonight either." Jay sighed into the phone sounding as if she'd rather be talking to anyone but him.

What the hell? He wanted to question her, find out if their little relationship deal had already died a quick death, ask if she had found someone else. But he didn't want to run the risk of coming across clingy or needy. He needed her to feel like this could work with no strings.

"Damn, Jay, I was really wanting Italian, a movie, and some Pixie lovin'," he attempted a light-hearted smile, even though he felt anything but.

"Call up someone else, I'm sure you've got plenty of girls on speed-dial." Jay sounded tired, irritated, and defeated.

"Well, the speed-dial of Kendrick Jordan *is* pretty legendary, but I only use it when I'm not in a relationship. And even a no-strings attached relationship counts in my mind, so it looks like the only people I may be eating and watching movies with this evening are my cousins if they are available." He pretended to sniff, "But no Pixie lovin'."

"Kendrick, about that...maybe we jumped into this thing

too quickly. I don't do relationships, I don't even know how, and now things could be all kinds of screwed up. Don't feel like you've got any commitment to me."

"No deal, Pixie. I'll give you tonight, but tomorrow I want to see you. Come over any time. Let's talk about what's going on. Doesn't have to be because we're attempting this relationship thing, it can just be because we're friends and you need to talk. Hell, I've done enough talking in therapy this week, the least I can do is listen to what's going on with you. Promise me you'll come over." Kendrick wheedled, amazed at how badly he wanted to see her, be close to her.

"I don't know. It's not really something you can help with, it's my responsibility. And I'm all kinds of fucked up right now."

Kendrick's ears perked up. "Jay, are you okay? You're not having crazy thoughts are you?" *Please don't let her be in a place as dark as Sarah was, I'm not sure I could handle it.*

"No, Kendrick, I'm not suicidal. Maybe it would be better if I was, but I've always felt like suicide was selfish, an easy way out. No, I'll deal with my own screw-up."

When the call ended, Kendrick immediately texted her.

Kendrick: Here's the address, please come over. I'll be here all day.

Jay: We'll see. Thanks, Kendrick. It's nice to know you're there if I need you.

Kendrick: You could thank me by telling me your name. June? Jill? Jolie?

Jay: No. No. No. Although, I do like the name Jolie.

Kendrick: I'll keep guessing.

Jay: I'm sure you will.

8

"Man, toss me a beer from the fridge."

Kendrick looked up from his bent position under the Mustang's hood to see his uncle, Kyle, walking into the garage. Cocking his head at the man, Kendrick wiped his oily hands on a rag and headed toward one of the four mini fridges in the garage. When the four cousins returned to Torey Hope from college, they decided there was no reason at the time to purchase a large fridge, they just stacked the four mini ones in a square shape and kept them stocked with beer, water, pop, and anything else that wouldn't fit in the kitchen refrigerator.

Handing Kyle the beer, and taking one for himself, he waited momentarily. Once they'd both taken a long drink from their bottles, Kendrick cleared his throat.

"So, to what do I owe the honor? I thought no one was coming over until later this evening for weekly dinner."

Running his hands through his stylishly messy dyed hair, Kyle caught his hands together at the top of his head. Hands clasped, elbows raised, head down, he breathed deeply.

"Thought we could talk. About the baby."

"Yeah, I figured as much." Kendrick's whispered words drifted through the garage.

"What's wrong with the car?" Kyle nodded toward the raised hood.

"Nothing. Just changing the oil. I know I can take it to Mikael down at the garage, but I thought I'd do it myself today." Kendrick picked up a wrench and continued what he was doing.

"Here, you get under her, I'll work from the top. We'll get it done quicker that way." Kyle motioned under the car.

Fifteen minutes later, the oil was changed. Draining the rest of their beers, the men wiped the majority of the grime from their hands and arms.

"The oil blends in with all of your ink." Kendrick nodded at the multitude of tattoos on Kyle's arms. The man was a walking canvas.

"Yeah, I could probably get by without washing before coming over for dinner, but I doubt the oil would do much to mask the sweat." Kyle laughed.

"I need to come see you sometime, have you work something up for me. I've always wanted a couple tattoos, but I just can't decide on something meaningful enough to permanently ink my body."

"You'll know when you think of something that's just perfect. Or you may never feel like you've got the right image. Some people get tons of tattoos and they all have a special meaning, or the recipient just liked the image. Others spend their whole life wanting one but just never figure out exactly what they want. Come see me sometime, I can work something up for you. Or you could always join me with the piercings." Kyle wagged his pierced eyebrow at his nephew.

"Nah, ink intrigues me, piercings just seem like too much to care for and too much of a chance at catching on things. Makes me a little nauseated to think of it getting ripped out." Kendrick shuddered.

The men each opened another beer.

Several silent moments later, Kyle spoke.

"My first wife, Izzy, was pregnant when she died."

"In a car accident, right?" Kendrick had heard the story a few times over the years.

"Yeah. We didn't know she was pregnant at the time. I didn't find out until after she was already gone."

"And you guys had been trying to have a baby, right?" Kendrick wondered how much more intense the feelings of losing a baby would be if they'd been trying to conceive.

"For quite a while, yes."

"Do you ever stop wondering about that baby?" The what-ifs were part of what was driving Kendrick insane.

"No, not really. You know the story of how Izzy spoke to Josie and me in the beginning, right? She told me our baby girl's name was Addyson Rose. For some reason, having a name to remember and mourn was helpful for me. Every year, I think about what she'd be doing, the milestones, you know?" Kyle voice was thick with emotion. "When Zoey and Asher were at certain stages, I'd find myself wondering what Addyson would have been like at that stage."

He stopped speaking, either because he was gathering himself, or because he wanted to give Kendrick the chance to speak.

"So, I need to accept I likely will never *be over it*, right?"

"Honestly, I found it was easier to accept Addyson's death after I knew her name and mourned her properly. I'll never forget Izzy or Addyson, they are in my heart forever, but I also have so much to be grateful for because losing them brought me to Josie and, eventually, Zoey and Asher. Instead of clinging to the sadness, I choose to celebrate the time I got to spend with Izzy and cherish the fact that Addyson is with her mother for eternity. And I know I'll see them again one day. But, for now, I want to focus on the present, not lament the past I can't change." Kyle looked at him. "I know it sounds a lot easier than it really is. I'm not saying this can all be done overnight. It's taken me several years to come to grips with the loss of my wife and unborn baby. And there are days when a song or certain eye color or a scent will bring a memory screaming into my head so fast it almost drops me to my knees. But, I have a beautiful family, a job I love, and a bright future. I'll never stop missing them, but I choose to look ahead and not behind."

"I want that, man, I really do. I'm really looking forward to being at a point where I can look forward instead of wallowing in the past." Kendrick finished his beer, setting it to the side. "I feel a little guilty. You lost a woman you loved enough to marry, your soul mate. I lost a high school girl-friend. I mean, I loved her, but a fifteen year old doesn't really know a whole lot about love. Now that I'm older, I find myself wondering what would have come of us, but I don't feel like I lost a soul mate. Losing Sarah the way it happened is what eats at me. And losing the baby, man. I told Dr. Parks, I feel so guilty. It's not like we *wanted* a baby, not like you and Izzy. But, each year as I've gotten older and more mature, I can't help but think about that baby. I'm in a place now where I *could* be a good dad, and it makes me miss that little person I never got the chance to know." Kendrick spoke almost as if he'd forgotten Kyle was there.

"Man, the guilt will eat you alive if you let it. You've got to let it go. Maybe look up some quotes or scriptures or lyrics, I find that's helpful when I'm struggling. And, here's something that I had a hard time coming to terms with. It's not that I'm happier with Josie than I would have been with Izzy, but I look around me and I see my wife, my children, my friends and family. If I'd never met Josie, Zach wouldn't have Zoey, and it hurts my heart to think of those two not together. I can't change the past, even if I wanted to, so I had to finally stop fighting it." Kyle glanced at his watch. "I better get going if I'm going to be cleaned up in time to get back over here for dinner. Seriously, let it go, man, no one blames you, and you shouldn't either. Let me know if you want to work on a tattoo."

Kendrick slammed the hood of his car after his uncle left. Cranking up the music playing through the garage speakers, he tossed a towel on the hood and propped himself up on it.

Jolting from a nap he didn't know he needed, he turned when he heard a voice at the door.

"Damn, if I wasn't already taken, I'd need help wiping the drool from my face. Seriously Kendrick, you could have a whole calendar all to yourself." Katie smiled at him. He felt a special connection to the girl after all the time they'd spent together when his cousin, Decker, was being an ass back when Katie had her own personal stalker.

"Thanks Katie-girl. Maybe I'll get some printed up, sell them at the local bookstore." He joked.

"They'd sell for sure. Sawyer's friend, Adam, would buy in bulk I bet." Katie winked.

Kendrick laughed.

"I came to tell you it's time to get ready for dinner."

"Shit, I didn't mean to fall asleep. I'll take a quick shower and then help with whatever is needed."

"No worries. We are just ordering subs for dinner. Sawyer and Luke are bringing different chips. Zach and Zoey are making crispy rice treats. Each family coming is bringing their drink of choice. Decker and I are going to go pick up the subs. Just didn't want you to sleep too long." She walked across the garage, pulling him into a hug. "I know it's hard, Kendrick. But you're going to get through this and move on. I have faith in you. Love you." Kissing him on the cheek, she left him to gather himself.

"Hey Kendrick, someone's at the door for you!" Asher yelled from the front room where he'd been playing video games with Luke. The family had been enjoying good food and easy conversation for a few hours, just enjoying their time together.

A look of dawning passed over Kendrick's face, and he glanced around at the twenty-something people filling his house. His eyes grew wide.

"Shit, I didn't really think she'd come. I mean, I wanted her to, but I sort of wasn't thinking about this when I invited her. Damn, she's going to think I set her up. Okay, guys, can you all just be cool?" He scurried out of the room, leaving amused smiles plastered on the faces of most of his family. Audrey quirked an eyebrow at Jeremiah, and he winked back. Seeing Kendrick worked up over a girl wasn't a regular occurrence.

Katie's grandmother had come to the get together with Jack and Judy. Never one to hold her tongue, she spoke, "That boy isn't just thinking with the head between his legs. Nope, whether he'd admit it or not, his heart's involved in whoever is standing at that door. I sure hope whoever it is is ready for all that comes with loving someone larger-than-life like Kendrick."

Katie blushed at her grandmother's words, and everyone else laughed.

"I don't think we've ever seen Kendrick worried about a girl. In fact, have we ever been introduced to any of his girls?" Jack smiled as everyone else wondered just who the girl was to have Kendrick so flustered.

When he got to the door, Kendrick immediately noticed Jay looked like shit. Still beautiful, her nose was red and those huge brown eyes were rimmed with red.

"Jay, what's wrong?" He started to reach out a hand, but drew it back when she stiffened.

"I shouldn't have come. I didn't know you had people over." She started to back down the stairs.

"No, Pixie, wait. It's just a casual family dinner. Seriously, it's subs and chips, nothing fancy. Come in and grab a bite, then we can talk." Kendrick motioned her in, fighting the urge to wrap her in his arms.

Noting that Asher and Luke were completely absorbed in their game, he directed her toward the kitchen. "I'd like for you to meet my family, just to say hi, but if you don't want to, you can stay out here, and I'll grab you some food."

"Kendrick, I'm not a complete bitch. I don't want to *meet the family* in a relationship type way, but you're my friend. I'm not going to come over to talk to you, eat your food, and ignore your family. Please, introduce me." Jay rolled her eyes at him, and he felt his heart flip-flop. Knowing how hard this was for her hit him two separate ways. One, he loved that she was willing to meet his family, even just as a friend. Two, he worried just what was going on that was bad enough to have her willing to meet his family just to talk to him.

With a hand hovering at her back, he led her into the kitchen.

"Hey, guys, this is my friend, Jay Keller." Kendrick tried to sound casual, but even to his own ears he heard his voice shaky and breathless.

Kyle murmured, "Excuse me," and turned to leave the room abruptly.

His wife, Josie, and Kendrick's dad, Jeremiah, smiled apologetically at Kendrick, shook Jay's hand, and followed Kyle out the door.

What the hell?

Shaking it off, Kendrick turned Jay toward his mom first. "This is my mom, Audrey. You just met my dad, Jeremiah. The dude with the wild hair and tattoos was my dad's best friend, also known as my uncle Kyle. His wife is my mom's cousin, Josie."

"Hi, Jay, it's nice to meet you. Your hair is fabulous, where do you get it done?" Audrey shook the girl's hand, and sincerely inquired about her hair.

Patting her hair self-consciously, Jay blushed, "Oh thanks, I actually do it myself."

"Really? That's impressive. The cut and color both?"

"Yeah. I may go to school to become a hair stylist some-day. I like messing with cut and color." Jay appeared at ease around his family. He wondered what it would be like intro-ducing her as a girlfriend. Probably freak her the fuck out, he chuckled in his head.

Kendrick pointed the rest of the family out, naming names and relations, knowing it was a lot to take in. He loved that his family was so warm and welcoming. Part of him wanted to think it was because they recognized the broken-ness in Jay like he did, but he knew his family was warm and welcoming to most everybody.

Handing her a plate, Kendrick grabbed one of his own and they filled up with subs, chips, and drinks.

Taking a swig of her water, Jay smiled somewhat sadly, "Of course you'd choose milk."

"Nothing wrong with milk, Pixie."

She rolled her eyes as they headed out to the garage.

On the way out, they passed Kyle, Josie, and Jeremiah coming back.

"Sorry for rushing out like that, Jay."

She smiled genuinely at Kyle. "No worries. Now, if the whole room had cleared out, I would have felt bad."

Kendrick looked askance at his dad, but Jeremiah just shook his head.

"I'll talk to you later tonight, right Kyle?" Kendrick pointedly asked his uncle.

"Sure thing. I'll be here for a while, after that I'll probably be at the studio or home. Come find me." Kyle nodded, silently letting Kendrick know he'd share whatever was going on later.

They made their way to the garage.

"Wow, this is a pretty impressive garage. Do all of these homes have a nice big garage like this one?" She took a seat at the table against the open wall. Biting into her sandwich, she waited for him to answer.

"No, we definitely lucked out with this one. We park in the parking at the front, but when we need to work on the cars or have a place to escape to, we come out here. It works out well." Kendrick had already eaten a sub before she arrived, but he was worried she wouldn't eat if he didn't, so he chomped into another.

They ate in comfortable but anxious silence. He really hadn't expected her to show up when he asked her to come over. Between the two nights of canceling on him, and showing up today, he had a feeling something bad was going on.

"Jamilyn?"

She smirked, shaking her head. "No."

"Jodie?"

"Nope."

"Judith? Jillian? Jason?"

"No, no, and *really*? Jason?" She giggled.

"Well, there are some girls with boy names. Maybe that's the angle I need to take."

"Josh? Jimmy? Julian?"

She just rolled her eyes. "No, now give it up. You won't guess it. No one has ever guessed it. Aside from my parents, some other people who also don't matter, and my grandma, no one has ever known my real name. It's not a big deal. I like Jay better, so there's no need to tell. But your guesses have been entertaining to say the least."

"So, your parents and some others didn't matter? Sounds like a story, Pixie." Kendrick pressed his luck.

"It's a long, ugly story. One I have no reason or wish to relive, so I don't tell it. Ever." Jay answered firmly.

Well, okay then.

They sat silently for a few moments as she chomped on the last of her chips.

"So, Pixie, I'd love to think you just couldn't be away from me any longer, but since I sincerely doubt that's true, as much as that bruises my ego, what brings you by?"

"I didn't come here to ruin your night, drag you into something that likely isn't your problem, or hurt you." She spoke mechanically.

"Seeing you at my door tonight guaranteed my night wouldn't be ruined. If you have a problem, I'm happy to make it mine if it helps you out. And unless you tell me this is completely over, I don't think you'll hurt me." He reached for her hand, gripping firmly when she tried to pull away. "Just let me. Talk to me, Jay."

Taking a deep breath, she whispered, "I'm pregnant."

9

*T*wo words rocked his world.

He stared at her for what seemed like eternity, but his brain snapped into gear quickly when he realized his reaction was important.

"Okay. So let's work this out." He wasn't really sure what the hell he was saying.

"I feel like a complete slut saying this, but I doubt it's yours, so you don't have to worry." Tears glistened in her eyes.

"Tony?" Hot jealousy clinched his gut.

"Maybe. There was another guy right before you."

"So, do you want to figure out who the father is?" Even as he spoke, he knew deep in his heart he wanted the baby to be his. And if it wasn't, he would claim it as his in a heartbeat.

"There's no need to figure it out. I can't keep it."

His head spun, the remnants of dinner threatened to reappear.

"What do you mean *can't keep it*? Adoption?" He tried not to let his voice shake.

"No, I mean termination. I'm not mother material. I can't carry this baby to term. Hell, I don't even know who the father is. I can't bring a child into this."

He walked to the fridge to get a beer. Swigging it down, he worked hard to gather his thoughts.

"Can you give me some of your time?" He asked pleadingly.

"Time for what? You don't have to do anything here, Kendrick. I just wasn't sure who to talk to. I almost went to the clinic yesterday, but you called and I changed my mind. I'm not even sure why I came here tonight."

"You came here tonight because you needed someone to talk to, you needed a friend, and you need to hear what I have to say." Kendrick sat facing her, knees touching hers, and grasped her hands.

"I know this is your body, your decision, but will you listen to my story before making a final decision?" He wanted so badly to lean in and kiss her at that moment, but he held himself back.

"Sure, Kendrick. Tell me your story."

"When I was fifteen, my girlfriend committed suicide."

Before he could continue, Jay reached a hand out to

stroke his cheek. "I'm sorry, Kendrick. That had to be so hard."

"It was, but the hardest part is she was pregnant. I didn't know. I'm not sure if she knew or not. For the past ten years, I've fallen deeper and deeper into depression wondering about the baby that was taken away from me. I didn't want to be a teen father, but the older I get I can't help but imagine what being a dad would be like." He lifted desperate eyes to her.

"What are you saying, Kendrick?" She pushed back from him. "You expect me to believe you want to be a father to this baby? A baby that is likely not even yours? Be a father to a baby born to a mother as fucked up as I am? A girl you've known for a very short time, and mostly just for sex?" She shook her head bitterly, "I don't buy it, Kendrick."

"Stop. Not another word. Whether this baby is biologically mine or not, I would raise it as mine, with you, because it feels like I'm being given a chance at something that was stolen from me ten years ago. And, Pixie, you're not fucked up. We all have a past, heaven knows I do. And what we have isn't *just sex*. Yes, we've had a lot of fun in that department, but I think I started falling for you the first moment I laid eyes on you in that bar."

He pulled her chair back towards his so their knees met again. Leaning into her, he rested his forehead on hers.

"Jay, I'm serious as hell about this. Please, at least carry the baby to term. You can decide then if you don't want to keep it. But don't end something before it's even had time to begin."

Tears poured from her eyes.

"I'm not fit to be a mother, Kendrick. I don't have a warm, loving family like you. I came from nothing, and I basically have nothing. A baby doesn't deserve that."

"You are a beautiful person inside and out. You hide yourself behind the sex and detachment, but I've seen you take care of people at the café. You are kind, warm, and have a caring touch. You fuss over the elderly folks, you make the kids laugh, and your eyes are drawn to the tiny babies. Don't tell me you're not fit to be a mother. Fuck that shit."

No words were spoken for several moments, the silence building between them.

"What if it's Tony's?"

"I'll respect that, but I'll still want to be a part of your life and the baby's. I don't see Tony wanting to get married, unless you suddenly morph into a man, and I don't think you'd ask him to settle down with you for the baby." Kendrick caught her tiny grin when he mentioned Tony's sexual preference being much more toward the male persuasion.

"I'd never ask him to do that, just like I'd never expect it of you."

"What if it's not mine or Tony's? Is the other guy in the picture?" Kendrick fought against gritting his teeth against the jealousy.

"No, he's not in the picture, and I wouldn't want him to be."

"So, give this a chance. You can move in here, or I'll move in with you. We can get to know each other, even if it's not romantically, we should work on our friendship before the baby arrives." Kendrick spoke, realizing he'd never been so serious about something in his life.

"You're serious aren't you?" She shook her head in awe. "What if the baby is born and I want to give it up for adoption? Would you fight me?"

"If it's mine, I'd keep it. If it's not mine, I'd petition to adopt. But, I want to believe you won't want to give it up once you come to terms with this and see your baby for the first time." He rubbed her thumb with his. "Whatdya say, Pixie? Please? Let me do this; let's do this *together*. I feel like today has lifted a weight from me and offered me a second chance. I want this. I want you, the baby, us, I want it all. Please?"

He knew he was begging, but he didn't care.

"You want to take all of this on even when you know the likelihood of anything romantic or serious happening between us practically zero?"

"I'll take my chances, Pixie." He kissed her cheek.

"Fine, I won't terminate the pregnancy. But I can't promise you anything about adoption. I need you to know, keep it in mind the whole time that I will likely give the baby away. I don't want a child to have to grow up like I did."

"And how is that?" He pushed.

"Nice try. It's not open for discussion."

"I want to take this to the next step. My place or yours?" Kendrick's face felt hot with excitement.

"Can you give me the week? This is a lot to take in." She walked to him, tipping her head up. "And, Kendrick, I need you to guard your heart. I'm not made for love. I never really experienced it, and I don't have it to give. Please don't get your heart set on there being an *us*. We can be friends, even friends with great benefits; we can attempt to be parental partners, but a romantic relationship isn't in the cards for me."

Her eyes looked so solemn and sad, he knew she believed every word she spoke.

"I'm a big boy. I'll keep my heart safe." He tweaked her nose, "Hey, I need to update those parameters we set earlier."

"Yeah?"

"Oh, yeah. That part about bringing in a third? Hell to the no. No thirds, male or female. It's you and me. Only." He immediately reached down and gently touched her stomach. "And this little one, but I doubt she'll care to share too much right now."

"She?"

"Yep, our own little pixie."

Swallowing tears, she smiled at him. "I need to go, Kendrick. I'll talk to you through the week. We can visit the living situation next weekend."

Watching her car pull away, he looked to the sky. Stars

winked down at him. His chest filled with a feeling he'd not experienced for a while. *Hope.*

Turning and walking into the house, he knew his entire family would still be there, waiting on him to return.

"MAN, I'm so sorry I bailed like that." Kyle ran a hand over his face.

"What happened?" Kendrick really wasn't upset, just curious.

"Have you ever seen a picture of Izzy?" Kyle asked.

"No."

"Here, I've got a picture of the three of us from high school." Jeremiah pulled out his wallet and produced a faded snapshot of the three friends.

"Oh wow, the similarity is eerie, huh?" Kendrick could see how seeing Jay for the first time would knock his uncle off kilter. Jay was almost a perfect replica of Izzy.

"Yeah, I was just shook up, thrown for a loop a bit when I saw her. It's almost like Izzy has her hand in things again." Kyle smirked slightly.

As Jeremiah put the picture back in his wallet, Kendrick continued, "Well, here's one to really throw you for a loop."

When all eyes turned toward him, he swallowed before speaking.

"She's pregnant."

It was almost comical to watch the dropped jaws and bugged eyes.

"And it's yours?" Decker spoke.

"Not sure. Probably not."

"So what's the plan? Are you two serious? How are you feeling?" Audrey reached out to pull him into a hug.

"Honestly, I feel like I'm getting a second chance. Whether it's mine or not, I want that baby, and I want Jay."

At the raised eyebrows, he proceeded to tell them much of the conversation he and Jay had had in the garage.

At the end, he knew many had reservations and doubts.

"Guys, I know it may not be the perfect situation, but today is the first day I've felt the weight lift from my chest in a very long time. I need this. I need her. Can you stand by me? By us?"

"As long as you keep up with your therapy, and as long as she doesn't hurt you, I'm willing to stand by you." Audrey spoke to him, giving the eyeball to the rest of the family encouraging them to do the same.

"I worry about what happens when the baby is born. What if she gives it up? You'll be heartbroken." His aunt, Libby, voiced her concern. "But, I'll support you in every way I can. We all will."

By the time the group had broken up, Kendrick felt like he was walking on cloud nine, but he also had a nervous feeling building in his stomach. Was he doing the right thing?

Had he thought this through? Would he end up hurt worse than he already had been?

Drifting to sleep that night, he felt a peace and knew he'd made the right choice. Day-by-day, they'd take it slowly. He slept with no nightmares for the first time in several months.

10

The week went smoothly, although Kendrick was on edge. He saw Jay at lunch a couple days during the week, but she didn't have time to talk. He wondered how long she'd be able to work the busy lunch rushes as the pregnancy went on. Her inability, or was it an unwillingness, to talk worried him day-to-day. Was she changing her mind? He knew she needed room and time to take it all in, but he wanted her to know he was completely sure about it all.

Therapy with Dr. Parks had been different. Kendrick had told the doctor about his and Jay's relationship, the pregnancy, his desire to keep the baby.

The doctor was quiet for a long time as he scribbled his notes.

Looking up at Kendrick, he cocked his head to the side and studied his patient.

"How far have you thought this through, Kendrick?"

Kendrick started to speak, but stopped. How far *had* he actually thought this through?

"Let me ask something else, and please know I'm not attempting to change your mind, I'm just trying to get into your head."

Kendrick smiled at the doctor wanly, "You sure you want to do that, Doc? It's sort of a mess in there."

"That's what I'm here for, to help straighten up that mess."

"And you think this whole baby scenario is going to cause more of a mess?" Kendrick sighed.

"Not necessarily. Let's just talk about it." Dr. Parks shifted in his seat before continuing. "Feeding the baby every two to three hours, diapers, fevers, crying all through the night. Babysitters, school, book fees, new clothes, day-to-day necessities. Mouthy teen, dating, sex talks, drug talks, growing up, saving for college."

The doctor paused in his list and studied Kendrick.

"What do you feel when I mention just some of what raising a child entails?"

"Excited, nervous, challenged, grateful to be given a second chance." Kendrick spoke definitively.

"Not a lot of men your age would feel the same. You've not been home from college long, you have a whole world ahead of you. And you want to take on the addition of a partner and a child? Because even if you and Jay don't end up in a romantic relationship, you're going to have to be in a good place to raise a child together." Dr. Parks waited for Kendrick to think through his answer.

"I know there's a chance Jay and I won't work out. I know there's a chance she won't want to keep the baby. But there's also a chance I will end up in love with a beautiful woman, sharing a life with her while we raise a child together. I've lived the partying, the screwing around, the not-a-care-in-the-world life, Doc. I have a solid, loving, supportive family, a great job, a bright future; I want to build that future with Jay and this baby. You're right, a lot of guys my age would shirk this responsibility even if the baby was definitely theirs. But I'm not most guys. My cousins and I were raised to love, support, and care for our family, friends, and others. We know how to face tough situations, and we know we're blessed to be able to live this way. I want this, Doc."

Dr. Parks was quiet for a very long time. As Kendrick began to squirm, the man finally spoke.

"Then we'll incorporate Jay and the baby into the things we work on weekly. If you'd ever like Jay to join in our sessions, just say the word, she's always welcome." He stopped speaking and jotted a note. "For the record, I think this will be good for you. Not easy, but good. It's a challenge, it's a second chance in a way, and I think it will help you move on from the losses in your past. My only concern is that it could lead to more loss in ways you can't predict or control. But, like everything in life, there's no use in fearing the unknown, we'll deal with it if it happens."

Kendrick left the therapist's office feeling buoyed knowing he had his family and his doctor on his side. If he could just get Jay more sure of things, he'd be feeling great.

ONE AFTERNOON, Kendrick popped in long after the lunch rush at The Café. He waved and winked at Jay's boss, grabbed them both a milk and slice of pie to share, and ushered Jay to a shielded booth.

"Wow, you just think you own the place now, huh?" Jay smirked and jabbed the pie with her fork.

"What? Barry is a good guy; he knows you need a break; he doesn't care if I grab a couple things. It's not like a bunch of people were here to watch me break the rules." Kendrick sat beside her and tweaked her nose.

They ate the pie and drank the icy milk. Then silence fell over the booth.

"Kendrick, I'm really not sure I can do this."

"This?"

"This. You, me, the baby, all of it."

His heart dropped in his chest.

"Talk to me, tell me what you're feeling." Kendrick held her hand.

"Do I want to be pregnant? Do I want to raise a child?" She shifted in the seat and looked directly at him. "Beyond that, do I want to live with you? I seriously doubt you and I would have moved past a few more quick fucks if this baby hadn't come into the picture. I feel so very conflicted. It's like my body, heart, mind are in this constant struggle. Part of me wants to run far, far away. But there's a little inkling of me, probably the part being ravaged by these damn hormones, that wants to lean on you, give us a chance, see where it all goes."

His heart soared again.

"Cling to that inkling. That inkling is likely the real you speaking. The other stuff is all fear of the unknown. It's okay to be afraid, but we can't let it rule us. Please, Pixie, let's be scared together and see where this all goes." He held both her hands in his larger one.

"I don't know. It's not like we're trying to see if we can raise a dog. We're talking about another human being. A real live person who will be dependent on us for eighteen years. I don't know that I'm made of what it takes to have people dependent on me."

"Okay, here's the deal. Let's take it one day at a time. Let's not think of all the things we know will be heading our way. We'll break it up into smaller segments. Get through the pregnancy first. Period. Then we'll work on getting through her first week, month, year. By that time I plan on you being madly in love with me and there won't be anything we can't conquer."

She looked at him with incredulous eyes. Whispering, she said, "Okay. One day at a time."

"KENDRICK, I'm glad you're so sure of yourself and us and the future, but you're moving like a speed boat thundering down the river. I need time. Time to accept what's going on with my body, time to accept the changes that are coming, time to accept that my plans have been crushed." Jay sat at her kitchen table, hot mug of tea in front of her, legs drawn up as if protecting herself.

Kendrick sat across from her, wanting to reach out and grab her hands, but knowing she had to work through a lot, and he needed to slow down. It seemed every time he got her convinced of the plan, she would go home and let her fears talk her out of it.

"Listen to me, Pixie." He stopped long enough to take a sip of the strong Irish Breakfast tea she'd brewed for him. "I know I can't sympathize or even empathize with the changes your body and mind will have to deal with due to the pregnancy. I do know that I have two grandmas, four aunts, and a sister who have been through it and will be great supports for you, along with Dr. Parks and the talk therapy Zoey is resurrecting down at The Center+. I know changes are coming, but changes are always coming. We can't stop life, we can't even slow it down. I'd rather we face those changes together. Let me hold you as we meet the changes and challenges head on; you don't have to do it by yourself. As far your plans being crushed, you can't tell me that you've not dreamed at least once or twice in your life of falling in love and having a baby with the man you love. I don't know what shit you've got in your past to have you so jaded against love, but I can see your heart, and I know deep down you have that dream." Kendrick stopped, knowing he was pushing her, but wanting to get a reaction from her.

She stood abruptly, stalking across the kitchen to place her mug in the sink with a heavy thud. "I don't love you." Her voice was barely a whisper, and it sounded like a very weak argument to Kendrick's ears.

Turning suddenly, she walked towards him with fire in her eyes. Standing defiantly in front of him, she jabbed his chest with a dainty finger.

"Fine, yes, that's what I want. I want it all. The cute little house, white picket fence, adoring husband, two kids, and a dog. But it would take a miracle of fairy tale proportions to make that happen, so I don't even let myself wish for it. I don't have the happy family like you. You're so very lucky. I deal with the shit life dealt me and try to make the best of it.

But wishing for things I can't have is pointless." Her voice caught on the last words.

Shifting to open his legs, he pulled her effortlessly into his body. With his hands resting gently on her waist, he rested his forehead against her chest. As if drawing strength from her, he breathed deeply and sat silently for several moments. When her arms came up to wrap around his shoulders, he looked up at her.

"Let me in, let me help you forget your past. We can have that dream, the house, the kids, the dog. It may not happen right away, there will be twists and turns, ups and downs, but that's life, Pixie. I just want that life with you. Maybe we don't have mad, passionate love between us right now, but it can grow. I like you, like spending time with you, care about your well-being, want you as part of my life, that's a good start." He knew his feelings for her were likely much stronger than hers for him at that point. But he got the feeling hers were a lot stronger than she wanted to admit.

She scoffed, "Right, I'm supposed to believe you're all of a sudden falling for some girl you met in a bar and had a three-some with? Your past sexcapades are just over?"

"Whether you want to accept it or not, I've been falling for you since the first time I saw you. It threw me for a loop, I've never reacted to a girl like this before. You're different, you're beautiful, you challenge me, you have a heart of solid gold even if you don't like to admit it. I agreed to your *no strings* deal only to stay close to you. I figured I could bide my time, charm you, let you see how good we are together. I hoped you'd fall for me the same as I had for you. Now, I'll be honest, I didn't plan on the baby thing, but you know what I think? Bring it."

She laughed through the tears threatening to fall.

"Seriously, *bring it?*"

Kendrick's thumbs brushed the tears from her cheeks. "Yes, *bring it.* Life is full of challenges. I, for one, think you and I were ready for this challenge even if we never would have asked for it. You were content to just be. Detached sex, decent job, just rolling along letting life happen. I was running from the past, hiding, refusing to deal with it. I'm ready to move on I'm ready for a distraction. I'm ready for this."

"So this baby and I are just a distraction to you? What happens when you get tired of your shiny new baby? You just pack up and leave? What happens when I don't fit into your mold of the perfect mom? You grew up with all of these perfect women, how am I supposed to compete with that?" By the end of her little outburst, angry, fearful tears poured down her heated cheeks. "I'm sorry, I don't know why I'm acting like this. You're being so wonderful, and I'm lashing out like a total bitch. I feel like a yo-yo the way I'm going up and down, back and forth. One second I think this is a great idea, I want to do this with you. I picture our sweet life together with a beautiful baby. Then I feel like my heart and soul are being ripped out, I should save this baby and save you from the hell we could all be facing."

"Pixie, stop." He moved her to the couch, pulling her down on his lap. "One, I think you've got some massive hormones going on here. We need to get some of those pregnancy books so we can read them to know what to expect. Two, I didn't mean you and the baby were just distractions. I meant I'm happy to have something take my mind off the suffocating blackness of guilt and anger; having you and the baby to focus on gives me light, gives me hope. And, yes, my family is great, but we are so far from perfect. Many of my family members have either screwed up royally or overcome some really bad shit. No one is perfect, but I think you'd be in awe to hear about all the bad we've overcome."

Jay snuggled into his chest. "Tell me about them."

"My Aunt Carly lived a nightmare, but she's strong and she fought through it so she could later meet my Uncle Nicky. You've met Nicky, you know he has a lot of issues. He's dealt with challenges since birth, but he's one of the most resilient, sincere, perceptive men I've ever met. He doesn't let the negativity he experiences get him down. My Uncle Nate was a lot like me, sleeping around, no strings, real slut if you want to know the truth. Until he met Aunt Libby. Aunt Josie had a horrible upbringing, in fact, I bet she'd be a good one to confide in about your childhood. She lived through a disastrous marriage and made it here to Torey Hope. It was fate because Uncle Kyle had also just come to

Torey Hope to escape a haunting past of losing a wife and baby. My own mom is probably one of the most screwed up. You likely wouldn't believe all the crap she did to Aunt Libby and Uncle Nate even if I told you, but she also had a terrible past to overcome, and look at her now, she's amazing. Katie had a stalker. Zoey was attacked by a mentally ill man who had been stalking her. Luke was abused severely while growing up and lost his mom, his one true support. Sawyer survived a pretty brutal attack because of his sexuality. My sister, Megan, got pregnant before she was married. One of the things I wish most is that she and her baby and husband would move back here to Torey Hope. My brother, Beckett, had a lot of the same type of challenges to overcome as my Uncle Nicky. And Kenja, Beckett's wife, also escaped a hideous past before meeting Beckett."

He paused and lifted her chin. "So you see, you couldn't ask for a better family to be a part of. We aren't perfect, but we *are* a *perfect mess* of mistakes and haunting pasts, but we mix that with our ability to keep an open mind, love and support those we love and care about, and cherish the blessings we've been given. There is nothing more important to me than my family, I would never do anything to purposely hurt them or risk losing them. I want you to be a part of that family, you and the baby."

"I think I'd like that. I don't know how to be part of a family. I can't promise I won't screw it up, but I want to do this. Just be patient with me." Her body relaxed into his.

His heart soared, threatening to beat out of his chest.

"Well, I *do* know how to be part of a family, and I still can't promise I won't screw it up. I'll be patient with you if you can be patient with me. We'll have to learn about each other, learn to live together, learn all about what a baby is going to bring to us." Kendrick dotted kisses along her jaw. "Does this mean giving up the baby is off the table?" *Please let it be off the table.*

"I don't want to take the option away completely, but I can say it's not one of my top options right now." Jay moved her head so his kisses could travel down her neck. He did chuckle slightly to himself how up and down she was. Hormones must be a very strange and powerful thing. He'd have to remember to yield to the hormones, and maybe talk to the older guys who had lived through pregnancies.

"What are your top options right now?" His breath whispered against her ear.

"Mmm, probably better let Tony know there's a chance the baby is his, let him decide how he wants to handle things. Get some books, set up a doctor appointment, get to know your family better..." She moved to straddle his lap. "And find out if pregnant sex is truly all that much better."

He gripped her hips, "Oh yeah? What is this pregnant sex you speak of? Better? Holy hell, I may die if it gets any better."

"Well then, let's test the theory. You know the way to the

bedroom." Jay laughed as he stood and scooped her up, quickly making his way to her room.

Laying her gently on the bed, Kendrick stood back and watched her momentarily. He made quick work of his own clothes, then slowly removed the tiny camisole top and barely there shorts she'd been wearing. Joining her on the bed, he traced a finger lightly on her skin.

"So, what's something that's supposed to be different with pregnant sex?"

"Well, I think the fact that I want to jump you every time I see you is one of the main differences."

"That sounds promising." He leaned in, feathering hot little kisses on her mouth. "Wait, does that mean you didn't want to jump me every time you saw me *before* you were pregnant? I think I'm offended." He smiled at her.

"Oh, no, I think I always wanted to jump you, it's just much more intense now."

When his finger traced lightly over her chest, her breath caught.

"And that." Her voice was breathless.

"That? What?" He smirked as he trailed his finger around a nipple.

"Certain areas being more sensitive to touch." She arched her back, whimpering.

"So, if I were to do this," he lowered his mouth, taking her in.

"Oh, yeah, if you were to do that I'd probably almost jump out of my skin." She held his head close to her chest.

"Mmmm, I wonder if other sensitive places are extra receptive these days?" He let his tongue travel slowly down her body until he reached the spot he had in mind. When her body almost came off the bed, he chuckled, "Yeah, I'd say *everything* is more sensitive. This should be fun."

Several moments later, Jay had barely come down from orgasm number two when he knelt between her legs. Reaching for a condom, he paused. Their eyes met.

"I got tested last month. All clear." Kendrick spoke softly.

"I was tested right after Tony left. All clear for me too." Jay's huge brown eyes were heated and longing.

"Well, since I can't get you pregnant, I guess we can go without. If you're okay with that." Kendrick moved to nestle himself between her legs.

She strained, trying to meet him.

Taking her head in his hands, he forced her eyes to look into his. "Before we do this, I need to know this is only us. No one else invited in, no one on the side, just us, Jay."

At her teary-eyed nod, he took her mouth slowly, gently before sliding his length deep.

Pausing to let her adjust and to catch his breath himself, he rested his forehead on hers.

"Oh, God, has it ever felt this good? I've never gone without a condom since the whole Sarah thing. Damn, it's so good."

She whimpered when he started to move. Slowly, forcefully, he took her to the stars before she crashed and shattered around him.

By the time they both came back to the ground, he could only laugh softly in her ear. "Yeah, I vote for more pregnant sex. Lots more."

"I think I can make that happen." She smiled, kissing him soundly.

Moving in with Jay went smoothly. Kendrick's family helped him move a couple things, but he was mostly going to use Jay's things due to the small size of her place.

They immediately started talking about plans for the little spare room to be the nursery. It was too early to start on it, but they had ideas for when the time was closer.

Kendrick continued his lunches at The Café and they set up weekly date nights.

"Once a week, no matter what, I want us to go out on a date. The other nights we can veg out and watch movies in our pajamas, but once a week we hit the town for dinner, dancing, a movie, something. I also want to set up a standing cousin night so you can get to know the guys and their partners. And, of course, there's the weekly family dinner." He leaned in to kiss her, "Is that all going to be too much at once?"

"I'm used to juggling multiple orders at The Café, I think I can handle it. But, I promise to let you know if it's too much."

Holding Jay in bed quickly became one of his favorite pastimes. One night, after a fun evening with his cousins, he rested his chin on top of her head, rubbing a hand softly up and down her back. "You don't ever have to share, but I'm here if you ever want to tell me about your past, you know that, right?"

Sighing deeply, she nodded. "I know you'll listen, it's just ugly and it makes me feel bad. Maybe someday."

Kissing her temple he prodded, "And maybe someday you'll tell me your real name? You know, since I'm like the live-in baby daddy now?"

She laughed. "Maybe. If you're lucky."

"Mmmm, I'm thinking I'm very lucky." Cupping her breast, he caressed the nipple knowing it would set her on fire.

Jay rolled over, pushing him to his back, and straddled him, "You're about to get even luckier."

Kendrick spent the next hour wondering if he'd died and gone to heaven.

11

"*I*'m going to pee while you get the popcorn." Jay gestured toward the restroom.

Kendrick watched her cute little butt walk away, smiling to himself while he waited his turn to order her popcorn with extra butter. He really wanted a large glass of cold milk, but he'd settle for the caffeine-free cola Jay needed to stick to for the sake of the baby. He'd learned caffeine was a no-no during pregnancy. The day after he read that in the pregnancy book he'd gone out and bought four types of decaf tea bags so Jay could still enjoy her hot tea.

He had also thrown out all the processed lunchmeat in her fridge, and called the grandmas and moms to make sure they all knew Jay couldn't have processed lunchmeats if they planned subs for weekly dinners anytime in the next nine months. During his tea buying spree, he also stocked up on three types of ice cream. So far, he'd been the only one to break into the frozen treat.

"I thought you were supposed to be throwing up sick in the mornings and craving ice cream at night." Kendrick asked one evening around a mouthful of rocky road.

"Maybe I'll get lucky and not get morning sickness. Although, I caught a whiff of eggs at work today and got a little nauseated. As far as cravings, nothing really sounds delicious right now. But, if you keep eating ice cream like that you're going to gain as much pregnancy weight as me if not more." She'd laughed at him as he popped one more bite into his mouth and sulkily returned the carton to the freezer.

Jay was wary of the pregnancy books they'd bought. She wanted to make sure she was doing the right thing for the baby, but a lot of the information weirded her out. Kendrick on the other hand was fascinated by the facts, graphs, time-lines, and photos.

"Whoa! Check out those ti...ahem, breasts," he'd exclaimed while thumbing through a full-color book one evening. "Damn, those are like porn star boobs."

Rolling her eyes, Jay had lifted her shirt, exposing her bare chest. "You're a nut, you know that? I hope you don't think *mine* will do that. Her boobs were likely three times the size of mine *before* she got pregnant. Mine will likely get fuller, but they aren't going to grow to the size of my head."

She had knocked the book out of his hands, straddled

him, and leaned in to kiss him. "I just don't want you to get your hopes up and then be disappointed."

"Noted." His hands had automatically claimed her small, perfect breasts as his mouth had trailed hot kisses along her jaw. "Is this one of those *I wanna jump you* moments where I feel like the luckiest guy in the world?"

"Yes, yes it is." Jay had giggled against his mouth.

LOST IN THOUGHT, he jerked in surprise when hands came around his eyes while he waited in line.

"Guess who!" A high-pitched voice echoed in his ears as a cloying scent enveloped him. He recognized the sickeningly sweet perfume, but couldn't place which former fling it belonged to.

"I give up." He reached up to remove the hands and turned to find a tall, buxom brunette standing next to him with a seductive smile. *Shit, what's her name? Brandy? Amberly? Madison?*

"Hey, baby, long time no see. Are you here by yourself? I could be convinced to ditch my friends and join you for the evening if you're interested." The girl ran a finger down his arm.

Damn, he still couldn't remember her name.

"Nah, I'm actually here with someone." Should he add in

a *good to see you?* It really wasn't, but should he try to be polite?

The decision was made for him when the brunette's eyes narrowed cattily.

He felt Jay next to him before he saw her. Turning, he wrapped an arm around her.

"Ah, here she is. We were just grabbing our popcorn before the movie starts. We better move up so we don't lose our place." He desperately wanted the girl to get the hint and leave.

"I've got a few minutes. I'd love to catch up on what you've been doing. I didn't even know you were back in town. I thought you would have given Brandy a call." She pouted her lip out.

Brandy. Yeah, that was it.

As Brandy flipped her hair, a gush of perfumed air blasted his face.

A slight moan slipped from Jay as she ran back towards the restroom.

"Who *is* that Kendrick? Are you offering pity dates these days? That girl is totally not your type." Brandy sidled up beside him. The girl practically straddled his leg as he waited his turn.

Ignore her, ignore her, ignore her. His main thought was getting Jay her popcorn and making sure she was okay.

Paying for the large popcorn and caffeine-free drink, he maneuvered his purchases to the butter station. He pulled out his own brown paper bag, poured half the popcorn into it, drenched both bags with butter, tossed them around, then mixed them back together. Kendrick was nothing if not proficient with buttery popcorn.

"Seriously, Kendrick, is she your girlfriend? I never thought I'd see you slumming it like this." Like a damn dog in heat, Brandy had yet to take a clue.

"You know what, Brandy, I've been in town since graduating from college. The fact that I've *not* contacted you should let you know that we had nothing worth contacting you about. Jay is my girlfriend, my friend, my partner, and she's beautiful inside and out. She doesn't have a judgmental bone in her body, she's special, and she's worth my time." He turned from her quickly, not wanting to be any ruder than he'd already been.

Brandy's gasp behind him was secondary to Jay's look of surprise directly in front of him.

Those big doe eyes looked at him softly, curiously. She silently took the drink from him. Turning without a word, she led the way into the theater.

Picking the corner seat in the last row, Jay settled against the wall. Once the drink and popcorn were positioned, she turned her face to him.

Biting her lip, her face shadowed in the darkened theater, she bit back a smile.

"So, your girlfriend, huh?"

Damn, he didn't realize she'd been behind him that long.

"Yeah, I mean, well...if you're okay with it. If not, that's okay, she can think you're my girlfriend."

"I don't know. Part of me wants to be totally okay with it, but the part of me that wants to be fair to you says I should call an end to this farce and let you go back to dating the types of girls you like. She's obviously much more your type than I am. I feel bad that I'm limiting your social life with baggage that's likely not even your responsibility." She ducked her head, "But selfishly, I want to be your girlfriend. I've never been that before. It must be these damn hormones, but I want that so damn badly."

"First, yes, I had a type before I met you, but I obviously wasn't doing a great job with that type because none of them knocked me off my feet the way you did. Second, you're not forcing any baggage on me or limiting my anything; biologically mine or not, this baby is *mine* just like you are." He leaned in to kiss her, "Third, I think I love these hormones because they make you a bit sappy. I want you to be my girlfriend so badly too." He kissed her again, "Fourth, where did you run off to?"

"Ugh, I think my morning sickness decided to pop up as evening sickness when I got a whiff of her perfume. I truly thought I was going to upchuck on her designer boots." Jay cringed.

"I don't like that you felt sick, but I would have laughed to see you vomit all over those damn boots. Who wears that to a movie theater? She looked like a hooker." Kendrick shook his head.

"You used to like that look. Now you're stuck with me in my vast and varied wardrobe choices, chopped, messy, colorful hair, and standoffish attitude. You sure you're making the right choice?" Jay looked up, sincerely questioning him.

"Never more sure of anything in my life." Sealing his decision with a kiss, he waved the bag of popcorn in front of her. "Still feeling sick, or does popcorn sound good?"

"Do you drink milk every chance you get?"

Confused, Kendrick answered, "Yeah..."

"Well then, there's your answer. *Of course* popcorn sounds good." She dug her hand into the bag and removed a large handful of buttery kernels.

They'd eaten their fill by the time the previews ended. Kendrick moved the drink to her right, lifted the arm rest between them, and pulled her close to him as the lights dimmed.

He'd never enjoyed a movie more than the ones he watched with Jay tucked under his arm.

THERAPY WAS GOING WELL. He hadn't been able to completely erase the guilt, anger, hurt, and confusion, but he was making great strides. Having the baby, Jay, and work to concentrate on was helping too. Kyle had proved invaluable in helping him through the hard parts; the two men spent many an evening in the garage or at Kyle's tattoo shop, beers in hand, just talking.

"Gotta tell you, man, if I didn't know Izzy had no family other than her parents, I would seriously wonder if Jay was a long-lost relative. Izzy was always a force to be reckoned with when she was alive. After she died, she didn't let up on Josie and me until we were together. Having Jay look so freakin' much like Izzy leads me to believe it's in the cards or fate or whatever you want to call it. I'm not saying it's going to be easy, but there's no way Jay can look so much like Izzy and it not be *right*." Kyle had mused one day while they talked.

"Izzy did a great job getting you and Josie together, so I think I'd be lucky if she was leading Jay and me together."

"Izzy was a spitfire. As much as I'm a black sheep and march to the beat of a different drummer, Izzy was even more so. My parents encouraged me to be myself, Izzy's parents did *not*. Maybe that's why she stuck out more than me, I don't know. But if Izzy decided she wanted something to happen, she didn't let up until she got her way."

"It's funny, I've never looked at you as a *black sheep* in the family. Maybe because we all have our own personalities and we've always been encouraged to be ourselves, but you've never stuck out as different to me." Kendrick commented.

"Really? Pierced all over, ink covering over half my body,

different hair color each week, none of that made me stand out to you?" Kyle laughed.

"Nah, you were just always Uncle Kyle. You are who you are. No one ever made a big deal of the differences, so I never thought about them. Besides, you're pretty kick-ass, we used your name to threaten people at school quite a lot growing up." Kendrick smirked at the memory.

"Ah, now I see. I hope you were at least using *crazy Uncle Kyle* against the bad guys."

"Of course, of course, we were always crusaders for the good, supporters of the weak."

KENDRICK WAS pleased Jay had agreed to lunch with his mom and aunts recently. They didn't invite the grandmas that first time, didn't want to overwhelm the girl. But another lunch was already planned and his own three grandmas, as well as Katie's grandma, were all invited. Oh to be a fly on the wall that day.

He peeked into the bedroom to check on Jay. She'd had a rough lunch rush at work, so she decided on a nap before showering and heading to the guys' house for their weekly cousin thing.

Glancing at the clock, he realized they still had a couple

hours before they needed to shower and head over, so he shucked his pants and curled up behind her.

"Shhh, keep sleeping, I just want to hold you." He whispered in her ear.

"Mmmm, I like when you hold me." Her groggy answer warmed his heart.

He watched her for several moments, a shock of platinum blonde hair battled with a streak of inky black for position on her forehead. Long black lashes rested on porcelain cheeks. Pink lips parted slightly as she breathed deeply in her sleep. *I love you.*

How in the hell could he love her? He couldn't. Could he? He knew nothing of her past, didn't even know her whole name, yet his heart ached at the thought of losing her. If this wasn't love, he didn't know what it was. But he knew he'd damn sure never felt anything like it before. And he never wanted the feeling to end.

Jay HICCUPPED through peals of laughter. "Oh my God, Kendrick, you were too much."

Kendrick couldn't help but smile as his cousins regaled her with stories of his childhood, and even some more recent tales.

His school days mischief, his high school shenanigans, his

utter ridiculousness throughout college, the reaction he had when Sawyer announced he was gay, the sex toys he sent along with Zach and Zoey on their first out-of-town trip, his constant barrage of sexual innuendos involving food and animals.

"What can I say? I like to keep people on their toes." He blushed slightly, but felt his heart swell to watch Jay laughing with his cousins.

"No wonder you didn't even flinch that first night Tony and I met you in the bar." Jay winked at him. "I would have loved to hear the conversation as it unfolded on that camping trip." She referred to the camping trip where Sawyer had told them all he was gay.

"Damn, I've got to piss. Be right back." He kissed Jay's temple without thinking. Freezing he caught her eye with a questioning look.

She just smiled, "I'll be here, learning all about you from those who know you best."

"Kendrick has always been the outgoing, charismatic, larger-than-life one of the group..." Katie started as he left the room.

"Don't forget brilliant, sexy, and most likely to bring on instantaneous orgasms." Kendrick yelled from the hallway. "What?" He feigned innocence when they all groaned and rolled their eyes.

Katie waited until she heard the bathroom door close.

"As I was saying, Kendrick is all of that, but he's also one to love with his whole heart, sacrifice for the good of others, and put his own feelings aside to protect his family." Katie finished her thoughts. "You've brought something out in him we've never seen before, Jay. I've seen him vulnerable a couple times, recently when he shared about Sarah and the baby, and I saw another side of him when he stayed with me during the whole stalker debacle. But, I've never seen the interest, the sparkle, the determination in his eyes that I'm seeing now. About family, yes, about a girl, never."

Jay blushed and smiled. "I hope we're making the right decision, I hope I'm worth it."

"Worth it? Worth what?" Kendrick returned to the room and looked around curiously.

"Worth the effort you're putting in. Worth the sacrifice you're making." Jay sniffed, clearly embarrassed to be caught teary-eyed in front of mixed company.

"Every second, every minute, every hour of what we have so far has been worth it and so much more. Remember, Pixie, we don't have to be perfect, don't have to have everything completely figured out. We just have to stand strong togeth- er." He put his arm around her and pulled her close to his side.

They lost themselves in the moment, and the other couples surrounding them seemed pulled into it as well.

Finally, a throat cleared, and the spell was broken.

"Something we've always prided ourselves on in this group is calling bullshit when we see it. We keep each other in line, on track, honest. If we see someone screwing up, we call them on it, we offer advice and support." Decker was letting Jay know she was accepted into their group, allowing her to see a little bit of how the family worked.

"Yeah, it can cause a few heated arguments, but knowing these people have my back no matter what, it means the world and makes it easier to face the tough stuff." Kendrick nodded.

"Like Kendrick stepping up, telling Decker he was being a complete douchebag when Katie had the stalker. Decker wasn't ready to pull his head from his ass, so Kendrick took care of Katie until Decker was ready and able to take over the role again." Zach grinned at Decker, clearly loving the fact that he got to point out the nearly-faultless man's screw up.

"Like when Katie convinced me I was being an idiot thinking I couldn't confide my secret in my brother, my cousins, my family. Yeah, there were a couple family members who needed more time to come around to the idea than others, but Katie had been telling me for years that I could trust my family to love me no matter what. I was a little slow on the uptake, but I finally listened to her." Sawyer reached for Luke's hand and smiled.

"Like all of us confronting Kendrick and convincing him to come back home and face his shit once and for all. Sometimes it's hard, sometimes it hurts, but we are here for each other. Always." Luke spoke then. As the newest honorary member of the crew, Jay seemed to brighten when he spoke of being a part of the group.

"Even when you want to scream, curse, punch someone in the face, when you stop and think about the fact you've got this whole family backing you, it's a pretty damn good feeling." Kendrick looked around at the members of the group.

"Okay, it's time for dessert. Zoey, Jay, come help me please." Katie popped up from the couch, likely sensing that Jay was ready for something a little less serious.

In the kitchen, the girls worked quietly plating up the Snickerdoodles Jay had brought.

"Jay, these cookies are so good." Zoey popped one in her mouth. "Seriously, I could eat like fifteen of them."

"Aww, thanks. The recipe is easy, let me know if you want it." Jay smiled.

"Coffee, decaf tea, milk...think we need anything else?" Katie listed the drinks.

"You don't have to do decaf tea for me, I can drink milk." Jay protested.

"Nonsense, Kendrick brought a whole box of decaf tea just for you so you can have it anytime you're here. Plus, we all know how Kendrick is with his milk, he may fight you for it." Zoey laughed.

"That man should never have any calcium deficiencies that's for sure." Jay rolled her eyes.

"Hey, Jay...," Katie spoke softly.

Jay stopped at the door, turning around with the plate of cookies in her hands.

"Yeah?"

"We're all really happy to have you here. Kendrick is... well, he goes all out, full speed ahead. Which means he plays hard, and I think he'll love hard. But I also think it means he'll likely screw up hard as well. Be patient with him. He's one of the best guys I've ever known, but he doesn't always get things right." Katie's eyes glistened with tears.

"Yeah, we all screw up, but a guy like Kendrick doesn't do anything half-assed, so he's probably going to make plenty of mistakes. Don't hesitate to put him in his place, call on the guys and us for back up, and kick his ass all the way across town if he messes up...but just know you guys are good together, his eyes are bright, almost on fire when he looks at you." Zoey took the plate from Jay. Placing it on the table, she pulled the tiny blonde into a hug. "Welcome to the crazy house, Jay."

The three girls laughed. Katie joined the hug.

"Hey, I'm missing a hug fest, what the hell?" Aly popped her head into the kitchen.

"Get over here, we're just welcoming Jay to the loony bin. Glad you got to come." Zoey brought her best friend into the circle.

"Ugh, work was a bitch, but I didn't want to miss the cousin thing. I brought your brother with me. He was at my house playing video games with Dad, so I let him tag along. I think he likes to feel like he's part of the group even though he's so much younger than most of the group." Aly smiled at Jay. "Welcome to the family."

The girls headed back to the living room.

Within minutes, the plate of cookies looked as though it had been demolished by hungry locusts, only a few crumbs remained.

"Damn, those cookies were good." Sawyer savored his coffee. "You've got to share the recipe. I need Luke to make them for me." He smiled at Luke and winked at Jay.

"They are super easy. It's one of the recipes I wrote down from my grandma." Jay glanced quickly at Kendrick before sipping her tea.

Reading her look as *please don't try to get me to talk about my family*, Kendrick let the comment go. He took a final gulp of milk while making eye contact with her. He hoped his look conveyed *fine, I won't ask right now...but I'm going to keep at you until you break.*

She must have read him loud and clear because she sighed and rolled her eyes before smiling slightly.

Aly had to leave early, wanting to get cleaned up from her shift at work. She took Asher with her so he could be home by his curfew.

The girls decided to chit chat in the living room while the boys headed to the garage.

Kissing the side of Jay's head, Kendrick whispered,

"About an hour then we're out of here. I think we have bedroom things to take care of." He winked.

"Bedroom things? Is that what we're calling it these days?" Jay laughed.

"One hour. Be ready." He tweaked her nose.

"Oh, I think it's you who better be ready." She bit her lip, causing heat to shoot through his veins.

"SHE SEEMS LIKE A REALLY GREAT GIRL." Zach knocked his beer bottle against Kendrick's.

"Yeah, she is." Kendrick mused quietly.

"What's up, man?" Decker questioned.

"Nothing, everything, I mean...," he started, then trailed off.

"What is it? You know you can tell us anything. Are you having second thoughts about the baby?" Sawyer cocked his head to the side, watching his cousin.

"What? Oh hell no. No, I'm one hundred percent convinced that Jay and the baby are my future. I just...," he stopped again.

"Oh hell." Luke laughed.

"What?" Sawyer looked at his partner with sincere curiosity.

"He loves her. Or he thinks he does. He's not sure, he's

never felt this way before." Luke smiled as he spoke. "Am I right? Is that what's got you all tongue tied?"

"Fuck you, man." Kendrick's retort was less than forceful. Rubbing a hand over his face, he sighed, "Yeah, yeah, you're right. I don't know if it's love, but I do know I've never felt this way before in my life."

"Thinking about her at all times of the day?"

"Wanting to tell her funny things that happen during your day?"

"Smiling like a goof anytime you think about her?"

"Knowing your life would go to hell if you had to live without her?"

"Dreaming of holding her and kissing her, not needing sex, just wanting to be close to her?"

"Thinking about the future and making her a permanent part of your life?"

His cousins offered detailed descriptions of what he'd been feeling.

"Yes, yes to all of that." Kendrick turned exasperated eyes to the men he trusted with his secrets, his life.

"Yep, he's got it bad."

"For sure."

"No turning back now."

Sawyer walked to Kendrick, motioning to the others to join him. Laying a hand on his shoulder, Sawyer pretended to wipe a tear and sniffed his nose. "Dearly beloved, we are gathered here today as our dear Kendrick says goodbye to his former self. No more serial dating, debauchery, and meaning-less sex. Today he becomes a real man, a man in love."

"Our little Kendrick is growing up. I never thought I'd see the day." Decker patted his shoulder.

"Fuck you all. I don't remember making fun of you when you fell in love." Kendrick knocked their hands from his shoulders.

"Oh really? You don't remember giving me a hard time about Luke?" Sawyer scoffed. "I seem to remember a huge scene at work where you and Zach had a few good laughs at my expense. And you definitely put Luke through the ringer when he came to you for some advice."

"Okay, maybe a little bit."

"And you don't remember the incessant teasing you tormented me with when you found out Zoey and I were finally taking that next step?" Zach reminded him. "Pre-tending your eyes needed bleached when you saw me kissing her?"

"Fine, fine, I get it. Paybacks are a bitch." Kendrick chuck-led. "But, what do I do about it? I don't think she's ready for the *I love you* stuff just yet."

"Just love her through your words and actions, even if you don't think she's ready to hear the actual words just yet." Decker offered.

"Yeah, man, I watched that girl tonight. She's completely taken by you. And not just because you're helping her out with the baby. Her eyes were only for you, she hung on your every word. Now, don't get me wrong, I think she'll kick your ass if and when you screw up, but I don't think she's as far off from loving you back as you think she may be." Zach clapped him on the back.

"Now, with all of that out of the way, Luke and I are going back to his place. We've got a night of hot...," Sawyer started.

"Whoa, that's a bit more than we need to hear." Kendrick held up his hands.

"What? I was just going to say painting. We're painting the living room at his place. Now *after* the painting...," Sawyer laughed, pulling Luke close to his side.

"Alright, let's all head to our respective homes, rooms, beds. Merry Sexmas to all, and to all a *great* night." Kendrick wagged his brows at them.

Later that night, he enjoyed unwrapping Jay like a gift, and it was definitely a *great* night.

A FEW NIGHTS later he stood in the garage at his dad's house with his father, Uncle Nate, Uncle Kyle, Uncle Nicky, and all three grandpas.

"So, how's Jay? The pregnancy getting her down?" Grandpa Jack spoke after a sip of beer.

"She's doing well. Seems things are going just how the

books say they will. She had a doctor appointment, we could hear the heartbeat. She started taking some prenatal vitamins. Right now all is good it seems." Kendrick took a drink of his beer. He felt guilty drinking at home, knowing Jay couldn't drink, so he saved his beer time for evenings in the garage with the guys.

"Does she have horror-mones?" Nicky asked.

At first, Kendrick thought his uncle had just gotten the word messed up. Nicky had always had some challenges, he probably didn't realize he said the word wrong.

"Yeah, the hormones seem to be making her a little crazy." Kendrick chuckled.

"No, call them the horror-mones because they will make her a horror. Carly always said she felt like a horror, and horrible, because of them. So we started calling them horror-mones. She was bad with Zach, but much worse with Aly. Like they were zombies coming back with a vengeance." Nicky spoke seriously, not joking around at all, but it made the others laugh.

"I'd second that moniker. Libby was pretty crazy throughout the pregnancy with Abby, but the twins were like double trouble with the ups and downs and tears." Nate chuckled remembering his pretty, sweet wife during two pregnancies.

"Ugh, yeah, Audrey was pretty much psycho for nine months with Megan. She actually was a little more centered with you Kendrick." Jeremiah got a faraway look in his eyes.

The grandpas all nodded in agreement.

"Yep, just be ready for irrational ups and downs, back and forth, tears and smiles all at once. Don't take most of it personally. It will be directed at you, but it mostly won't be the real her." Grandpa John advised.

"Yep, it will be like a zombie taking over her body and mind, eating her brain." Nicky nodded sagely. "I guess it's more like a little baby zombie taking her over from the inside out."

"Josie was so shocked to find out she was pregnant after being told she couldn't have kids, she reveled in every single bit of it. She was mostly just weepy the whole nine months. And she almost ate us out of house and home." Kyle chuckled.

Kendrick and the guys spent a few more minutes talking about what to expect. When they finally broke up, the Captain patted him on the back.

"Just be there for her, hold her hand, rub her feet, let her cry or scream. Come drink a beer with us if you need to."

Kendrick headed home that evening with a nervous excitement about facing the next several months.

12

Kendrick pulled his car onto the freeway heading back to Torey Hope. He'd been visiting a high school baseball coach a few towns over. He was hoping to get enough interest in a summer baseball camp, and wanted to tap into the neighboring towns' school sports programs. His long term plans included The Center+ being where several high schools sent their students during the off-season to train. Along with that, he had plans for The Center+ to feed local talent directly into the high schools and nearby college programs.

His meeting had gone well, but he was ready to get home to Jay. He smiled when he thought of how cute she looked sprawled out in bed that morning. The sheer camisole she slept in left nothing to the imagination. Her abdomen had started to swell slightly, and he couldn't resist spooning behind her to rest his hand on her teeny tiny baby bump.

"Good morning, baby." He'd whispered in her ear as he rubbed her belly.

"Mmmm, good morning." She mumbled.

"Oh, yeah, good morning to you too, Pixie." He leaned down to trail kisses along her belly. "Silly mommy thinks all my sweet nothings are for her. She better learn I've got to share my words between her *and* my baby pixie these days."

He'd looked up to find her a mixture of fire and tears.

"Damn it, Kendrick, you can't say things like that." She sniffed and wiped her eyes.

"Why not, Pixie?" He smirked.

"Because it makes me cry and want to jump you at the same time." She sniffed again, "Stupid hormones."

He'd kissed her thoroughly and made her promise to tell him all about her lunch with the girls when he got home later that night.

He was four miles from the Torey Hope exit, less than ten minutes until he was pulling up to his new home with Jay. Dinner, cuddling on the couch, listening to her giggle about her lunch, whispers to the baby he was certain was a girl, and hot fast sex followed by sweet slow sex...the evening awaiting him was promising.

The horn blaring to his left shocked him from his smiling daydream. A semi-truck, screeching tires, rolling that seemed to never stop, pain, fear, blackness. The promising evening ahead of him had just taken a devastating turn for the worse.

THE INCESSANT BEEPING was beginning to piss him off, but the soggy wet blanket surrounding his brain wouldn't lift enough to allow him to figure out where the damn sound was coming from. Giving in to the heaviness of his head, he slipped back into the darkness.

THE FUCKING BEEPING HAD to stop. His left arm was pressed against cool metal. Trying to breathe deeply made him feel like he was drowning. Eyes which may have been glued shut attempted to open, if only long enough to find the damn beeping and beat the shit out of it. But it was no use, the current of darkness swept him under again.

AT LEAST THIS time he could hear voices over the beeping. Warmth covered his body, a blanket maybe? He felt a heaviness in his right hand, a presence at his right side, but his damn eyes felt as if cement had been poured into them. The voices seemed near, but only murmurs reached his ears, interrupted by the never-ending beeping.

THIS TIME he was going to fight through it, he was going to overcome the darkness, stop the beeping, and open his eyes. But the pain shooting through his body had other plans. His stomach lurched, the beeping increased, and a moment later the ever-present blackness was back invading every corner of his mind.

"IT'S BEEN THREE DAYS, Doctor, how much longer is he going to be like this?" Decker's voice was a life preserver, Kendrick clung to it.

"I'm glad so many of his family are here today, I wanted to explain again about what Mr. Jordan is going through." An unknown voice, maybe the doctor, spoke in an assured tone.

Still unable to open his eyes, Kendrick focused his strength on keeping the pain at bay by not trying to move and fighting off the blackness threatening to devour his mind again. He focused on the voices, trying to make out the ones he recognized.

"Mr. Jordan suffered several injuries in the accident. He was very lucky; had he not been wearing his seatbelt the accident could have had a very different outcome. He has a couple broken ribs, broken bones in both his leg and arm, a bruised spleen, a dislocated shoulder, and a punctured lung. Our most immediate concern, however, was the head injury." The doctor's list seemed to go on forever, and Kendrick felt as though each injury began to throb even more as the man's words were spoken.

"So is he in a coma from the head injury?" *Sawyer*. Kendrick felt his heart squeeze to hear another familiar voice.

"He's heavily sedated, but not in a coma. It's possible he can hear bits and pieces of what we are saying right now, but we are keeping a steady stream of pain medication flowing for two reasons. One, we need to keep him still due to the extensiveness of the injuries. If he were feeling the pain right now he'd be more apt to toss and turn, be agitated."

Agitated. Yeah, that's a good word. If the damn beeping would just stop maybe I could relax a little.

"What's the other reason?" *Zach*. He had a feeling his entire room was packed full of as many family members as would be allowed in to see him.

"His body needs rest to heal, and we especially wanted to be able to monitor the head injury. At this point, we feel it's a concussion, but no bleeding of the brain. We'd like to keep him sedated another twenty-four hours, then we'll begin to decrease some of the heavier medications to see how he handles being more conscious. He may come out of sedation quickly or slowly, he may fight and struggle, or he may not. It's sort of a waiting game at this point."

"So the head injury is bad, but not severe. What about the punctured lung, is he in immediate danger from that?" *Katie.*

"No, the puncture luckily is only affecting a very small portion of his lung. At this point, we feel safe taking a wait and see approach with that injury. He has the extra oxygen on as a precaution, and we'll watch for complications, but it appears the rib barely nicked the lung tissue."

Ahh, oxygen, that's what's on my face making my damn nose itch like crazy. I wonder how much it would hurt if I tried to lift my hand to scratch my nose.

"I'll let you all visit a bit longer, but the nurses will be kicking most of you out fairly soon. They usually let one person stay if the patient isn't critical. After today, I'd say Mr. Jordan is in serious, but not critical, condition. If you have any other questions, please don't hesitate to ask the nurses, or save them for me when I make my rounds tomorrow morning. Like I said, I feel like Mr. Jordan will make a full recovery, and while he may not feel lucky for a while during his recovery, he's a very lucky man to have escaped that accident with non-life-threatening injuries."

Kendrick felt the air in the room move as the doctor opened the door, and the remaining bodies shifted. His head felt heavy, throbbing, and he knew if he gave in to the quick-sand pulling at his mind he could escape the beeping. But he wanted to hear the voices around him. Maybe just a brief moment of letting it take him under.

He became aware of his surroundings again. Had he slept through the nurses kicking them all out? And who all was there? He forced his brain to block out the beeping which was like a tiny knife to his senses over and over again, and just listen for the words being spoken around him.

"The police talked to several witnesses. What they've been able to gather so far is that one semi-truck driver fell asleep at the wheel, crossed the line making another semi-truck swerve. When that truck swerved it crossed into Kendrick's path, bumping the front of his car just enough to send him skidding and rolling. The first impact was into the guardrail, but a lot of his injuries likely came from the several times the car rolled down the embankment." Decker relayed the details of the accident to those in the room.

Ah, so that's why I feel like I've been run over by a steam roller. I basically have been.

"Both truck drivers stopped, the one who fell asleep called 911. Seems he has a new baby at home, had been up late with her, just didn't get enough sleep. Only took a split second for his eyes to be off the road, and there wasn't much the other truck could do. By the grace of God, Kendrick's car stopped rolling before it hit the water at the base of the embankment."

Kendrick listened a bit longer, gathering enough to realize almost every single member of his family was in the room. What about Jay? He hadn't heard her voice, but he felt like she was there with him. If only he could wash the sawdust from his eyes and take a look around. He longed to see that beautiful pixie.

Fighting to stay awake when his eyes were already closed proved more difficult than he could have ever imagined. He felt as though several members of this family spoke to him as if in a dream, but when he finally woke from the deep darkness again, he could only remember bits and pieces like he was in a thick fog.

He listened. *Beep, beep, beep.* He hated that sound, but it had become the background music to the little drama playing out in his life, so he decided he needed to just accept it. After all, the beeping was likely tracking his heartbeat, so at least it meant he was alive.

"Here, sweet girl, I brought you a decaf tea. The nurse is going to bring you a cot to sleep on. You know he wouldn't expect you to stay, you can go home if you'd be more comfortable." *Mom.* Even as a grown man, hearing his mom's voice was comforting.

Decaf tea. It had to be for Jay. His sweet Pixie was with him.

"No, I want to stay." Her voice was tired, scared, but it was there with him and that's what mattered.

"Okay, I know he'll be happy to see you when he wakes up." His mom's voice was to his left then. She leaned in close and he wanted to wrap her in a hug, but instead he just relaxed into the hand she cupped on his cheek. "You get some rest, baby boy. Tomorrow you're going to start waking up a bit more, and you need your energy to start healing from this. I love you. Be strong." A kiss feathered on his forehead, and then she was gone.

Before he had time to focus on Jay, a wave of blackness swept over him again.

HE AWOKE TO A GIGGLE. *Jay.*

"So your mom and aunts are fabulous, your grandmas are so sweet, and Katie's grandma is a hoot. I think this baby is going to be the most spoiled child in the world, but I feel lucky to have so many people here to support us through it."

She stopped, and the silence threatened to invite the darkness to take over again.

Her sniffle helped him fight it off.

Why was she crying?

"Kendrick, I was so scared. I was waiting at home for you to get there. I'd been watching the clock, just waiting on you. But when you were forty-five minutes late without a call, I knew something was wrong. About that time, Decker, Sawyer, and Zach showed up at the door. Good thing they are quick and strong because I'm pretty sure they are the only things that kept me from collapsing to the floor. I immediately thought you were dead. They assured me you were very much alive, just hurt, and got me here as quickly as possible." She stopped again, but her thumb stroking his hand gave him enough to focus on so he could stay awake. At least for a while longer.

"Before you're completely awake they want to set your arm and leg. You're lucky you don't need any pins or surgeries. They already relocated your shoulder, I'm so glad you were completely out for that part. It's strange to me, but the nurse said the whiplash and dislocated shoulder will be the longest and most painful part of your recovery. The lung, spleen, and broken bones should heal much faster. At least according to the nurse."

He wanted her to keep talking, but she laid her head down on the bed and yawned. The poor girl was exhausted. Selfishly he wanted her to stay by his side, but he also wished someone would have forced her to go home to sleep. Sleeping in the hospital at his bedside couldn't be all that great for her or the baby.

HE WOKE AGAIN when she roused from her own sleep. He tried to grip her hand, but he felt as weak as a kitten. She must have felt a little something, because she squeezed his hand and spoke, "It's okay, I just need to go pee. I'll be right back."

When she returned, he felt her straighten his blankets, adjust his pillow, and stroke a hand along his face.

"Can you hear me? I wish you'd open those damn sexy eyes of yours and say something crazy, but I know you need your rest. If I wasn't so afraid of hurting you, I'd crawl in this bed and cuddle beside you, but I'll let you rest comfortably."

He felt her perch herself at his bedside again.

He wasn't sure if he slept, or if she was just quiet for a very long time, but she eventually picked up his hand, bringing it to her lips.

"It's Jaymison. Jaymison Marie Keller. I'd give anything for you to be awake right now so I could tell you my full name." Her whisper choked on tears.

Jaymison. A beautiful name, for his beautiful girl.

"Kendrick, I was so scared. Yeah, I'm terrified of the future, having this baby, being a mom. But I was just getting used to the idea of doing it all with you, and to think you'd been ripped away from me, I felt like I couldn't breathe."

He knew that admission took a lot on her part.

"Can you hear me at all? I feel like you're trying to wake

up, you seem more alert under those eyelids tonight than the last couple days, and your hand is twitching more." She squeezed his hand. "So, because I want to give you something to wake up for, how about we make a deal?"

He tried to squeeze her hand, tried to flutter his eyes open, but he wasn't sure he succeeded in either attempt.

"I'll take your silence as agreement." Wry laughter laced her exhausted voice.

"How about I tell you about my past if you agree to wake up and start your road to healing as soon as tomorrow? Deal?" She sighed with a shuddering sob. "I'm going to take that as a yes."

And with that, his sweet Pixie launched into a story sure to break even the stoutest of hearts.

"I WAS BORN IN CALIFORNIA. My parents were Jimmy and Marla. They were likely nice people, but they sucked as parents. I remember watching the family across the street all the time when I was seven or eight. The two perfect kids played in the yard with their perfect little dog. The mom brought out snacks, the dad washed their already pristine car, then he sat on the porch reading the newspaper with a proud look on his face and a loving smile for the mom. It was like the fucking Cleavers lived in that house. It was a stark contrast to my life. My mom would be out partying it up, or doing drugs at the house until all hours, then she'd sleep until 3:00 or 4:00 p.m. only to wake and do it all over again. My dad would spend most of the day in the basement practicing his music. He'd come up, curse at my mom, chuck me on the shoulder, and leave for the night. He played guitar and sang in local bars. He was actually pretty good. I'd usually heat up leftover pizza or Chinese and spend the rest of the night in my room, trying to block out the sounds of my mom getting high or trying not to be scared of the sounds in an empty house."

She stopped. His heart squeezed. He had a feeling it was going to get worse before she reached the end.

"My mom died when I was eight, almost nine. My dad always said it was a heart attack, and it likely was, but as I've gotten older I've realized it was probably a weak heart due to all the drug use." She sniffed and laid her head gently on his hip. Even if it had been painful, he would have welcomed the pain if it meant comforting her in some way.

"I think a paramedic who came to the house when my mom died must have filed a report about me. With the drugs around, my age, just the general appearance of the house, he probably had no choice. But that landed me in foster care for several months. I'm really surprised Jimmy fought to get me back. Foster care was both good and bad. It was good because I was away from the drugs, I was never alone, and my case worker checked in on me often. It was bad for so many other reasons. I went through three foster homes in those months

away from my dad. None of them were the dream foster
parents you hear about in those feel-good movies on televi-
sion. They were all just in it for the check. Luckily I already
knew how to fend for myself with meals because there were
no happy family meals going on. One of the foster moms
actually did do my laundry which was really nice. I was going
on ten towards the end of my time in the foster homes. None
of the other kids paid much attention to me. No one was
mean, they just ignored me. At the time, I felt sad that no one
wanted me as a friend. Looking back, I realized they had their
own shit going on. Some of the foster moms homeschooled us,
but I went to school when I was with other ones. It was a
different school than when I'd lived with Mom and Dad. I
basically was in and out of four different schools in less than a
year. No one had the time or took the time to get to know me
well enough to know if things were okay with me."

Jay stopped talking again. She stood and walked to the
bathroom. He smiled in his mind, the tea must have gone
right through her. When she returned, she switched to the
other side of the bed, taking up his hand in hers again.

"The last home was the worst. There were a couple older
boys, about sixteen or seventeen. They were total creepers,
but the foster dad was even worse. I saw them watch the other
girls. They seemed to like their long hair, the start of curves
and breasts. I purposely whacked my hair off, slopped some
black on chunks of it, and thanked my lucky stars my chest
was flat as a board. I knew those boys were hurting the girls,

and I knew the dad was too. By the time Jimmy proved he could take care of me, I was so scared they'd come to me during the night I was barely sleeping. When my case worker picked me up to take me back to my dad, I told her what I was seeing happen. I've always hoped it was enough to get those girls away from that hell hole."

She reached for the remains of her tea. It had to be just barely warm now.

"So Jimmy and I moved to Indiana. He had a friend there who offered us the basement to live in. My life didn't get better, but it didn't really get any worse. I wasn't abused, I wasn't starved, I was just ignored. During summers he would take me to the local bars with him, he called it our bonding time. He'd convince the owners to let me hang out in the back with a book. He'd toss them a few dollars to feed me a cheeseburger and fries. It wasn't ideal, but I blocked most of it out. There was one really nice lady who owned one of the bars. She had a comfy office where she spent most of her time; I learned to love tea because of her. She would brew us a nice hot cup of tea every single time I was there."

"School was nice because I got free meals; we lived in an area of high poverty so every student in the building qualified for free breakfast and lunch. My dad had to make sure I was in school or he would have been in trouble. So he would leave at night, leaving me alone with a microwave meal and the tv. I loved school, so I'd work hard on my homework and read books cover-to-cover each night. I got myself up for school, got to the bus stop, and spent the day reveling in any attention school staff could give me. I was quiet, never caused any trouble. I didn't make friends easily; I think I was too conditioned to think it wouldn't last after all the moving from foster home to foster home."

"As I got older, I started to worry more about my appearance. Dad would leave me a bit of money here and there. I'd take the city bus to the local thrift store and stock up my wardrobe. I learned how to cut, style, color my own hair. When I started high school I started acting out a bit. I was pissed. I didn't have a mom, my dad was as good as dead. Jimmy was really good at his music, but he drank away any profits and slept his way through every bar fly in Indiana. I kept my grades up because I'd heard about a trip to Paris for the top percentage of students. I had no plans on college, but I wanted to go to Paris so badly I could taste it. But in addition to keeping my grades up, I became pretty kinky with the boys. No one ever believed it because I was so quiet, and I didn't let any rumors get to me, but I was definitely a sure thing most Friday and Saturday nights. I never touched drugs, and didn't drink much because of what I watched my parents go through. By the age of sixteen, I was the perfect little student during the week, and a wild child on the weekend. But it was fun, and I thought I deserved some fun."

By this point, Kendrick's injuries were starting to scream, but he blocked the pain out, determined to hear her story through to the end.

"Then my dad died, and the foster care nightmare started all over again. I was in three homes during that time. Again, not the dream foster home where the mom and dad just want to share their love with unfortunate kids. But these were somewhat clean, didn't have tons of kids, and were all in an area where I could at least stay at my high school. I got to travel to Paris the summer before my senior year. It was the best time of my life. The food, the architecture, the people, the history, it was all so beautiful. I took it all in. For the first time, I was on my own, but it was by choice, not by necessity. No one was forcing me to be self-sufficient, I was doing it because I enjoyed it. When I returned to the States, I vowed I'd graduate high school and figure out how to live on my own as soon as I was eighteen. But the state found my grandmother, Rebecca, first. She was living in Illinois. I had no choice; she was next of kin and willing to take me in, so I moved to Illinois."

"I had never met this woman before, but I was immediately pissed at my parents for never allowing me to know her. She was amazing. She showed me love for the first time in my life. I think she knew I'd been ignored and neglected, so she pampered me and spent every waking moment with me. We had tea every day. She taught me to cook and bake. I didn't love it, I wasn't great at it, but she said it was a skill I needed to learn. The best thing she taught me to make was snickerdoodle cookies."

"I was settling in, feeling like maybe I could lead a normal life. My grandma had shown me that love existed, good people were out there, and I didn't have to distrust everyone. But then she died. She was old, but not super old. I know it is irrational, but all I could think was that she left me too. Everyone in my life who was supposed to love me or care for me or support me had left me. I was truly on my own again. After she died, I had to move away from that little town. She had only rented her little apartment, she had nothing much to leave to me. I took her recipes, some sweaters, a picture of the two of us, some of her books, and a suitcase. I jumped on a bus and stopped in Torey Hope for the night. The Café was open so I walked in for dinner, saw the Help Wanted sign, and never looked back."

She laughed with no humor.

"So there you have it, the whole sordid tale. Raised poor, no one to love me, everyone leaves me, no real future. And *that* my dear Kendrick is why I'm scared shitless to have this baby and attempt living my life with you. Nothing has ever worked out for me in the past, what's to say it will now?"

What's to say it won't, Pixie?

Damn, he wished he could wake up enough to talk to her.

"But as much as I want to keep up the wall, fight against it all, I can't help but feel pulled in by you, your family, and the thought of us having this tiny baby to love. In the beginning, I was convinced I didn't know how to love a child because I was never shown love. But, the longer I'm around you and your family, the more I realize that I maybe, just maybe, *can* show this baby love because I know what it's like to live without it, and I'd never do that to any child, let alone my own. I feel doubtful every day that you think you can love a child who likely isn't your own, but then I see your own mom and how much she loves Beckett. She's not his biological mom, but she loves him as much as she loves you. Your grandma Janie may not be the biological grandma to any of you, but she loves you fiercely, so maybe you really can love this baby even if she's not yours."

"Now, I need to pee again and get some sleep. Don't forget we had a deal. Tomorrow you start waking up and we get you on the road to healing. If you're good, I'll even see if they'll bring you a big glass of milk." She leaned in to kiss his forehead. "Please get better soon, Kendrick. I need you more than I ever planned to need anyone ever again."

Her words were barely a whisper, hard to hear over the roar of pain in coursing through his body, but he clung to them valiantly before the blackness overtook him again.

13

*A*s he was wheeled back into his room, he became aware of the heaviness encasing his left arm and right leg.

"Jaymison." He thought he spoke aloud, but he couldn't be sure. "Jaymison."

An unfamiliar voice spoke near him as a hand patted his good arm. "You looking for that pretty little girl who has been camped out here? I'll go get her for you, sugar."

Several moments later he felt the door to his room open. Forcing his eyes open, he blinked through the scratchiness and tried to focus.

"Well, she didn't answer to Jaymison, but she's the one who's been by your side the whole time. I hope this is who you're asking for."

He saw the nurse bustle from the room and Jay make her way to the bedside.

"So, I tell you my real name in a moment of desperation and you sell me out to the first ear who will listen?" She tried to sound pissed, but he knew she was just happy to have him awake.

"It's a beautiful name." His voice was gravelly, it made talking harder than he expected.

"Here, take a drink." She put a straw to his lips while brushing a hand over his forehead. "How are you feeling?"

Clearing his throat the best he could, he scanned his mind down his body.

"Like I've been run over. Seems like everything hurts. Did they just put these casts on?" He indicated his arm and leg.

"Yes, you started to wake a little, so they took you down to get the casts on before you were completely awake. You're lucky the casts are just up to your elbow and knee. And since they are on your left arm and right leg you can use a crutch instead of a wheelchair; that should make things a lot easier once you're back at work." She pulled a chair up and sat beside his bed, holding his hand.

"Your family is on their way. I promised I'd call as soon as you woke up."

He watched her, saw the fatigue in her eyes.

"Climb up here and lay with me?" He patted the mattress on his right side.

"I may hurt you." Her eyes were huge with concern.

"Pixie, it hurts more not having you close to me. Just come rest with me for a bit. We can sleep until everyone gets here. Then I want you to sleep at home tonight." He held a hand out to her.

"Okay, but use that button over there to push some pain meds before I climb up there. You can push it every fifteen minutes I think." She indicated the red button to his left.

He pressed the button and almost immediately felt a rush through his body. The pain wasn't gone completely, but it took the edge off.

"Thanks, that's helpful. Now climb up here." He shifted slightly, allowing her room to cuddle up beside him.

Cradling her in his good arm, he kissed her head. "Ahh, this is the best medicine I can get. Any idea when I can bust free of this place? And how about a shower?"

"The doctor wants you up and moving around first. And you have to be off all IV medications. Oh, and you have to eat a certain amount of food and start in on some physical therapy. Probably a day to three days. Then you'll be off work for at least a week, but more like two weeks." She cuddled closer. "No showers until the cast is completely set. It's waterproof, but you'll still have to cover it in the shower; we'll have to figure out a system at home. Until then, it's sponge baths."

"Mmm, I think a sponge bath is in order." He kissed her again. "As soon as we sleep."

She giggled, "And as soon as you brush your teeth."

Feigning offense, he pulled her closer. They immediately drifted into a comfortable sleep.

"Even a car wreck can't stop his mojo."

"Damn, got the girl into his bed even with a head injury."

"I'm thinking those casts are going to put a major crimp in his sexcapades."

Kendrick came awake slowly as the voices drifted around him.

Without opening his eyes, he knew his cousins were in the room. Slowly he extended the middle finger of both hands in response to their words.

"Ah, good to see the bump to the head didn't mess him up too badly."

Jay shifted and awoke slowly. He glanced at her, loving the blush coloring her cheeks.

"Hey, Pixie, do me a favor and go home. Take a shower, eat, sleep until morning. You can come back tomorrow. It will make me feel better knowing you're comfortable at home instead of trying to sleep in a chair here. Please?" He tacked on the please for good measure when he saw she was starting to protest.

"Fine. A shower and bed sound really good. I'll be back tomorrow." She leaned in and kissed him. "Don't wear yourself out with this group, you've got a lot to do before you get to come home."

He watched her leave the room and felt like she took a piece of him with her.

He spent the next several hours chatting with his cousins, the girls, and his parents. Later, his aunts, uncles, and grandparents all came in. Luckily the nurses were cool because they were *way* over the visitation limit.

By that evening, he knew he'd overdone it a bit. His arm and leg throbbed, but the hot, searing pain was in his shoulder and neck more than anywhere else. He'd pushed his little red button more times than he could remember, but it wasn't taking the pain away.

"Hey, baby boy, you okay?" Audrey brushed the hair from his forehead.

"The pain is just really bad." He winced as he tried to shift in bed.

"We're all going to leave. Let's call the nurse and see if there's something she can give you to help with the pain and help you sleep."

Goodbyes were said as the nurse administered the glorious elixir of pain meds.

"Luckily, the doctor says the punctured lung is healing nicely, so you don't have to worry about that one much. Tomorrow we'll take these IVs out and you'll start taking the medications orally. If you can tolerate those and keep food down you'll be one step closer to heading home." The nurse patted his knee. "Sleep tight."

He barely noticed her leave the room as his eyes grew heavy and drooped shut before he could respond.

THREE DAYS LATER, a little woozy from the pain medication concoction he'd swallowed just that morning, Kendrick hobbled from the edge of his bed to the waiting wheelchair.

"I'm not a complete invalid, you know. I can walk to the car. Why do you think they gave me the crutch?" Kendrick tried to joke, but came across as a pouting child.

"Kendrick, you've been in bed for almost a week. You're under the influence of some pretty strong drugs. You have a cast on one leg, and another on your opposite arm. Yes, you'll get the hang of maneuvering yourself around, but let's get you to the car in one piece first, okay?" Sawyer edged the wheelchair closer, nodding toward it.

Sulking, Kendrick wobbled himself around to flop into the chair. "Get me the fuck out of here."

The nurse came in with his prescriptions.

"Now, you'll be on this one for a couple weeks. You can't drive with this one, so even if you're up to going back to work, you'll need a ride. You'll take it two to four times a day as needed. It has one refill."

She shook the little bottle at him. "This one you can take up until the casts come off in four weeks. It also has one refill. You'll want to take this one with milk if it upsets your stomach."

She handed the bottles to Zach with a look of *make sure he takes these correctly*.

"This last one you can take *as needed* up to four times a day, but you may have days when you don't need it at all. I'd suggest staying on it up until the casts come off, but then start trying fewer doses. It has up to three refills, and you can talk to your doctor about more if he feels you need them."

Zach took the final bottle as Sawyer wheeled Kendrick from the room. Luke stood with Zach until the other two were out of sight. Turning to the nurse as she completed something on her computer, Luke cleared his throat.

"Excuse me. Can I ask about the pills? What are they for? Are these medications dangerous or addictive?"

The nurse smiled. "He's lucky to have you guys on his side. He won't be on them long term. He's going to be in a lot of pain, so the pills will help. He's got short term sleep aids and muscle relaxers. For the longer term he has the pain medication. As long as he sticks to the directions on how to take them, he should be fine. My biggest concern would be drowsiness while driving, so I hope you're ready to taxi his grumpy butt around town." She winked as she left the room.

Luke grabbed a piece of paper and wrote down the exact instructions from each bottle. When Zach looked at him questioningly, he shrugged his shoulders, "Just want to make sure he takes them right, ya know?"

Decker had Zach's truck waiting downstairs. With the backseat empty, Kendrick was able to position himself at least somewhat comfortably.

"Let's go. Get me home before the pain meds wear off or before I puke them all back up." His last words were slurred as he slipped into a foggy sleep for the drive home.

"Jay? Jaymison?" His groggy voice filled the room.

"I'm here, just went to the bathroom." She padded across the bedroom. "How are you feeling? It's about half an hour until your next dose of pain medication. Why don't we sit up and talk to make the time go faster. Then I'll get you a big glass of milk and you can head back to la-la land."

"Funny. I wish to hell I didn't need these damn pills. They make me feel weird, my stomach hurts, and I can't stay awake worth a damn." He groused as he tried to sit up in bed.

"It's only been a couple days. Give it some time. You'll be able to stop taking some of them in about a week." She soothed while fluffing his pillow and helping him get situated.

"I'll be right back. I'm getting milk and your pills."

She returned with a glass of cold milk, and a handful of pills. Placing them on the bed, she turned to assess their seating arrangement. Crawling into bed with him, she settled on his right side so she wouldn't have to fight with the cast on his other arm.

"So, what should we chat about? Weather? News? Religion?" He pulled her close.

"Religion? Hmmm, I'd never thought of that. I didn't go to church growing up, mom and dad were never available or coherent enough to get me there. But your family goes to church, right?"

"Yeah, we've always gone. Well, the four of us didn't go while in college. Probably should have, but Sundays were spent nursing hangovers and trying to politely convince Saturday night's girl to go home." He snickered.

"You were a total whore." She shoved at him lightly.

"Ouch, go easy. This reformed whore is injured."

"So, I think I'd like the baby to grow up in church. I think we should start going with your family."

"Whatever you want, Pixie." He leaned down and kissed her nose.

"Okay, next topic up for discussion. A shower. I've done the best I can with sponge baths, but it's time you get an actual shower or bath. We need to ask one of the guys to help."

"What the fuck? No way I'm having one of them wash my balls, Pixie. Hell to the no." He attempted to sit up from the bed, but winced in pain.

"Shhh, it's almost time for the medicine. Sit still. I would offer to help, but you're too big and awkward in those casts for me to feel safe washing you."

"Damn straight I'm too big." He chuckled with his eyes closed against the pain as he grabbed his crotch.

"And still cocky as they come." She shook her head, smiling.

"Still wanting to talk about my cock, Pixie? Anytime."

"You're ridiculous. Even if I wanted sex right now, in the dead of night, I don't think you're up for it. Here, take your pills." She handed him the glass of milk.

Swigging a large portion of it, he popped all the pills in his mouth at once, and washed them down with the rest of the milk.

"Mmmm, milk." He tried to pull her close again, but the pain in his shoulder and neck were too strong. She helped him get into a sleeping position, and crawled up next to him.

"I'm up for it you know. Feel this." He cupped his junk again, then frowned. "Hmmm, maybe not so much. I think I dreamed that hard-on. Another day maybe." His voice drifted.

"Yeah, another day for sure." She smiled into the dark.

"Jaymison."

"Yeah?"

"Nothing, I just like to say your name."

"Well, say it after you sleep."

His breathing evened out, but before he went under completely, he spoke again.

"Jaymison."

"What?"

"I *like* saying your name, but I *love* you. I really do." He spoke in a dreamy voice.

"Yeah, well, I'll believe that when the pain, exhaustion, and pills aren't all working together." She laughed a bit.

"S'true. Love you. Really do." The medication brought slurs to his words, and he was out.

Pressing up on an elbow, Jay traced her finger along his jaw. Leaning in to kiss him, she whispered, "And I love you, I really do. Don't know how, don't know why, never saw it coming. You were supposed to be just a fun time, but you're so much more than that."

SITTING IN THE GUYS' living room, leg propped up on the ottoman, Kendrick looked at the group in disbelief.

"You're fuckin' with me, right?"

"Nope, look, I even got bubble bath." Zach held up a bottle. Opening the flip-top lid, he breathed deeply. "Mmmm, milk and honey. Awww, our big man will smell so sweet."

"Shut the fuck up. How am I supposed to take a bubble bath? I can't get into or out of the tub by myself and Jay is too tiny to help. Unless Katie and Zoey want to join with her to get me in and out." He wagged his eyes at the other girls.

"Yeah, I'm going to have to pass on that one." Katie smiled as she rolled her eyes.

"Zoey? You like naked cousins." He tried to dodge the fist Zach landed on his good arm, but had nowhere to go from the couch. Kendrick loved giving Zach and Zoey a hard time about their relationship being *taboo* even though the two weren't really related.

"I only go for pseudo cousin nakedness, not full-on cousin nudity. Sorry." Zoey laughed.

Jay cleared her throat to cover a laugh.

"So, like I said last night, I think maybe the guys could help out with the bath." Her big brown eyes twinkled, but he could see she was serious.

"Do I seriously stink so badly I'm going to be forced to let my cousins close to my junk?" He winced as he spoke.

A chorus of *Yes!* and *You really do* filled the air.

Kendrick frowned and tried to sniff his armpit, but the pain in his neck was too much.

"Damn, I can't even sniff my pit. Okay, okay, fine. But why a bath? Why not a shower?"

"Well, we figured a shower would take a lot more balance and maybe wear you out quicker. A bath should be easier. You just need someone to help you into and out of the tub." Decker spoke confidently, as if he'd planned the whole bathing scenario out perfectly in his head.

Fucker probably wrote up a proposal for this, complete with illustrations, Kendrick thought.

"And, you can soak in the hot bath for as long as you'd like. Jay can even visit with you. You just need one or two of us to help you in and out. So, who's it going to be?" Zach waved the bubble bath in front of him.

"Well, shit. I've not given much thought to which cousin I want up close and personal with my junk." Kendrick seemed to truly be thinking about the decision.

Decker checked his watch. "Make up your mind quickly. We've got two hours before your next medicine doses, so you need to be out of the tub and ready to sleep by then."

"And don't act like we've not seen you naked before. You've run through many parties clutching your crotch as an angry girl chased you because you called her the wrong name. And don't forget the texts you've sent us with things like, 'Check out the size of this thing' or 'Don't you wish your boyfriend were hung like me?'" Sawyer rolled his eyes.

"Yeah, I'm pretty sure you sending me a picture of your dick saying, 'If he's not as big as me, let him go. I'll keep you satisfied' when I started dating Sawyer negates any feelings of awkwardness you could be feeling right now." Luke blushed a bit.

"Ugh, the pressure. And to be fair, most of what you're referring to was done in a drunken state. This is highly sober, so I have the right to feel awkward." Kendrick used his one good arm to push himself up in the seat a bit. Then, putting on his playful act, he pretended to weigh his options.

"Well, Decker is the controlled one. He'd likely be able to

keep any feelings of jealousy or lust completely hidden, even when up close and personal with my massive piece."

Decker shook his head and rolled his eyes while the others laughed.

"Zach is all lovey dovey with his soulmate, so he'd likely not be interested in my junk. But, once he sees it, up close and personal, he may throw caution, and Zoey, to the wind and go all man-on-man on me."

"Dear Lord..." Zoey snorted.

"Sawyer is all about the male body, he likes it up close and personal. He's used to seeing that part of a man. Same with Luke. They may have to fight off their jealousy, but they are the most accustomed to dick."

More head shaking and eye rolling.

"Make up your mind, or I'm calling our dads over here." Decker was not amused.

"Fine, fine. I choose...," Kendrick tapped his finger on his chin. "Sawyer and Luke."

"Ha! You guys lose!" Zach laughed.

"Why the hell would you choose us?" Sawyer almost whined. "We're gay, why would you want us all up in your junk?"

"Nope, no backing out. He chose you fair and square. Go get our boy in the tub." Decker fist bumped Zach.

"What the hell, did you all place bets?" Kendrick let Sawyer and Luke help him up from the couch.

"Yep. Decker and I thought you'd choose Sawyer and

Luke, but they were for sure you'd pick the heteros." Zach laughed again.

"Well, I figure neither of them have ever come on to me, so my virtue is safe with them." Kendrick smirked.

"What the hell, neither of us have ever come on to you either!" Decker huffed.

"I know, but Sawyer is all up Luke's ass, literally. And Luke isn't related to me. So, if he were to get all lusty with me, it wouldn't be gross." Kendrick waved away the conversation. "Let's get this show on the road."

Luke and Sawyer helped him toward the bathroom, leaving the rest of the group standing in awed silence.

"Do you ever finish a conversation with that man and fear for your brain cells?" Decker wondered aloud.

"All the time." Zach shook his head.

"Let's blame it on the meds this time." Jay laughed as she headed to the bathroom as well.

Fifteen minutes later, Kendrick was settled in the tub.

Sawyer and Luke came out of the bathroom looking like they'd just wrestled an animal to the ground.

"Give Sawyer and Luke some private time. I think the physical exertion and close proximity to my cock got them all worked up." Kendrick laughed from behind them.

"Oh Lord, that man. Never lacking for confidence. Go on you two, take all the time you need, I'll tend to him until his water is cold." Jay laughed, then spoke louder over their shoulders, "And *maybe*, if he's lucky, I'll call you back to help him out before the cold water shrivels *everything*."

"Get your pretty little ass in here. And lock the door. We've got a short amount of time before they drug me up again." Kendrick's eyes were heated when Jay entered the bathroom.

"Strip."

"Say what?" Jay's eyes were wide with curiosity.

"You heard me. I'm awake enough, the pain isn't bad because the last ones haven't worn off and the warm water really helps. Strip down and join me in here."

"And where exactly am I going to sit? You're taking up the whole damn tub, you oaf." Jay rolled her eyes, but she had shimmied out of her pants.

"I have the perfect place you can sit." Kendrick reached down to adjust himself under the bubbles.

Climbing into the tub, Jay straddled his hips. "Is this okay?"

"This is beyond okay. Thank God I brushed my teeth before my bath. Kiss me, Pixie."

With one leg over the side of the tub, and one arm over the other side, he was pretty much immobile, but he made very good use of his one good hand. Trailing a finger over the tiny baby bump, he palmed the slight protrusion.

"How's my baby?"

In answer, she rocked her hips against him.

"Baby is good. But Mommy needs you."

His heated eyes sought hers as a hand trailed up to engulf a breast. Flicking at an already pebbled nipple, he growled.

"I meant what I said during the night. *I love you, Jaymison.* It may have happened quickly, it may not make a lot of sense, but I've been told true love isn't restrained by rationality or time. I love everything about you. I'm going to bury myself deep inside you and make love to you right now, but later I'll still love you because of your heart, your sass, and for being the perfect anchor for me." His large hand guided her hips toward him, allowing her to slide down his length slowly.

"Oh, shit, that's so good. The warm water is amazing. We need bathtub sex a lot more often." Jay moved up and down his length, unsuccessfully trying to keep the water from splashing.

"Reach back and drain a little water. And then I hope you're ready to work for this one, because I'm not going to be able to do much but lay here." Kendrick rocked his hips into her leisurely.

"Not a problem, I think I can handle the work for both of us this time." Jay stopped the water from draining, and began a slow up and down rhythm.

Reaching between them, Kendrick offered the only assistance he could at the time. Jay didn't complain.

Several moments later, Jay was dried off and dressed. The water was draining to hide any evidence which may have been floating. And Sawyer and Luke were called back in to help him out.

"Did you two have a nice little sexual relief session?" Kendrick smirked at his cousin.

"Did you?" Sawyer quipped without pause.

"What? I'm in two casts, recovering from a motor vehicle accident. My beautiful girlfriend was simply here to cleanse me and keep me company. I find your accusations offensive." Kendrick attempted to keep a straight face, but busted out laughing at Sawyer's quirked eyebrow.

"Fine, we learned that bathtub sex can be quite enjoyable." Kendrick winked at a blushing Jay.

"Oh my God, Kendrick, is nothing private with you?" Jay laughed.

"What, there's water all over the floor, we're both flushed and relaxed, and I'm sure they could all hear most of our interaction in here anyway. There are no secrets between friends and family."

"Although, if you wanted to keep a little bit to yourself so we had to employ our imaginations, that would be okay." Zach hollered from the hall as he walked by.

"Yeah, next time you need a bath, we're investing in ear plugs first." Luke winked.

"Alright, alright, you're all just jealous I was getting more action than you even in my injured state. Now get me the hell out of here before my balls shrivel up and we can't find them until the next bath." Kendrick reached up an arm and let Luke and Sawyer heft him from the tub. Jay wrapped a towel around him.

"I'll get him dried off, boys. Thanks for your help." Jay winked.

As the door closed again, Jay rubbed Kendrick dry with another towel.

"Let's get you dry and dressed before the pain starts up again. Are you sleeping here or at my place?"

"Let's head home. Will you sleep with me?" He held onto the counter while she helped him into his clothes.

"You know I will." Jay helped him with deodorant, and pulled a sock over the toes on his casted leg. Looking up at him, hands around his waist, her eyes watered as she said, "You know I love you too, right?"

"Yeah, Pixie, I heard you the other night. But I'll never get tired of you saying it." He kissed her before they headed to say goodbye to the crew.

14

"The hell I will!" Kendrick attempted to shoot up from his chair. Legs and arms flailing as he fought to gain some semblance of balance, he winced when pain shot through his body.

The look on Decker's face was one of smug satisfaction.

"You okay?" Decker asked dryly. When Kendrick nodded angrily, Decker continued. "While you've almost knocked yourself flat just trying to get out of the chair, you proved my point precisely. You're not ready to return to work full time. You're not able to drive yet because of the medication and the casts. If you can get someone to bring you into work a couple hours a day, you can do some desk work. But, I want you to take at least two more weeks off."

Decker crossed his arms across his chest signaling the conversation was over.

"Deck, I'm going fucking crazy at home. The medication has me in a fog, I've not felt this high since smoking pot back in school. Jay works every day, so I'm just sitting there watching soap operas. I haven't watched Days of Our Lives since college, but I turned it on last week and can still mostly follow the storylines after just a few episodes. My life is a blur of pills, pain, daytime tv, and naps."

"Sounds pretty nice to me. Enjoy it while you can. It's just a couple more weeks, three at the most. I know I won't be able to keep you away once you get the casts off." Decker walked around to sit at his desk.

"Can I at least come in here and hang out? I can staple papers or make coffee or run copies. *Something*. Please?" Kendrick pleaded with his cousin.

Decker watched him for quite a while before shrugging. He sighed heavily, "Fine. But you have to get a ride in. If you get tired, take a nap in someone's office. And if I think it's too much, I'll send you home, no questions asked."

"That's fine. It won't be a problem. I just need to be out of that house. I'll have someone bring me each day. Thanks, man. You're saving me from going insane."

"Whatever." Decker started to go back to his work, but looked up thoughtfully. "You know, Dr. Parks is here a lot lately helping Zoey with the therapy sessions she's running. Maybe you could get him to do your sessions here so you don't have to find a way to his office. Just a thought."

"Yeah, man, that's a good idea."

Kendrick checked his watch. Thank God, it's almost time for another pill. My neck and shoulder are fucking on fire.

"Hey man, one last question," Kendrick had gingerly heaved himself from the chair and hobbled toward the door, but he turned with a shit-eating grin on his face.

Decker raised an eyebrow, waiting on the question.

"Can I get a ride tomorrow morning?" Kendrick laughed at Decker's eye roll.

"Only because you're on my way. But I'm not going to be late for you, asshole. Be ready or you can find some other way to work."

"Aye-aye, Captain Tight Ass." Kendrick tried to offer a mock salute, but he misjudged the angle of the cast and ended up beaning himself in the forehead. "Fuck!"

"Serves you right. Now go home." Decker laughed before turning back to his paperwork.

KENDRICK WAS able to meet with Dr. Parks at The Center+ which allowed him to spend more time in the place he loved, with people he loved even more.

Dr. Parks still had him working through the loss of the baby, but the accident and new baby had somewhat distracted Kendrick from his anger and guilt.

"Doc, I know Sarah's suicide and the baby's death weren't

my fault. I guess I'm starting to understand it's just one of those sucky things in life we all face at some point or another. I mean, my uncle Kyle did nothing to deserve to lose his wife and baby, it was just a really shitty thing that happened. So I don't think I feel so much guilty now, but I'm sad. I just wish I could have gotten to know him or her."

"I think it would be good for you to have a memorial for the baby you lost. It would likely bring you closure. You've said Kyle found a lot of peace once he was able to name his lost baby and officially say goodbye to her. No pressure, but keep it in the back of your mind as something you may want to do." The doctor made notes as he spoke. Looking up again, he continued. "How are things with Jay?"

"Good, really good. You'll probably make notes that I'm crazy, but I'm in love with that girl. Never expected it, don't really know what to do with it, but I love her. And, maybe even crazier, I love that baby. I don't care if she looks like me, looks exactly like Tony or some other guy, or comes out green with orange hair, that's *my* baby." Kendrick spoke confidently, but then looked up hesitantly to see what the doctor would say.

"No judgement here, Kendrick. No one can control who they love or when it happens. As far as the baby goes, I think as long as you and Jay keep the biological father in the loop as much as he wants to be included, things will be okay and that baby will be lucky to have you for a dad. And a girl, huh?" The doctor smiled with eyebrows raised.

"We don't know for sure, but I want it to be a little girl. *Daddy's little girl,* I can protect and spoil. If it's a boy I'd worry I'd corrupt him and he'd turn out too much like me. The world wouldn't know what to do with a little me running around." Kendrick laughed.

"How's the neck and shoulder? You have that pained look around your eyes. You doing okay?" Dr. Parks asked as his therapist, but his concern came across like a friend.

"Yeah, the pain's still pretty intense. The pills help quite a bit."

"Be careful with the pills, huh?" Dr. Parks gave him a pointed look.

"No worries, Doc. They are *take as needed* for the pain, but I don't go over the dosage." Kendrick didn't feel the need to share he'd maybe doubled a dose here and there, or taken a pill earlier than the allotted time period. He tried to shake off the guilt. Could the doctor tell he was hiding something?

"Well, to be honest with you, it's that *as needed* that gets most people in trouble. Just let me know if you start to feel like you're needing the pills too often."

Dr. Parks glanced at his watch. "I've got to scoot, Zoey has a therapy group coming in and I said I'd help her lead it."

Kendrick watched the doctor walk away. The ever-present pain began its ascent from dull to throbbing to searing within moments. Looking at the time display on his phone, Kendrick swallowed thickly to see it was still an hour until his scheduled dosage. *Fuck it. I'll just take the meds now and push the next dose off a bit longer since I'll be asleep.* He popped the two pills in his mouth and swigged his water. Next week he would be down to just one prescription. He was really hoping the pain was more under control by then.

"ARE you sure you're feeling up to this?" Jay turned concerned eyes toward Kendrick as they walked toward the baby superstore in a neighboring town.

Glad he'd taken the extra pain pills that morning because he knew he had about four to six hours free of excruciating pain, Kendrick smiled down at her before kissing her nose. "Yep, let's go get our baby some bling."

Jay laughed. "I don't think registering was designed to get *baby bling*, but if that makes you feel better about it that's fine."

Once inside the store, the two of them stood in awe taking in the vast and varied products lining shelf after shelf after shelf.

"Whoa. Baby supply overload." Kendrick whispered. "Maybe you should have brought one of the moms with you to do this." Doubt crept into his words.

"Nope. All the moms and grandmas swore up and down this was something we needed to do together. They said it would be a fun bonding time, and we needed to register for the products *we* want, not for what others suggested to us." Jay grabbed his arm and marched up to the registry desk.

After the bored-looking teen had introduced herself as Hannah, she showed them how to input their information into the computer and how to use the scanners to mark the items they wanted to apply to their baby registry. Assuring them it was as easy as it looked, but promising to help if they needed it, Hannah went back to her perch behind the desk and glued her face back to her phone.

"Okay, first things first. Our names. I guess this is so any family or friends outside of the Torey Hope clan can look it up if need be. But, I have no one, and almost everyone you know is in Torey Hope. But, it's a required step, so..." Jay started typing in the information.

Mother's name: Jaymison "Jay" Keller
Father's name: Kendrick Jordan

"I don't like that." Kendrick stated.

"Like what?" Jay wrinkled her nose at his words.

"Keller and Jordan. I know it's maybe old-fashioned, but I'd like to see our last names matching on there. And the prospect of the baby's last name...it's just something that eats at me a bit I guess." Kendrick shrugged.

"People have different last names even when they are legally married sometimes. We've got time to figure it all out. Let's just take it one step at a time." Jay worried her lip slightly before returning her attention to the computer screen.

Once all of the pertinent information was entered, they picked up their scanners and started around the store.

Kendrick knew Jay had been reading and researching certain products, so he let her call the shots on the big pieces. Stroller, car seat, bouncy seat, bassinet, carrier, and breast pump were all on Jay. Once she had scanned those, they started in on the smaller items.

"Do you like this color? I mean, this is the diaper bag I like, but I figure you should like the color too since you'll be carrying it as well. I don't want something too girly in case it's a boy." She held up a nice-looking bag that appeared to have more functions than most adult carry-all bags.

"It's nice, I think it would look hot slung across my chest." He put it on and did a model-like walk down the aisle. "I'm going to be a DILF." He winked at her. "You know, *Dad I'd Like to Fu...*" he stopped when her hand covered his mouth. Biting at her hand, he let fiery eyes travel down her body as he nipped at her fingers.

"Shhhh! That's enough. I know what DILF stands for." She tried to sound stern, but couldn't keep the laughter from her voice. "And while I agree you'll be a very sexy dad, I don't think we need to announce it in the store."

"We should get t-shirts. Yours could say *I'm a MILF* and mine would say *I'm a DILF*. It's a good idea. Think about it."

He laughed at her eye roll, and they continued down the aisle.

"Diapers, and onesies, and booties, oh my!" Kendrick sang as they went section by section. "Wipes, and bottles, and butt cream, oh my!"

Jay laughed at him and compared two boxes of diapers. "How the hell are you supposed to decide on a type? Maybe we can register for a small box of several brands and try them all out before deciding which we like best?" She mumbled more to herself than to him. Beginning to scan various packages of diapers, she didn't appear to notice when he wandered off.

Several moments later, she looked up to find she was alone. "Kendrick?" Shaking her head, she took off to find him.

After one lap around the store, Kendrick came strolling from the book area with a smirk on his face.

"Where'd you disappear to?" Jay asked suspiciously.

"Nowhere, just doing some scanning of my own."

"Oh, Lord. Do I even want to know?" She couldn't help but snigger at the thought of Kendrick scanning items like a madman without her there to keep him in check.

"I just got some things to keep our buyers laughing. It's not like I can get into much trouble in a store dedicated to baby items." He wrapped an arm around her. "Now, if you want to go to the adult-themed store a few blocks over, I'm sure we could have a good ol' time picking out items for future sexcapades." Wagging his brows at her, he kissed the top of her head.

"No, I think we're good for now. Let's get a few more things scanned and then we'll grab something to eat before heading home. You can take some medicine with dinner if you need it, and I'll drive so you can sleep."

They chose a few outfits, blankets, and other essentials before returning to the counter to turn in their scanners.

"You guys want a printout of your registry?" Hannah asked.

"Yes, please." Jay turned wary eyes to Kendrick as the papers shot from the printer.

Walking to the car, Jay scanned down the list. "Ah, here we go. Let's see what Kendrick added. *Butt Paste? Anti-Monkey Butt? Baby Butz?* Did you think we needed an assortment of diaper creams?" She smiled at him, knowing why he'd picked those items.

"What? Those are funny. Maybe we'll give the Anti-Monkey Butt to Sawyer and Luke, tell them it's for the morning after their rough ridin'." Kendrick laughed out loud.

"Nipple cream?! You put nipple cream on our registry?" Jay smacked at him.

"What? The hemorrhoid pads and nipple cream are to take care of two of my favorite spots on your body. Our family will like to know their gift is going toward the well-being of our sex life." He edged away from her, laughing, when she smacked at him again.

"Kendrick! You don't put nipple cream and hemorrhoid pads on a registry! Oh my God, I'll be so embarrassed when people see this. And if they actually buy these things I'm going to punch you. These are things I send you out for, late at night, so you have to ask the pimply kid at the pharmacy to look up a price and he shouts *'Need a price check on nipple cream and hemorrhoid pads please.'*" She couldn't help but laugh through her blushing cheeks.

Continuing to scan down the list, she found the section of books.

"Oh! Books. I didn't even think to register for those yet. That's such a good idea, Kendrick." She kissed his cheek. "<u>Love You Forever</u>, <u>On the Night You Were Born</u>, and....Kendrick, tell me you didn't register for a book called <u>Go the F**k to Sleep</u>."

Jay looked at him in exasperation.

"What?" He tried to look innocent. "I'm sure there will be nights when we want to scream that. I figured having the book might help."

She could only shake her head at him. "I don't know how you do it, but somehow you make me love you a bit more each day." Popping up on tiptoes she kissed his lips, "Thank you for loving me and this baby. Now, let's go eat, I'm starving."

Their drinks and food arrived just in time for Kendrick to take another pill. By the time they'd eaten and paid their bill, he was beginning to feel the effects of being on his feet all day, but he had no intention of letting on he was in pain.

"I'll take you up on driving, I don't want to drive when I've just taken that pill." He stretched out the best he could in the front seat and made small talk with her as they drove.

The last thing he remembered before giving into slumber was Jay squeezing his hand, "Thanks for today, Kendrick. It was fun."

See. I can deal with the pain my way, and still give Jay the things she deserves. I just have to stay on top of the pain.

"WHAT THE FUCK is up your ass, Kendrick?" Katie poked a finger at his chest.

"Sorry, Katie, I didn't mean to snap at you." He felt bad for responding the way he did when Katie had only asked a simple question about the paperwork he had handed her.

His casts were off and he'd returned to work. He really wanted to start weaning from the medication, but fuck if the pain wasn't more than he could handle.

If he took the medication, the edge came off the pain and he felt a lot more mellow. If he didn't take the medication, his mind was a bit clearer, but he was snappy and the pain seemed to sear through his body. So did the people around him want a foggy, mellow Kendrick, or a snappy, stressed, prick Kendrick?

Katie finished thumbing through the paperwork, then

slapped it back against his chest. "Well, figure your shit out, I don't need you snapping at me."

Her eyes softened. "Kendrick, you look exhausted. Go home, take a hot shower, and get some sleep. Tomorrow is a new day, and as long as you're not biting my head off, we will be just fine."

Kendrick smiled slightly as she turned to leave. Heaving himself down on the chair, he took out the pill bottle he'd taken to carrying with him. *Take one pill up to six times a day as needed for pain.* Well, he wouldn't take them while he was sleeping, so he could push the every four hours instruction. And he damn well needed them for pain. He shook a pill into his hand. Damn, it wasn't even officially time for another one, but he'd obviously waited too long if his hands were already shaking. Swallowing the pill and washing it down with water, he headed to his car. He had to get home before the pill made him too drowsy to drive.

By the time he got home and took a hot shower the medicine was starting to ease the pain and he felt a lot less on edge. He'd just take a nap while he waited for Jay.

Before stretching out on the couch, he wrote her a note:

Hey Pixie,
Wake me when you get home. I'll be all rested and ready to play with you and Pixie Baby.
Love you,
Me

Someone was watching him. He slowly opened his eyes and shifted. Pain screamed through his body when he tried to sit up. The room was dark, his vision blurry, but he could feel the presence of someone in the room with him.

"Pixie?" He finally reached the lamp. "Why are you sitting in the dark? Why didn't you wake me up? Oh, fuck, I need to take some medicine, I slept through my last dose." He knew very well it wasn't late enough for him to take another pill, but he couldn't face climbing into bed with the red-hot pain lancing his senses.

He reached for the pill bottle, grabbed one, and swallowed it dry before reaching for water to rinse it down. Only after he'd taken the pill did he start to feel less anxious. And only then did he realize Jay hadn't answered him.

"Jay?" He watched her. She sat in a chair facing him. "Jaymison? You okay?"

The look on her face was one of being lost in a distant memory. He moved closer, touching her hand. At the contact she roused herself from her trance.

"Hey, Pixie, what's wrong? You were really zoned out there." Kendrick took her hand in his.

"Oh, yeah, sorry. Didn't mean to *scare you*." Her voice was sarcastic and edged with a venom he'd never heard.

"Whoa, where's the attitude coming from?" Kendrick tried to keep it light, but he felt a bit defensive.

"The attitude? You're right, I have no right to have an attitude when I come home to find the man I love passed out on the couch in a drugged-up stupor. So sorry to overreact, Kendrick!"

She stood and paced the room, taking a deep breath. When she turned to him, tears sparkled in her eyes. "When I couldn't wake you up, I had some bad recollections of my dad trying to wake my mom up after her benders. I was scared, Kendrick. I don't like what's happening, it's like reliving past nightmares." She turned accusing eyes towards him.

"Damn, I'm sorry. I must have overdone it at work today, I was really out of it. I promise I won't work so hard, I can't come home so exhausted and not be here for you and the baby. Won't happen again." He didn't like the accusation in her voice, but he didn't want to wade into the subject any further, so he smacked a sound kiss on her lips and leaned down to kiss her belly. "Now, let's head to bed."

In his mind he had every intention of spending quality time loving on Jay before they both slept. But, by the time she emerged from the bathroom to climb into bed, he had given into the drug-induced sleep. The worried look in Jay's eyes and the sick feeling in the pit of her stomach, were lost on his slumbering body.

15

"So, Kendrick, what brings you in today?" The robust, rosy-cheeked doctor entered the room with a smile on his face.

"I, uh, just needed a refill on my prescription." Kendrick's voice stammered.

It had been four months since the accident. His leg and arm seemed to have healed fine. All internal injuries were forgotten. But his shoulder and neck were still causing him a lot of pain.

The doctor read over his chart. "On a level of one to ten, what's your pain like on average?" The doctor glanced up.

"If ten is the worst, then it's a ten. I can't seem to shake the pain in my shoulder and neck." Kendrick's hands shook. His last script had ended yesterday. He'd finished the pills a whole day early. He'd lived in a hot bathtub for the last 36 hours, trying to ease the pain while waiting to see the doctor for a new script.

"I'm a little hesitant to give you another script this time, Kendrick. This pain is something that should have started to abate by now. I'd like to set you up in some physical therapy for your neck and shoulder."

"Well, it maybe *should* have abated by now, Doc, but it most definitely hasn't. I'm dying here. Give me another month, if it's not better by then, I'll do the physical therapy." Kendrick knew his eyes had to have the look of an alcoholic looking for his next shot, but he was desperate to get the pills to ease his pain and calm the craving in his body.

"Okay, one more month, but then we've got to take a different course of action. Last thing you need is to become dependent on pain medication." The ruddy-faced doctor laughed.

Kendrick smiled tightly, his only thought on getting to the pharmacy and how fast they could fill the script.

"So, the doctor gave you another refill?" Jay's voice held concern, but Kendrick heard judgment.

"Yeah, Jay, he did. He knows I'm still dealing with a lot of pain." Kendrick snapped. He had finally gotten the pill bottle opened in the pharmacy parking lot. He took two pills at once, thinking he could ease the pain quicker than with just one. Once the pain was back under control somewhat, he would skip a dose here or there.

Now standing in the kitchen, Jay watching him closely, he stared into the pill bottle and almost obsessively counted the pills, trying to plan how many he could take each day before he'd need a new script.

But the doctor said no more refills.

Fuck that. I'll find another doctor.

He felt the moment the medication began to enter his bloodstream. His body began to relax, he felt calmer than he had in a couple days. This is why I need the pills. If I'm in pain, I'm an asshole no one wants to be around. This way, I get rid of the worst of the pain, and I stop snapping at others.

"No need to get shitty, Kendrick. I just worry that you're taking a lot of pills and the pain isn't getting any better." Jay's brow creased. "This baby will be here in a few months, I'll need your help. I just don't want you to have to keep dealing with this pain." She lowered her voice, "And, honestly, I don't think I could take it if another person in my life chose a substance addiction over me."

"Pixie, I love you. Thank you for your concern, but I'm fine. The pills help, and I think the pain is getting better a bit each day." He hated lying to her, but he didn't want her to worry. "I'm even going to start skipping some doses of the medication, wean down from the higher dosages. I'll be here for you and the baby, no worries."

~

BUT SKIPPING doses didn't work. Without the medication he was grumpy, unfocused, and overwhelmed with pain. So he spaced the pills out as much as he could in hopes of saving them for as long as possible. But he knew the pills would be gone soon. He needed to get a new script. He contemplated this at lunch while sitting in the employee lounge.

"Hey, man, where'd you go when you broke your leg last year?" Kendrick tried to sound nonchalant while asking the question of one of his employees. The man's name was Billy if he remembered correctly. He'd broken his leg in a nasty fall during a staff football game last year.

"Well, I was still living in Whitley, so I went to a local doctor there." The man leaned in conspiratorially, "To tell you the truth, I still go over there from time to time. Let's just say Dr. Smith doesn't mind writing scripts for pretty much anything I ask for. He's very generous in his prescribing if you know what I mean."

Kendrick tried not to look pleased. He had only hoped to find a new doctor, never planned on finding one who was passing pills out like candy. Attempting to keep the excitement from his voice, he asked, "Yeah? What do you usually ask for?"

"Vicodin, oxy, anything I can get a nice little high from, you know?" The man seemed to register what he'd just said to *his boss* and had the presence of mind to at least look somewhat guilty. "I mean, not that I'm ever high at work. Just evenings and weekends, to take the edge off. Know what I mean?"

"Yeah, man, I totally know what you mean. People who haven't been in pain just don't get it." Kendrick inwardly rolled his eyes. Had he lost all of his integrity stooping low enough to discuss pain pill highs with a man who logically shouldn't even be his employee any longer? No, he just needed to get a few more pills so he could keep working and be there for Jay. If this round didn't do the trick, he'd for sure look into that physical therapy.

"Hey man, here, let me give you a few extras." The man rattled some pills in a bottle and tossed them at Kendrick. "And be sure to look up Dr. Smith in Whitley. Tell him Billy sent you, he'll hook you up."

"Uh, yeah man, thanks. Not sure I need to see him, but thanks for the suggestion." Kendrick nodded at the man, shoved the pills in his pocket, and headed out of the room. Before he'd even reached his office, he had his phone out looking up the number to Dr. Smith in Whitley.

16

He had an appointment with Dr. Smith scheduled for the end of the week. The sympathetic receptionist had worked him in the best she could, but it seemed Dr. Smith was an extremely popular guy. Until then, he would just have to space the pills the best he could. And hang out with his family and friends in hopes of keeping up appearances, when all he really wanted to do was hide in his room and shut out the world.

"Hey man, pause the game, I've got to piss." Kendrick rolled his stiff shoulders, hoping the pain would stay at a dull ache and not rage to searing with the movement. He laid the controller down and headed toward the bathroom while Zach moved to the kitchen to get them each a drink and a bowl of chips.

Before leaving the bathroom, he glanced in the mirror.

He'd not taken a good look at himself recently; he didn't exactly like what he saw. Did he really look as disheveled and disconnected as he felt, or was that just his imagination.

For no other reason but nosiness, he opened the mirrored cabinet above the sink. It's not really nosiness. I used to live here. Hell, I probably even left some of my stuff here.

He didn't know why he felt the need to rationalize opening that cabinet, but the thoughts played through his head as he stared at the variety of items filling the shelves. Toothpaste, tweezers, hair gel, Band-Aids, pill bottle, mouthwash, floss, qtips. *Pill bottle?* The opaque orange called to him.

Doesn't matter, it's not yours. Probably not even pain medication anyway.

He scolded himself, but even as he thought the words, his hand slowly reached into the cabinet to turn the bottle slightly so he could see the label.

ZOEY MARTIN *was written boldly on the sticker. Vicodin. The date on the bottle indicated it had been in the cabinet since Zoey's attack out in California. The bottle was over half full. Zoey never really dealt with a lot of pain, but the doctor probably prescribed the medication for the bump to her head. She's barely taken any of the pills. I bet she's even forgotten they're in here.*

He grabbed the bottle, clutching it tightly in his hand.

Zach's voice and the creak of the door registered a

moment too late, and Kendrick looked up guiltily with the pill bottle still in his death grip.

"You okay, man? You've been in here forever." Zach eyed the pill bottle then looked back up at Kendrick.

"Um, yeah, shit sorry about that. Um, it's just that I forgot my prescription and the pain's starting to get really bad. I was just looking to see if there was something in here I could take to lighten the worst of it for now." He shook the bottle and tried to joke. "Looks like Zoey's not using these. Think she'd mind if I borrowed one?"

"Oh, um, yeah. I guess that would be alright. She never really used those." Zach stood at the door, waiting.

"Okay, thanks." Kendrick reached for the door, pushing it shut as he spoke, "Just going to finish up in here. I'll be in to kick your ass on that game in just a second."

Confusion and worry flickered across Zach's face, but he backed away from the door and headed back to the living room.

Feeling like a complete jackass, Kendrick quickly opened the bottle and poured a majority of the contents into his hand. Making sure there were some pills left, he replaced the lid and put it back in the cabinet. Plucking one from his hand, Kendrick looked disdainfully at the little white pill. *Looks like a damn bullet. Like a bullet straight through the pain. My magic bullet to make everything better.*

He pocketed the rest of the pills. Swallowing the pill with

water from the sink, he gritted as it caught in his throat. *Oh, guilt, you're one tough bastard to swallow.*

Returning to the living room, he drained the water Zach had gotten for him. He walked to the kitchen to grab a tall glass of milk before they finished the game.

BY THE END of the week, things were looking up. Dr. Smith was true to Billy's word and hooked him up with a month of pills, and included three months of refills.

"Hey man, thanks for the recommendation. Dr. Smith seems like a great guy. This pain just isn't going away, so being able to get a new script was really helpful." Kendrick nodded at Billy the next week in the lunch room.

"Yeah, and the mellow high isn't half bad either, right?" Billy snorted.

"Nah, man, just need them for the pain." Kendrick's words sounded unconvincing even to his own ears.

"Whatever you need to tell yourself, man." Billy winked. "Want some advice? If there's ever a time when you've missed a dose and need a really quick shot, grind the pills up and snort them. Works within seconds."

Kendrick stood staring at the man in disbelief. Was he really having a conversation about snorting pain pills with one of his employees? He should march his ass down to Decker's office and turn Billy in for drug abuse. The Center+ ran a respectable family business, they didn't need a drug user on staff. *But, if you turn Billy into Decker you'll have to admit to how you know Billy is doing drugs. And Billy will likely have no qualms about telling Decker you've visited Dr. Smith. If Decker fires Billy for drug use, he might as well fire you as well. Double-standards much?*

Kendrick grimaced as Billy went on and on about snorting the pills. "Uh, yeah, great. I'll keep that in mind."

He left the lounge with a strange sense of relief. I wouldn't actually snort the pills. It's just good to know it's an option, a last resort.

A *HIS AND Her* baby shower was being held for the entire family at Audrey and Jeremiah's home. Kendrick kissed his mom's cheek when they arrived.

"Mmmm, smells good in here, Momma. Whatcha cookin'?"

"Jay requested nachos and pretzels. The cheese and meat for the nachos are simmering, and the pretzels are baking. Everything should be ready for us to eat in about twenty minutes." Audrey hugged Kendrick and Jay.

"Thank you so much for hosting the shower for us." Jay had been touched when Katie and Zoey had offered to throw them a shower and Audrey had insisted they use her home.

"You know this group never turns down a chance to have a party. I think we'll mingle, then eat, then games, gifts, and end with desserts if that's alright with you guys. Head on into the living room. I was helping the girls with decorations, I think it looks great." Audrey pushed them into the living room which was bright with every color of the rainbow.

"Oh my gosh, you guys! This looks fabulous!" Jay held both hands up to her face.

"Do you love it? We wanted to keep it gender-neutral but still be bright and colorful and fun. Here, you guys come over here and we'll take some pictures." Katie ushered them around the room to stand by the gifts, the cake, the food table.

When the pictures were done, Katie and Zoey left the room for a bit, and Jay turned to Kendrick with tears in her eyes.

"What's wrong, Pixie? Too much? You don't like it?" He instantly brushed her tears away with his thumbs.

"No, no, it's so very perfect. I'm just thinking about what could have been."

He watched her as she searched for her words.

"I have never felt as loved as I do when I'm with you and your family. And I almost took that away from myself and this baby because I was scared and selfish." She sniffed her nose. "It's just ironic that I thought this baby would be the end of my life as I knew it, but it turns out this baby was the beginning of a life I had only ever dreamed of having."

She turned and looked directly into his eyes. "And the fact that you love and support me and *our* baby, even when we don't know if it's biologically yours..." She swallowed her tears. "You just blow me away every single day, Kendrick."

He kissed her deeply before whispering in her ear, "Genetics be damned, this baby is mine. I will love, support, and protect the two of you until my dying day. Good times, bad times, highs and lows, laughter and tears...I'll be beside you both through it all."

He meant every word he spoke. And he knew he could keep those promises as long as he kept his head above water with work, the pain, the pills, and keeping up appearances.

The shower was complete and total hilarity as was usual with the Deckers, Jordans, Morgans, and Martins. After they had stuffed themselves on nachos and pretzels, they moved to the games. The men had to race to drink milk from bottles. Kendrick was disqualified when he took the lid off and chugged the milk.

The next game had teams trying to guess the contents of dirty baby diapers. Strained peas, some sort of pureed meat, and a melted chocolate bar brought the most laughter. Decker turned a little green around the gills when Katie suggested he sniff the diaper to figure out the substance.

"Man, I don't know how a control freak like you will ever have a kid. You do know you can't schedule the baby's diapers and spit-ups, right?" Zach laughed at his cousin who quickly flipped him the bird with a wry smile before kissing Katie firmly on the mouth.

Kendrick watched them momentarily. He had a feeling those two would be making their relationship more official and starting a family a lot sooner than anyone had ever imagined Decker settling down. But Katie had mellowed Decker so much, and the two of them just fit.

The final game was for one partner to coach their blindfolded partner through changing a baby's diaper. Once the teams had chosen one partner to be blindfolded, Asher and Aly came in with squirt guns. Smiling slyly, they shushed the other members of the teams.

"On your mark, get set, GO!"

As soon as a person would get a diaper off their baby, Aly or Asher would spray them in the face with the water.

"What the hell is that?" Decker shouted.

"Well, with a *real* baby, especially boys, it *could be* pee. You and Sawyer used to pee on your dad and me every chance you got." Libby smiled as she watched her son struggle to diaper the baby in front of him.

"I definitely got the wrong end of this game." Zach grumbled as his sister sprayed him with water.

"You used to pee on me with every diaper change. I started putting a cup over you just to make it through without getting soaked." Nicky smiled as his son tried unsuccessfully to block the water raining down on him.

"Done!" Luke pulled off his blindfold and high-fived Sawyer.

Kendrick ripped off his own blindfold, "How the hell did you do it so fast?" He looked down at his own pathetic attempt to diaper his doll. His face dripped with water, the powder was spilled and getting pasty in the water, and the diaper was most definitely on backwards. Possibly upside down.

"We worked together as a team. Sawyer held my hands and guided them through each step." Turning, Luke kissed Sawyer. "Good job."

"So, I'm the one getting ready to have a real live baby in my care, but you two are the ones wiping, cleaning, and powdering butts like old pros. That's just great." Kendrick pouted as he looked down again at his own lackluster results. Turning to Jay, he shrugged and smiled. "You know what this means?"

She giggled, "We need to practice? A lot."

"Nope. It means Sawyer and Luke are the first official babysitters after the grandparents. Grandparents get first dibs because they've already successfully raised children without causing serious harm to them. But, Sawyer and Luke are the first on the backup list. At least until Decker and Katie or Zach and Zoey get better at diapers."

"What about until we get better at diapers?" Jay questioned.

Glancing at their doll, then at the perfectly diapered and

dressed doll in front of Sawyer and Luke, Kendrick shrugged. "You guys want to make some extra money? I'll pay per diaper. Double through the night."

The group laughed.

"No way, man. You'll get it. You and Jay will get your own little system worked out." Sawyer laughed while he drew Luke close to his side.

Kendrick watched the love that shone between those two men. Several months ago he would have envied that love as something he didn't think possible for himself. But now he knew just how it felt to be in love with your perfect someone.

"Okay, time for gifts. Jay and Kendrick, you guys sit there at the front. We'll bring the gifts to you." Zoey walked toward the gifts, and Zach trailed behind her. Kendrick couldn't help but notice how Zach pulled Zoey close to him, whispering in her ear as they prepared the gifts. Those two had waited such a very long time for their happily ever after. If ever there was a *perfect couple* it was Zach and Zoey, even though they were far from actually being perfect.

Ooohs and ahhhs sounded around the room as tiny baby clothes were unwrapped. Extreme gratitude filled the room as essentials were unwrapped. Hoots and hollers of laughter rang out when Kendrick opened the Go the F**k to Sleep book along with *Butt Paste, Baby Butz* and *Anti-Monkey Butt.*

"Hey, Sawyer, I was thinking you and Luke may want to keep some of the cream for yourselves." Kendrick winked at his cousin.

Ever calm and unflappable, Sawyer just smirked, "No worries, we bought ourselves a second tube to keep at home just in case."

The whole group laughed amidst some groans of "Whoa, too much information," and Kendrick dodged slaps from both Jay and his mother.

"Who is ready for dessert? I brought cake and an assortment of donuts." Grandma Janie not only baked the best desserts, but she was always bringing goodies from The Cakery.

Pulling Jay to stand up, Kendrick kissed her nose.

"I just have to take a piss. I want cake, and a donut, and whatever else looks good. Plus a big glass of..."

"Milk. I know." She grinned at him.

When he finished in the bathroom, Kendrick peeked out the door. When he was sure no one was nearby, he closed and locked the door. Cracking open the closet where he knew his parents kept their medications, he began to pilfer through the various bottles. Pulling a basket close to him, cradling it against his chest, he perused the label on each bottle. All OTC pain relievers, nothing he could use.

When the door opened behind him, he jumped like he'd been shot. Bottles and various items flew from the basket, raining to the floor. Immediately he knelt down and began picking up the mess.

"Ooops, sorry. Forgot to tell you the door doesn't lock anymore. Dad hasn't fixed it yet." Audrey looked at the closet to Kendrick and back to the closet with a confused look.

"*Shit, you scared me, Mom.*" *He sheepishly ducked his head, trying his best to look innocent. No, Mom, I wasn't digging through your medicine cabinet in hopes of stealing your prescriptions.*

"Sorry, you were in here such a long time I thought I'd check on you." Audrey's eyes held true concern as she brushed a hand over his face. "Are you feeling okay?"

"What? Oh yeah, Mom, I'm fine. I mean, my neck and shoulder still hurt like a bitch, but I'm surviving." He stood again, the basket of medication clutched to his chest.

Audrey looked at him pointedly. "Were you looking for something in particular or just snooping for the hell of it?" She smiled wryly.

Kendrick stared at her, trying to come up with a plausible answer.

He glanced down at the basket, inwardly sighing with regret that there were no prescriptions in it. "Oh, um, yeah. I've got a nasty hangnail. Just looking for the nail clippers." He rattled the basket, "Not in here." Chuckling he returned the basket to the closet.

"You weren't even close to finding them." Audrey smiled. "Here, Dad still keeps them in the sink drawer like he always has." She pulled the clippers out, handing them to him.

"Ah, should have known. They were so close the whole

time." Kendrick faked a laugh, pretending to inspect a hangnail before going through the motions of clipping it off.

Putting the clippers back in the drawer, Kendrick ushered
his mother out of the bathroom. "Let's go eat, Janie makes the
best donuts in the world."

Audrey smiled at him, wrapping her arm around his
waist. "That she does."

She looked up at him. "Are you happy, Kendrick?"

Taken by surprise, Kendrick stopped short.

He thought about the question. If he pushed aside the
pain, pushed aside the overwhelming worry of how and when
he'd get more pills to dull the pain, and pushed aside the
stress of keeping up the façade in front of his family...if he
ignored all of that and focused just on Jay and the baby and
his job and his family, yes he was happy.

Smiling softly at his mom, he nodded his head, "Yeah,
Mom, I'm happy."

Audrey's smile held relief, "That's all I can ask for. I love
you, Kendrick."

"Love you too, Mom."

"THAT SAUNA WAS the best addition to the gym area *ever*."
Kendrick clapped Decker on the back.

Decker smirked. "Glad you like it. Does it help with the pain?"

"Yeah, man, it really does." *The sauna helps, but the pills ain't half bad either.* Kendrick snorted in laughter at his thoughts.

Decker raised an eyebrow at him.

Feeling like a high school kid trying to hide his buzz, Kendrick tried to smother his laughter.

"You okay, man?" Decker eyed him suspiciously.

"Yeah, yeah, I'm fine. Just enjoyed the sauna a lot." Kendrick smiled like a fool while he checked the time. "Gotta split, man. I need to find Jay."

He left The Center+ and headed toward The Café. Jay's shift would be almost over. He was hopeful she'd be asking for some time off soon. He didn't think she needed to be on her feet as the pregnancy neared the end. She had a couple months still, but he would feel better knowing she was at home, safe, where he could protect her.

Walking into The Café, the jingle of the bells announced his arrival. Jay looked up and smiled immediately, but her brow creased within seconds. Pulling her into his arms, he kissed her deeply. Or rather, he *tried* to kiss her deeply, but she thwarted his efforts and he ended up just slobbering on her and himself.

"What the hell are you doing, Kendrick? I'm *working*. You can't come in here and just start mauling me." Jay pushed at his chest.

"Why not? Baby Daddy just wants a little lovin'." He spoke loudly, trying to cover his laughter. Grabbing her by the hand, he pulled her through the back exit, shouting to her boss that she'd be back after her fifteen minute break.

In the brightly lit ally, he pulled her to his chest. "Come on, Jay. We haven't had much time together lately. I miss you. I just wanted some kisses."

The scrutinizing look she ran over his face immediately made him feel self-conscious.

"How many pills have you taken today, Kendrick?" Her voice was shaky, tight.

"I took as many as I needed for the pain. You don't know how bad it hurts. The pills are from a doctor, I'm fine." He instantly felt defensive, backing away from her. "You need me there for you, you need me ready for the baby. No one wants to be around me when I'm being a complete dick, so I take the pills so I can function through the pain. You're not my fucking mother, so maybe you should back off."

Fire flashed in Jay's eyes. She gritted her teeth and looked at the ground for a moment before lifting her head and poking him in the chest.

"You know what? You're right. I'm not your mother. But I *did* watch my mother and my father both struggle with addictions my entire life. I'm no stranger to the glassy-eyed excuses, the snappy lows, the mellowed state, the happy highs. Speaking of your mother, what exactly do you think your mom would say if she knew how much that little pill bottle has come to mean to you?"

Guilt ate at Kendrick's soul, but anger was easier to deal with. He threw his hands up in the air and tried only half-heartedly to keep his voice at a respectable level.

"I'm guessing she'd be proud of me for being able to come back from a life-threatening accident to return to work, spend time with the woman I love, and prepare for her grandchild to arrive. But, maybe that's not enough for you, huh? Not enough that I'm working my ass off for you and the baby when all I really want to do is curl into a ball and escape the pain? Sorry to be such a disappointment." Guilt bubbled inside his gut, but he clung to the anger instead. Accepting the guilt meant admitting he was in the wrong. Holding onto the anger allowed him to cover the real problem and put the blame elsewhere.

Jay's eyes glistened. "Kendrick, I never asked you to be here for me or this baby. You took this position on your own, and as much as I've come to love you and look forward to our future and raising this baby with you, I have to tell you something."

His heart plummeted as she spoke.

"Almost nine months ago I never would have thought I could emotionally survive a pregnancy, let alone raise a child. But, thanks to your love and support, and the ever present support from your family, I know I *can* do this alone if needed. I would miss you terribly, but if you continue to choose drugs over everything else in your life, I *will* do it by myself. The best and worst part of that would be knowing each and every member of your family would stand by my side to help with this baby even as they stood by your side to help you through this rough time. Having your family without having you would likely almost kill me, but I'm strong enough to do it. This baby doesn't deserve to grow up with an addict for a dad. Hell, I don't deserve to spend the rest of my life in second place to drugs. Get your shit figured out." Jay's eyes held fear, hurt, and longing as she gave him one last look and walked away.

She hadn't said the words, but he heard the ultimatum loud and clear. If he couldn't get himself away from the pills, he'd find himself living without Jay and the baby.

He pinched the bridge of his noise, fighting the wave of nausea washing over his body. He had three months of pills. He couldn't just stop cold turkey, but he could space them out and wean himself down until they were gone. He'd just have to toughen up against the pain. And do a better job of hiding the side effects from those around him. He could do this. He had to. Losing Jay and the baby would be like living his worst nightmare all over again.

17

$\mathcal{J}$ay's palms were sweaty as she walked up the steps to Jeremiah and Audrey Jordan's home. She'd been to Kendrick's parents' home several times, but this time was different. Not long ago she'd been at the home to celebrate the upcoming arrival of the baby with Kendrick's family. But today wasn't for a happy celebration. She doubted there would be laughter or smiles, more likely anger and tears.

When she'd called Katie and told her she was worried about Kendrick, tears had filled her eyes when the other woman had agreed with her concern. Maybe Jay had been hoping she was seeing things that weren't there; having Katie agree with her was both a relief and a burden. Katie's concern for Kendrick meant Jay's concerns and worries were valid. And that meant something needed to be done.

Katie and Zoey met her at the door. She knew all the family had been invited to attend the get together, except Kendrick. He was at home, sleeping. Lately, if he wasn't glassy-eyed high, he was asleep.

She rounded the corner to the living room, decaf tea in hand thanks to Zoey, and found herself face-to-face with Kendrick's entire family. Over the past several months she had grown to love this group of people more than she had ever imagined possible. She loved them because they were real, they were all a part of Kendrick. They loved and protected and supported each other fiercely, and they called each other on their shit when necessary. It was all of those things which made her both nervous and confident about calling them together.

With greetings, tummy rubs, and general small talk out of the way, Decker took charge as usual. Jay didn't mind him taking the reins to get things started because she wasn't exactly sure how to begin.

"So, we all know Jay called us here today, and as much as it's great to see everyone and visit, I don't think she had a general social gathering in mind. Jay, the floor is yours." Decker nodded at her as the rest of the family took their places around the room.

Reminiscent of Kendrick sharing the nightmare of his past with the family so many months ago, Jay sat on the ottoman with Decker and Katie seated to her left, Zach and Zoey seated to her right, and Luke and Sawyer seated at her back. She hadn't been present when Kendrick had faced his family in exactly the same way, but the arrangement wasn't lost on the other members.

"First, I want to thank you all for coming. I also want to thank you all for accepting me and the baby into your family with open arms. I've fallen in love with all of you almost as much as I've fallen in love with Kendrick. I grew up thinking love was a mythical thing, only people in fictional stories got to know the love of family and friends. But, then I stumbled upon Kendrick and all of you; you've all shown me what it means to be strong, stand for what is right, and love beyond measure." Jay took a sip of her tea, calming her nerves as much as she could, knowing what she had to say next was likely to go over like a lead balloon. When Katie and Zoey both reached for her, she felt a renewed sense of strength.

"Because of all of that, what I'm about to say is not only extremely difficult, it's also terribly important." Taking a deep breath, she continued, "I think Kendrick is in trouble."

Every eye in the room was on her, every breath was being held waiting for her to go on.

"I think he's gotten himself in too deep with the pain pills he's been taking since the accident. I watched both of my parents struggle with and eventually die from substance abuse, and I'm seeing the same behaviors from Kendrick. It breaks my heart to admit this to all of you, but I'm truly scared for him." Jay stopped, and looked around the room.

"What type of things are you seeing?" The Captain spoke up gruffly.

"Glassy eyes, sleeping much more than usual, happy highs, snappy lows, and excuses left and right." Jay braced for a fight from those who didn't believe her. She didn't want a fight, but part of her longed for someone to come to Kendrick's rescue and save him from the accusations she was making.

"This is ridiculous." Audrey's eyes were narrowed, contempt flowed from her words. "You come into *my* house and accuse my son of substance abuse? The man was in a terrifying auto accident, he's still in terrible pain, he's working his ass off to be there for you and a baby that likely isn't even his, and yet you've called us all here to throw him under the bus? What type of person does that? What could you possibly know about Kendrick that the rest of us wouldn't know?"

Jay looked down. She didn't want to fight with Audrey, but she wasn't surprised Kendrick's mother was the one to defend him. It made sense on several different levels. No mother wants to admit her child is having problems. And admitting to Kendrick's problems would possibly be hitting too close to home based on Audrey's unsavory actions in the past.

Jeremiah seemed to sense his wife's distress, but also to recognize his son's dangerous situation. Laying a hand on Audrey's shoulder, he spoke softly, "Let's hear Jay out. If Kendrick's in trouble he needs us to be there for him, not

pulling blinders over our eyes instead of facing the truth."
Jeremiah pulled his angry wife close and nodded at Jay to
continue.

"I called you all here today in hopes of putting our obser-
vations and ideas together in a way in which we can help
Kendrick. I know from stories you've all told me that
Kendrick would be doing the same thing if he suspected one
of you was in trouble because he loves you all more than life
itself. I want us to come up with ways to help him. My hope
is our ideas and love can pull him out of this." Jay felt the
confidence wane from her as she finished her little speech.

But, within moments, many members of the family began
to speak and her hope was buoyed.

"Kendrick has been snappy at work over the tiniest little
things. He and I have had more than one run in over the past
several weeks since he came back to work full time." Katie
spoke up.

"I didn't think much about it until now, but Kendrick
seemed really weird at work the other day. Talking about how
much he loved the sauna and almost giggling. Sort of like a
kid who's drunk trying to hide the fact that he's drunk." Decker's brow creased in worry as he remembered the incident.

"Oh dear," Grandma Cindy spoke up, "I didn't think a
thing about it until you brought this up, but Kendrick was
over the other day. He brought over a piece of mail that had
accidentally been delivered to The Center+. He was asking
all about arthritis medication. Asked what I took for mine and

what Judy takes for hers. He was overly interested in it, something he's never even asked about before." Cindy looked worriedly at her husband.

A dismayed sound came from Grandma Judy. She closed her eyes as if to will herself to continue. "Kendrick came over the other day asking to borrow a tool from the garage. He excused himself to go to the restroom and was gone for a very long time. When he finally came out, he gave me a quick hug, grabbed the tool, and left immediately. Later that night, I noticed the medicine cabinet was a mess. I accused Jack of digging in it and not cleaning it up, but he said he hadn't been in that cabinet in weeks. If what you're saying is true, it was likely Kendrick looking for pain medication."

The entire family was silent while they absorbed this information.

Audrey laughed bitterly.

"So, a bunch of coincidental things happen, and because Kendrick's new flavor of the month is trying to burn him at the stake, you all just automatically assume the worst about the boy you've watched grow up? You take her side over your actual family?" She shook her head in disgust. "Unbelievable."

"Audrey, that's enough." The Captain spoke sharply. "You're likely a bit too close to this situation as both a mother and someone who has dealt with some traumatic past issues. But, if Kendrick is in trouble, we all need to put aside our feelings on the matter and help him." He sighed deeply. "You and

I both know the backlash that can come from not admitting to problems right in front of our faces."

Audrey's jaw clenched. She looked as if she wanted to say something, but she kept quiet.

"Oh, shit." Sawyer exclaimed. "I was cleaning out a drawer in my room about two weeks ago. I found an old prescription bottle of pain pills the doctor had prescribed after the attack in the park. It was empty, but I knew I hadn't taken all of them. I even asked Luke if he'd taken some. We didn't come up with an answer so we let it go, but now it seems more likely that Kendrick took them." Sawyer's face was tight with worry.

"So some pills go missing and it *has* to be Kendrick?" Audrey sneered.

"No, Aunt Audrey, it's not just missing pills and assuming it's Kendrick. I saw it with my own eyes. He was in the bathroom a very long time the other day. I walked in to find him holding an old pill bottle of Zoey's in a death grip. He said he'd forgotten his at home and wanted to know if he could borrow one of Zoey's. It was a really awkward situation. I'd bet money that the bottle is almost empty now, if not completely empty." Zach's face was etched in sadness and concern.

"So, Kendrick's in trouble, he needs our help. What do we do?" Kyle spoke up.

"I remember, after the attack, you all took turns calling me or stopping by to talk to me. Maybe we could all take some time to talk to Kendrick and let him know we're thinking of him. It won't stop him from abusing the pills, but it will let him know we're there for him whenever we figure out what the next step needs to be." Zoey spoke softly.

The gathering broke up somewhat awkwardly. Even though no one was happy about what was happening, they were all grateful to Jay for bringing it to their attention. Good-byes were said and most of the group had departed, leaving Jay with Audrey and Jeremiah.

"I'm so very sorry to have upset you like this." Jay attempted to keep the quiver from her voice.

"Audrey, I think you should tell Jay about the day of the baby shower." Jeremiah held his wife close to his side.

"That was nothing, J." Audrey tried to dismiss the subject.

"Angel, if it was nothing you wouldn't have mentioned it to me that night." Jeremiah nudged her again.

"Kendrick took a long time in the bathroom and I was worried about him. I walked in on him because the lock still doesn't work right..." She trailed off, trying to focus the attention on her husband for not fixing the lock.

"Go on." Jeremiah nodded.

"It was nothing. He jumped when I walked in, spilled a basket all over the floor." It was evident Audrey didn't want to continue the story.

Jeremiah took over. "He was looking in the closet where we keep all of our medicines. Told his mom he was looking for the nail clippers. It struck Audrey as odd because we've kept the nail clippers in the sink drawer since before Kendrick was born."

He stopped and looked at his wife. "You and I both know Kendrick knew where the clippers were. He wasn't looking for them, he was looking for prescriptions. Audrey, Kendrick is in trouble."

Jeremiah turned to Jay. "I'm sorry if you felt attacked tonight. It's really hard to hear your child is having issues with drugs. Audrey may not be ready to accept it and apologize to you, but on behalf of both of us, thank you for speaking up."

Audrey sighed and pulled Jay into a hug. "And I'm sorry for the nasty things I said in there. I just don't think Kendrick has the problem you're saying he does."

Audrey looked at Jeremiah over Jay's shoulder. When he nodded at her, she continued.

"And to be quite honest, it's putting a lot of guilt on me because it's very *like mother, like son* and that means bringing up my past sins which is not a lot of fun." Releasing Jay from the hug, she smiled slightly. "The only thing I can cling to right now is that you're wrong. Completely, totally, dead wrong."

Jay's eyes filled with tears. "Believe me, I wish I was."

18

Kendrick felt like he was in the movie Groundhog's Day.

The entire week had been on a continuous loop. He woke in pain, took the fewest pills possible, but knew he was still taking too many. He completed his work to the best of his foggy-headed ability, but he knew he was doing a half-assed job. Deep down he feared he was at risk of damaging the program he'd been working so hard to build. He did his best to stay awake to spend time with Jay, but usually a warm shower and a bedtime pill relaxed him so much that he wasn't able to keep his eyes open.

The other thing that played on repeat during his week, aside from the pain and the pills, was the strange occurrence of almost every single family member calling him up and asking to meet him for coffee.

The first day had been his mom and dad. It was a bit strange, but he figured they were just missing seeing him and wanted to check in on him. They'd sat around talking for about an hour, sipping their coffee at the local shop. His mom had held onto him tighter than usual when they'd said goodbye.

"You know you can always come to us for anything, right?" Audrey had looked deep into his eyes. "I love you more than life itself and would do anything to help you. Don't ever forget that, baby boy."

Kendrick had watched the two of them walk away, confusion crossing his face. If he had heard his mother's whispered words, "She's right. I can see it in his eyes," he would have been even more confused.

But, as it was, his confusion and suspicion just slowly grew as each day brought a new request for coffee.

Nate, Nicky, and Kyle had directed him to a corner booth in the back and seemed highly sensitive to his fingers tapping on the table. At one point he finally had to dismiss himself because Uncle Nicky staring intently at his eyes had made him extremely self-conscious.

When he returned from the restroom, the other three men had stood to leave. Glad to have the strange get together over, Kendrick had accepted the clap on his good shoulder and nodded when the three men declared he could call them at any time about *anything*.

By the time Zach, Zoey, and the Captain invited him for

coffee, he was getting slightly pissed. He'd had a fight with Jay that morning when she'd snapped at him about their failed attempt at sex the night before.

"Hey, Pixie, stay in bed a bit longer. You can be late." He'd nuzzled her neck and started his hand roaming over her body.

"No, Kendrick, you had your chance last night. You couldn't get it up and fell asleep halfway through that lame-ass attempt at foreplay. Maybe if you stopped the pills, you'd have a better chance at gettin' some. But, as it is, I'd rather be at work." He'd watched in angry disbelief as she'd walked from the room.

Feeling ashamed and guilty, he yelled from the other side of the bathroom door. "Thanks for kicking a man when he's down. I'll see you later tonight."

So sitting across from his cousins and grandpa, wondering if they knew about all the other family members planning secret little coffee shop talks with him during the week, he felt nothing but itchy and anxious.

"Let me guess. You all called me here today to let me know you love me, you'd do anything to help me if I was in trouble, and I should call you if I ever need anything. Is that about it? Because, unless you've got something new to say, I'm going to order my coffee to go and head back to work." He inwardly sneered at the looks on their faces.

Zoey chose to ignore his little outburst. "Kendrick, I know you're still in pain. I want to have you start some private yoga lessons with me. We can do it at The Center+ or at home. And the neurokinesis I'm trained in should be able to provide you with a ton of pain relief; it's a therapy that addresses the underlying cause of your pain and works to correct the dysfunctional movement patterns stored in your brain. We can set up multiple sessions and get that pain under control once and for all. And the therapy sessions at The Center+ are always open to anyone needing to talk about issues. I run a lot of them, but Dr. Parks is available too." Zoey ducked her head sheepishly, "I know you've been skipping therapy sessions and avoiding Dr. Parks. Maybe it would be helpful to get back into that routine?"

Kendrick could only glare at her, fearful if he opened his mouth he would say something he regretted. He looked to Zach and found the usually laid-back, affable man staring at him with a challenge in his eyes.

"You can think of the yoga and different therapies as payback to Zoey for the pills you borrowed from her the other day." Zach spoke in a soft, yet deadly serious voice.

Shit.

Shit, fuck, shit.

"Kendrick, you know I don't mince words with you boys. You need to get your head out of your fucking ass and fix this. You've got a girl you're about to lose, a baby who needs a daddy, and a whole family of people worried sick about you. Fix it yourself, ask for help, I don't care, just get it done." The Captain spoke gruffly before standing to leave.

Kendrick watched the three of them leave. Their words swirling in his head. His shoulder throbbed. Coffee splashed on the table when he violently grabbed his cup. Turning to leave, he took a sip but threw it in the trashcan. He wasn't sure which was more unappetizing, the cold coffee or the cold knot of dread and guilt forming in his stomach.

Sawyer was at least somewhat original in his attempt to talk to Kendrick. Instead of suggesting the coffee shop, Sawyer just showed up in his office.

Sawyer sat across the desk, staring at Kendrick for several moments.

Kendrick was shaky, on edge, almost looking for a fight.

"Got something on your mind, Sawyer, or did you just come in here to waste my time?"

Instead of blasting back, Sawyer took a deep breath. "You know, I wanted Luke in here with me, but he insisted it would make you feel like we were ganging up on you. But at this point I almost don't care how you feel."

When Kendrick raised an irritated eyebrow at his cousin, Sawyer continued.

"You stole from me. You've been a part of me, my heart, for my entire life. I would give anything to help you, protect you, support you, but you *stole* from me. I'm having a really hard time wrapping my head around that and reconciling it. You're my family, my best friend, part of my soul, but knowing you would stoop low enough to steal from me, I have to tell you, it hurts." Sawyer's eyes sparkled with tears as he stood to leave.

"Whatever you need, whoever you need to turn to, do it. Make this right. For Jay, the baby, the family, and most importantly for *you*."

Kendrick's stomach dropped as Sawyer left the office.

The final family member to address him was Decker. Of course it was. Leave it to Decker to think he could come along and clean up everything and fix it all.

When his phone rang, he groaned to see Decker's name. Accepting the call he growled, "Let me guess. You'd like to have coffee with me? We should meet at the little shop on the corner?"

"If that's what you want. Sure, I'll see you there in thirty minutes." Decker responded swiftly and confidently which only served to piss Kendrick off a thousand times more.

Before he left his office, he shook the pill bottle in his pocket. He wasn't in much pain, but he'd need the boost to get through a conversation with perfectly composed, perfectly in control Decker.

When he settled at the table with his coffee in hand, he laughed sarcastically at his cousin. "Did you guys all plan to use the coffee shop for all of my little mini interventions? 'Cause I got to tell you, I feel like Bill Murray in that Groundhog's Day movie. Every day it seems I'm back here drinking coffee with people telling me to stop being such a fuck up. Getting pretty old, Deck." He wasn't sure if his words slurred, but he knew his tongue felt heavy and he'd much rather be curled up sleeping than struggling to keep his eyes open to talk to his cousin.

"Well, how 'bout you stop being such a fuck up and get yourself off those damn pills? God, Kendrick. You're not a stupid man, how can you keep doing this to yourself? You've become a liar and a thief. That's not you. You've always been larger than life, a complete cut-up, but you've never purposely hurt anyone or lowered your standards of integrity when it came to your family or your job. Until now." Decker stared hard at him before air whooshed from his lungs. "Fuck, you're high now, aren't you? Damn it, Kendrick, what the *hell*?"

"You don't get it, Decker. I'm in pain. I need to work. I need to be there for Jay. I need to be there for the baby. The pills help me with all of that. They are legal drugs, prescribed by a doctor. I'm not a druggie; I'm not a criminal. I'm a man trying my best to keep up with all of life's demands." Kendrick spit his words out, steeling himself against the urge to topple the table and storm from the coffee shop.

"Yeah, well, how's that all working out for you? Gotta tell you, man, from my side of things it's not looking like it's working very well." Decker shook his head in disgust, standing to leave.

Kendrick stood as well.

The men were no more than a foot apart, eyes locked,

chests heaving. A glimmer of regret danced across Decker's face, then his eyes turned to steel.

"I didn't want to believe it, but I have no choice now. Fix this, Kendrick. Because if you don't, we will fix it for you." Decker watched his face closely.

"Oh really? Is that a threat?" Kendrick tried to sound uncaring, but he knew Decker was as serious as a heart attack.

"No, it's a promise. And you know it." Decker nodded curtly before turning on his heel to leave.

Fuck.

19

He smiled at Jay as she wandered into the nursery. He'd been putting together the nursery furniture for several hours, and they'd not shared one cross word. It was a rare day indeed.

Her belly looked like a soccer ball protruding from her body. She hadn't gained weight anywhere but her stomach, and he could hardly imagine a baby was cramped inside that tiny little bump. She grimaced as she placed her hands on her lower back before lowering herself into the newly assembled rocking chair.

She smiled at him. "You're doing a great job in here. Thanks for getting the guys to do the painting so quickly. Why don't you finish that piece up and then take a break. My back is killing me, and I've not been working nearly as hard as you, so you must be exhausted."

"Your back hurts? What's wrong? Should you see the doctor?" He spewed the questions quickly before crawling on his knees over to her position in the rocker. Large hands engulfed her belly, rubbing soft circles. Lifting her shirt amidst her giggles, he leaned in to kiss the tight skin stretched across her abdomen. Mouth right on the protrusion, he spoke muffled words.

"Hey there, baby pixie, you're making your momma's back hurt. Can you ease up just bit? I don't want her hurting for another whole month while waiting on you to make your appearance."

He placed more kisses around her belly before trailing upwards. Lifting her shirt over her head, he pulled her hips to the edge of the chair and settled between her legs. Flicking thumbs over her sensitive nipples before mouthing them through her bra, he continued the trail of kisses up her neck to her jaw and eventually to her mouth.

Eyes locked on hers, pushing the pain and edginess to the back of his mind, he spoke in a low growl. "Hi there, Pixie. I've sort of missed you, you know?" Lowering his mouth to hers, he kissed her deeply, pouring his entire soul into the melding of their lips. With a groan, he angled her head and swept his tongue across her bottom lip.

"Oh!" Jay proclaimed in surprise. "Ah, the baby either doesn't like that or likes it a lot. She's moving around like crazy and tap dancing on my bladder."

He pulled her closer, until her belly was flush against his

abs. He immediately felt the little bounces and prodding coming from deep inside her womb. Leaning back, he watched in amazement as her belly stretched and wobbled and rolled with each movement from inside.

"That is fucking unbelievable and beautiful." He leaned in to kiss her.

"Ah! Hold that thought, I've *really* got to pee!" Jay kissed him quickly and waddled from the room. Within minutes, she poked her head back into the nursery. "Hey, I'm going to take a warm bath in hopes of easing this back pain. Once you're done with that, meet me in the bedroom?" She wagged her brows at him.

"Sounds like a plan." He winked.

He had the last piece of furniture completed within minutes. His neck and shoulder screamed in pain. Washing his hands in the kitchen, he contemplated taking another pill. But, the pain was so bad he knew it wouldn't work fast enough to get him through sex with Jay. And if he took something now, he'd likely pass out before she was out of the tub.

"Fuckin' man up. She likes to be on top, let her. You can keep your neck and shoulder as still as possible, and then take something when it's over. Can't leave a horny pregnant woman wanting something she can't have." He popped eight ibuprofen in hopes of taking away some of the fiery heat searing through his body. Washing them down with a huge glass of milk, he headed to the bedroom.

Stripping down, he found he was actually hard, something that hadn't happened with a lot of regularity since the accident. Okay, if he was being honest, it hadn't happened much since he started taking so many pills.

Positioning himself flat on the bed, he gripped his length in his hand and hoped Jay would emerge from her bath soon. He needed to take something for the pain, but he was determined to be awake and able when she came to him.

She was like a fucking angel standing at the end of the bed. Skin damp and pink from the warm water, breasts full and pebbled, that beautiful baby bump on display for only him to see. Crooking his finger he motioned for her to join him as he kept hold of himself with his other hand.

She crawled languidly up the bed, straddling his body, and batting his hand away from his cock. Biting her bottom lip, she leaned down and took him in her mouth. Moments later, he felt the tingling beginning in his balls. He bucked under her.

"Pixie, you've got to stop or this will be over before you get what you're looking for." He pulled her up to kiss him. As their lips met, she slowly lowered herself onto him, hissing as he stretched her body.

Kendrick knew the vision of her rocking above him would be ingrained in his mind for the rest of his life. As she rode out the final bursts of her orgasm, he felt himself surge and explode inside her. Roaring his release, only barely cognizant of the pain ripping through his body, he held her close to his chest as they both breathed heavily.

"You okay?" She sat up, looking at him carefully.

"Yeah, just a little sore. I'll take a hot shower to ease the pain." He fought back the tears of pain as his body burned and the nausea threatened to overtake him.

"Okay, go take your shower. I'm going to read for a while. I'll be back in later." She kissed him, cleaned up quickly in the bathroom, and headed to the couch.

Once alone in the bathroom, shower running full blast, he let the scalding water pound down on his back. Washing quickly, he stepped from the shower with other things on his mind. Once dressed and hair fairly dry, he reached to the very back of the vanity drawer. He shook two pills from the prescription bottle he'd kept stashed in a plain OTC pill bottle. He knew Jay was watching his pills carefully as he tried to wean from them. Keeping them hidden from her had become priority number one. Looking around frantically for something to crush the pills with, he grabbed a brush and quickly went to work smashing the pills into a fine dust.

Don't think about it. It's no different than swallowing them. This will just get them to the pain quicker. He told himself if he didn't get the pain under control soon he was going to black out. And what kind of situation would that put Jay in?

He didn't think about the consequences of snorting the white powder up his nose, he just rolled up a receipt he dug from the trashcan and immediately put it to his nose. Bending over the sink, he caught his reflection in the mirror. Breathing deeply, he took in the first line before looking at himself. The effect of the medicine was instant. He felt his head float away, taking the pain with it. With the second line, his entire body was numb. Dropping the paper straw, he brushed the remaining powder into his hand and licked it. The bitterness coated his tongue while a stinging in his nose brought tears to his eyes. Sniffing, he pinched his nose and waited for the pain to subside. Feeling as if he was watching himself from outside of his body, he stumbled to the bedroom and fell face first upon the bed.

"DADDY? Daddy? You need to wake up. She's going to need you." The child's small voice echoed from somewhere very far away.

Kendrick looked around and struggled to understand where he was.

He was floating. Wispy, white clouds wrapped him in warmth. He liked it here. There was no pain here. This would be a nice place to stay.

"Daddy? Daddy, you can't be here. You need to leave." Panic laced the child's voice.

Kendrick looked around again. Where was the voice coming from? He let himself float through the soft clouds, content to just be comfortable and out of pain.

"Daddy, you need to go back."

Kendrick opened his eyes to find a young boy about ten standing in front of him.

"Who are you?" Kendrick asked the child, but the answer niggled at the back of his subconscious before the boy even answered.

"My name is Ricky. Daddy, you have to leave. You're not allowed to be here yet. She's going to need you. You have to go back." The boy seemed torn between being happy to see his father and desperate to make Kendrick leave.

"Who's going to need me, Ricky? How about I just stay for a little bit, buddy. I've wanted to know you for such a long time." He felt his heart clench in his chest, the pain taking his breath away.

"I love you, Daddy, and I'm so happy to see you. But the other baby needs you now. You need to go. Bye-bye, Daddy." The freckle-faced boy vanished, and Kendrick was left alone in the cold darkness.

"Hi, Katie. It's Jay." She attempted to keep her voice calm, but fear and pain were competing to take her out.

"Jay, what's wrong?" Katie was instantly concerned.

"Um, I think I'm in labor." Jay squeezed her eyes shut and tried to breathe through the pain radiating through her body.

"Oh my God, isn't it early? Wait, why are you calling me? Is Kendrick not home?"

"It's only about three weeks early. And, I, um, can't wake Kendrick up. He's passed out on the bed. He's cold and clammy, and I can't get him to even respond to me. I'm really scared, Katie." Tears poured down her cheeks. She sat on the edge of their bed, belly clenched in pain, and laid her hand on Kendrick's chest, praying that he was still breathing.

"Oh, God, Katie, it hurts." She moaned. Turning to look at the man she loved lying dead-still on the bed, she shuddered, "Please, Kendrick, wake up. I need you."

20

K atie practically dove from the car as soon as Zoey had slowed enough for her to get the door open. She ran frantically into Jay's place, yelling for her as she searched and tried to listen for her.

Finding her curled up on the bed, panting and crying, Katie dropped to her knees and took her hand.

"Oh, babe, it's okay. I'm here. Zoey and I will get you to the hospital." Katie grabbed a duffle bag from the closet and stuffed some clothes into it. Rummaging quickly through the kitchen she found Jay's purse. Hoping it had the needed insurance information, she threw it into the bag and started to help Jay to her feet.

"I can't leave him, Katie. He's so sick. I can't leave him." Jay wailed, looking desperately at Kendrick's unconscious body on the bed.

"The guys are on their way, they are probably pulling up now. They will take care of him. I promise you, they will be here to take care of him. And he won't die. Not yet at least because he's going to get his ass kicked severely by every single member of this family. Now, come on, let's go have a baby!" Katie's voice was confident, but her hands shook violently.

Jay seemed to relax as a contraction came to an end. She rolled to her side, kissing Kendrick's cheek and running her hand down his back.

"Kendrick, please wake up. I need you. Your baby girl needs you. Please, baby, don't leave me like this. I love you so very much." She broke down into wracking sobs as Katie helped her from the bed and led her toward the door.

They met the other four guys coming in.

"Where is he?" Decker demanded. He grabbed Katie and hugged her close, while Sawyer held a trembling Jay.

"He's on the bed. He's breathing. But he's completely out of it." Katie's eyes met Decker's, the fear evident on both of their faces.

"Hey, girl, we've got this okay? You just concentrate on how much Kendrick loves you, how much we all love you, and go have that baby. We will take care of Kendrick." Sawyer held Jay close, his worried eyes making contact with Luke's over her head.

"Okay, ladies, looks like Zoey has the car ready." Zach

helped Jay down the steps, Sawyer on her other side, Katie carrying the bag.

When they reached the car, Zach opened the back door. "Your chariot awaits, madam." He winked at her and kissed her nose, trying to stay upbeat. His eyes met Zoey's as he assisted Jay into the backseat so she could lay down if needed. Zach and Zoey shared a look of extreme worry.

"Okay, Audrey and Jeremiah are on their way to the hospital. I think Libby is coming with my mom and dad. Josie said Kyle and Nate were on their way here." Zach relayed the information to Katie as she got in the car. Thumping his hand on top of the car, he signaled to Zoey she was good to go.

Turning, Zach drew in a deep breath as he faced the uncertainty of what was waiting on him in that bedroom.

The four men watched Kendrick for a moment, assuring themselves he was breathing.

"This asshole is going to *wish* he was dead by the time I finish with him." Decker rolled Kendrick over and pulled him to a sitting position.

A small trickle of blood ran from Kendrick's nose.

"Oh my God." Luke voiced the terror they were all feeling.

Kendrick was cold. It was dark and wet, and he was all

alone. His stomach rolled, threatening to empty with every breath he took. His nose burned like a red-hot poker had been shoved into it.

And then he was drowning. Every which way he turned his head, water covered his face. He couldn't breathe, couldn't open his eyes, he was going to die.

"Wake up, mother fucker. Kendrick! Wake the fuck up!"

He knew that voice. The water stopped assaulting his face, he took a deep breath. Looking around in the dark world, he searched frantically for Ricky, but he was nowhere to be seen. The warm wispy clouds were gone. The pain was back, but it radiated through his entire body, not just his neck and shoulder.

"Open your eyes, Kendrick. Open them so we can see you're okay."

Another familiar voice.

Soon he was drowning again, ice cold water shocking his system, making him gasp a breath. As soon as he took that deep breath, he felt his body revolt. Waves of nausea rolled through him as his body purged itself of the poison.

A cacophony of voices surrounded him, he knew them all, but didn't understand where he was or what was going on.

"Turn him to the side, don't let him choke on the vomit."

"That's enough water for now, he's awake."

"We need to get him out of the wet clothes and washed off."

"Kendrick, can you get to your feet? Come on, man, this is really important."

"Dad! We're in here!"

"Fuck! What the hell happened?"

"Why is he bleeding?"

"If I had my way it would be because I punched him in his damn stupid-ass face, but his nose started bleeding when we rolled him over."

"I think he snorted something. There's white powder all over the sink."

"He crushed the pills, and spilled a bunch of them all over. I flushed them all."

"Save the pill bottle. If we can't get him awake, we'll have to tell the ER what he took."

What the hell is going on? His eyes cracked open to find himself in the bathtub, soaked to the bone, shivering cold, covered in vomit, with his nose gushing blood.

Looking around, he blinked hard, trying to wake himself from what had to be a nightmare.

Six men are in my bathroom. What the hell?

"What the hell?" His voice cracked when he tried to talk.

"Thank God. Kendrick, we need to get you washed off and dressed. If you can do that, you can go see your baby be born. If you can't, you have to go to the ER. What's it going to be, man?" Zach slapped Kendrick's cheek, trying to get him to focus.

"I'm going to go make him some coffee." Nate left the room quickly.

"He probably doesn't want to watch this. Reminds him too much of when he and Mom were drugged." Sawyer shook his head, "And that was done *to* them, this dick chose to do it to *himself*."

Kendrick tried to replay the words in his head.

Drugged?

ER?

Baby?

Wait, baby? Where was Jay?

He opened his eyes again, squinting at the men standing around his too-bright bathroom.

"What happened?" His voice cracked again, but he tried to stand up. The pain rushing through his body slowed him down, but he didn't give up. "Where's Jay?"

Once he was somewhat standing up, he looked around again. "Would someone please tell me what the fuck is going on?"

"Zach, Luke, be sure to hold him steady." Decker's voice was sure and firm.

The fist that slammed into his mouth was too.

"Mother fucker! What the fuck was that for?" Kendrick stumbled a bit, held up only by Luke and Zach.

"That was for being a stupid, selfish prick." Decker yelled right in his face. "You're snorting pain pills, passing out dead to the world, while your girl is in labor trying to have a baby. *That's* what's going on, Kendrick."

Sawyer moved Decker to the side. Standing in front of Kendrick he forced the man to look at him. "Kendrick, can you get cleaned up and let us take you to the hospital? Jay needs you, she's having the baby."

She needs you. The other baby needs you now.

Ricky's voice whispered in his head. Ricky, his son. He had spoken to his son.

Jay. Jay was having the baby. They needed him.

Fighting through the sludge traveling through his body, trying to pull him back down, Kendrick allowed himself to be stripped, rinsed in water that was almost too hot, and dressed quickly. Lukewarm coffee was handed to him, and he gulped it quickly. A bottle of water followed.

"You need to drink as much as possible to flush the medication from your body." Luke handed him another bottle of water and a warmer cup of coffee was poured into a travel mug.

"Can you handle this, Kendrick? Can you focus enough to go to the hospital? Because if they think you're high, they won't let you in and will likely call the police." Kyle looked directly into his eyes. Shaking his head, he looked at the others, "Maybe he should go to the ER. They could help detox him quicker."

"No. No way. I need to be there for Jay and the baby." Kendrick pulled himself upright. Downing the second bottle of water, he quickly began to take large gulps of the coffee. It burned as it went down, but he was beginning to feel less bogged down and somewhat more clearheaded.

"I'm going to pee, then we need to go." Kendrick turned towards the bathroom, confused when Decker followed.

"What the hell, man. I need to piss." Kendrick frowned.

"Yeah, well, sorry if I don't trust you right now. Just so you know, we flushed your pills. This isn't over Kendrick. You can see Jay and the baby, but this isn't just going to go away." Decker stood in the doorway and waited for Kendrick to finish.

Kendrick felt the loss of those pills as acutely as he felt the need to be near Jay. How would he survive the pain and hold it all together without the pills?

Decker snorted, and Kendrick realized he must have spoken that last part out loud.

"We'll figure something out. You weren't exactly doing a bang up job of it on your own, you know?" Decker clapped him on the shoulder as the men loaded into two vehicles and headed across town to the hospital.

ime seemed to stand still even as the scenery whizzed past. Kyle and Nate were waiting on Kendrick at the hospital entrance. Zach and Decker got out with him while Luke and Sawyer went to park the car.

In his head, Kendrick knew he was walking to the labor and delivery floor. He knew Jay was in labor. He knew the baby was about three weeks early. But, putting all of that information together into complete, coherent thoughts was proving difficult. He kept getting stuck each time he replayed the fact that he snorted pain pills and passed out cold onto the bed he shared with the woman whom he wanted to spend the rest of his life.

Would she forgive him? Could she? Should he even hope for that?

"What if she doesn't want me here?" He voiced the fear

which was pounding through his head. His heart thudded in his chest. If she turned him away, he didn't know what he'd do. More drugs? That's what he wanted. Right then and there, as Jay was having their baby, he wanted a damn fucking pill so badly he could barely think straight. Just one would take the edge off, ease the pain, calm his thundering heart. He reached for the pill bottle in his pocket, gut sinking when he realized it wasn't there.

"I don't know if I can do this." He felt wild with anxiety, his breaths coming too quickly. "What if she doesn't want me here?" He asked again to no one in particular as they rounded the corner into the waiting room.

His mom and dad jumped from their seats, pulling him into their arms.

"Oh, baby boy, what happened?" Audrey patted his face, tears in her eyes. "Never mind that right now, Jay is waiting for you. She's been asking and asking. Go on." She nodded toward the nurse who waited to take him into the delivery room.

"Sir, are you okay?" The nurse eyed his pale skin, shaking hands, and heavy breathing.

"Yeah. Yeah, I'm okay. Just nervous I guess." He tried to smile, but knew he looked like exactly what he was, a strung out junkie.

Just one pill, one pill would help me out so much. I can't be by Jay's side like this.

It appeared like he would have no choice. The nurse

pulled the door open and led him into a dimly lit room. Jay looked tiny and fragile laying on the bed. An IV ran from her arm to a bag of liquid suspended high above her head. A light beeping filled the room, and the rhythmic beating of what he assumed was the baby's heart made up the background noise. At the sound of the door, Jay's head turned.

Her face broke into a smile only seconds before she broke down into sobs.

He crossed the room in two strides, ignoring the throbbing in his head and the fire in his neck and shoulder. Dropping onto the bed, he reached for her. Holding her tight, he barely remembered to breathe. The only thing that mattered at that moment was holding Jay in his arms.

"Kendrick, I was so fucking scared. Scared you wouldn't be here for this, scared you wouldn't be here at all. Ever again." She sobbed into his chest.

"I know, Pixie, and I'm so damn sorry. I'm here now, and I'm not going anywhere." He tipped her face up to his, kissing her lightly. "I love you so much. So damn much it hurts. Right in here." He guided her hand to his chest.

She rested her head against his chest. "I love you too."

He glanced around at all that surrounded them in the room. "What's going on, is the baby coming?"

"Yes. They gave me an epidural to ease the pain. I begged them to wait a little bit before they broke my water. I wanted to give you time to get here. They agreed as long as the baby was tolerating the contractions well, and she is."

"She? Do you know something?" He looked at her curiously.

"No, just used to you calling it *she*."

At that moment, the door opened and a nurse entered. "Okay, now that Daddy's here, let's get the baby delivered."

The next two hours went by in a blur of activity. The nurse broke Jay's water and examined her cervix several times. Once the nurse deemed her ready, Jay started pushing while Kendrick held her hand and did his best to watch without passing out. One last hard push and Jay collapsed back onto the bed as a cry pierced the air. His daughter's cry. Kendrick watched in horrified fascination as the doctor handed him the scissors to cut the cord. A second later, their beautiful, clumpy, messy, *beautiful* daughter was placed upon Jay's chest. Tears streamed down his cheeks as he wiped tears away from Jay's face before they dripped upon the baby's tiny nose. Leaning in, Kendrick and Jay placed several breathless kisses on the baby's head before the nurse gently took her away to get cleaned up.

Kissing Jay firmly on the lips, Kendrick walked in a daze over to where the nurses were fussing over the baby girl. Suctioned, wiped down, weighed and measured, the baby was promptly wrapped up from head to toe and delivered to his waiting arms. He stared down at her tiny puckered mouth, button nose, and dark gunky eyes. He needed to sit down. No pill on earth could provide the high he felt at that moment.

Sitting on the rolling stool, he scooted across the floor.

The doctor was finishing up with Jay, but her attention was directed only on Kendrick and their baby.

"She's the most beautiful thing I've ever seen." Kendrick's voice cracked in emotional awe as he continued to stare at his daughter. Leaning in to kiss her, he whispered reverently to Jay, "Thank you, thank you for loving me, sticking by me, and giving me this beautiful gift. I love you so very much, Pixie."

Several things happened all at once. The door swung open, allowing almost every member of his family to enter the tiny room. The nurses looked at each other, then at the doctor, and they gave the family a stern look. "You've got fifteen minutes."

Jay pulled Kendrick close, nuzzling his cheek. "I know you love me. And I love you too. So very much. And that's why this is so damn hard." She sobbed against him, "Please, never forget that I love you. We all love you."

When he turned to look at his family, dread settled upon him.

"What's going on?" He knew the answer even before Dr. Parks entered the room, but he clung to the baby in his arms as if he could avoid the answer if he just never let her go.

"Kendrick, you know what you need to do." Kyle spoke tearfully.

Dr. Parks caught his eye and nodded an encouraging, supportive smile his way.

"So you're all here to gang up on me and take me away from my daughter?" Anger rose in his voice.

"Kendrick, you have to get better so you can be a father to that gorgeous baby girl." Katie spoke softly, flinching when Kendrick cursed loudly.

"What if I won't go?" Kendrick challenged.

Decker stepped forward with Zach, Sawyer, and Luke flanking him, Jeremiah and Nate behind him. Tears streamed down Decker's face. "Damn it, Kendrick, don't make me do it. If you don't go with Dr. Parks, I'll have no choice but to remove you from your position at The Center+." Decker's voice shook as he whispered, "Please, Kendrick, please don't make me do it. Go with Dr. Parks, get better, and come back to live a long, healthy, happy life. Please."

Libby stepped forward and took the baby from Kendrick's arms, soothing him with a slight whisper, "It's okay, Kendrick. We'll take care of Jay and the baby. Do this for them, for you, for your family's future."

He gazed helplessly around the room, his eyes landing on each and every family member standing there. He saw fear, sadness, and uncertainty, but he also saw determination, hope, and love. When his eyes landed on his mom, she broke down. He pulled her into his arms.

"I'm so sorry, Mom. I screwed up. Bad."

"Oh, baby boy, we all make mistakes. You and I just seem to make them bigger and better than others." She sniffled a laugh, hugging him closer to her. "Please know I didn't want to do this to you. I remember the pain and feeling double-crossed when your family presents you with an impossible decision. Don't fight it, baby. Just do it. Do it for you, for Jay, for my *granddaughter*. And never, ever think that this is being done out of anything but love. We all want so badly for you to be healthy and happy."

Kendrick backed away from his mom, glancing around the room again.

"Well, with the only options being to lose my family and job or go get myself better, I guess it's a no-brainer huh?" He attempted to laugh, but nothing felt very funny at the moment.

"I'll wait outside, Kendrick." Dr. Parks nodded patiently at him. "Take your time."

"Can I have some time with Jay and our daughter?" Kendrick timidly asked his family. He felt he had no right to ask, but he couldn't leave without it.

"Of course. We'll be outside waiting." Audrey hugged him close. "Before you leave, I'd like to know her name." She winked at him, kissing him soundly on the cheek one last time.

The hugs he received from every single member of his family buoyed his hope that he would survive this and come back better than ever. But when the room was empty and silent, he turned to Jay and felt every hope dashed. Could he ever fix what he'd done to her? Could he even get away from the pills? And if he did, would she take him back? Let him around their baby?

"I see what you're thinking, Kendrick. It's written all over your face." Jay smiled tiredly at him. His stomach clenched with guilt. Here she was, exhausted from giving birth, and he was putting her through an emotional wringer because of his fucked up choices.

"Stop. Yes, you made bad choices, but I love you. We aren't over. Far from it. You're going to go get yourself clean, get that shoulder and neck healed, and come back home to us. We'll be here waiting on you." Jay reached out to touch his hand. "Waiting to welcome you back, with open arms."

"It's not going to be easy." Kendrick stated the obvious.

"I know."

"I don't know if I'm strong enough to get through this." His voice broke.

"You are."

"What's her name?" Tears broke free, pouring down his face.

Jay handed the baby back to him. Head bent, he kissed the top of her head while sobs shuddered through his body.

"I was thinking about Bella Marie, after Kyle's Isabella and my middle name." Jay smiled at him. "We never knew Isabella, but she helped to make Kyle into the man he is today, and you have needed him so much lately. I felt like it was just fitting to name the baby after her."

"Bella Marie. I like it." He smiled back. Turning his attention back to the baby asleep in his arms, he whispered, "Hey, Bella Marie, Daddy has to go away for a little while. But I'll be back soon. And once I'm back, I'll spend the rest of my life loving and protecting you. Never forget how much I love you and your momma." He nuzzled her head again.

Handing the baby back to Jay, he watched in apt fascination as she began to feed his daughter. "Wow, you're really good at that." He smiled goofily at Jay while she laughed.

"I think it's just something babies know how to do." Jay shrugged.

He sat close to her, grasping her hand, breathing her scent. "I'm sorry I fucked things up so badly. I'll spend the rest of my life loving you and making this up to you." He kissed her firmly. "I love you, Jaymison Marie Keller."

He stood up with determination. Kissing her once more, he winked. "Now, if you'll excuse me, it's time to open a can of whoop ass on this addiction."

The sound of her giggle followed him from the room. It was a sound he would hold close during the hellish weeks to come.

Upon finding his entire family still waiting, he smiled at his mom, "I think Jay and Bella Marie are waiting for you." Audrey squealed and headed toward the room.

"Mom, wait." He turned to everyone seated in the waiting room. "I owe you all an apology and a thank you. Please watch over Jay and Bella until I can get back here. Thank you for forcing my hand. I know over the next several weeks I may not feel very grateful, just know that I am. I love you all."

Kyle walked forward, tears in his eyes and Josie tucked under his arm. "Bella?"

Kendrick smiled, "Yeah, since Jay looks so much like Izzy, and you've been such an instrumental part in helping me heal from losing my son, Jay and I thought it was fitting."

Closing his eyes and swallowing his tears, Kyle pulled his nephew into a hug. "Thank you. I can't think of a more beautiful way to honor Izzy."

Final hugs and goodbyes were given. With a small smile to his family, a nod to Dr. Parks, and deep fear of the unknown in his belly, Kendrick followed the doctor out to the car which would take him away from his heart and soul. But he'd be back, there was no question about that.

22

_J_ay and Bella were released forty-eight hours later. She went home with Katie. It was decided that living by herself would be too much at first, and living with Audrey and Jeremiah could cause more stress than necessary while Kendrick was detoxing.

Katie was absolutely thrilled to have Jay and Bella at her home. But her mother and grandmother were possibly even more excited.

"Oh, it's been so long since I've helped with a baby. This will be the most fun I've had in a very long time." Grandma grinned and clapped her hands.

The four women fell into as much of a routine as one can expect with a brand new baby in the home. Katie took the early morning feeding since she was already up for work.

Katie's mom and grandma took over afternoon feedings if Jay needed a nap. They all enjoyed daily visits from family members. Many came daily, some came on lunch breaks from work, others came to visit and hold Bella while the main care-takers ate supper, cleaned up, and rested a bit.

Jay blossomed as a mother. Her fears of not being able to care for her baby were drowned the moment Bella was placed on her chest, and those feelings grew more intense each day.

"I'm not saying there are no worries in my mind. Yes, I worry about her getting sick, making ends meet, raising her in this scary world. But, there's no doubt in my mind I'll protect her until my dying breath. My parents didn't look at me that way, and I was fearful I'd be more like them. But the moment Bella was in my arms, I knew there was nothing I wouldn't do in this world to keep her safe and protected and happy."

"That's because you're a wonderful person at heart, dear." Grandma smiled over her teacup as she watched Jay nurse Bella. "What else is on your mind?"

Jay looked up, startled.

"I can see something else there. You're in love with your baby, over the moon, but something is bothering you." Grandma poured herself and Jay another cup of tea. "I had my hair done yesterday, my teeth are clean and fitting well, and my arthritis is playing nice today, I've got all the time in the world. Talk to me."

"It's nothing really. Not big enough to bother you with it. I'm silly, it must be the hormones. I just need to focus on this beautiful baby and be happy." Jay's eyes sparkled with unshed tears.

"That's a load of poo if I've ever heard one. Yes, those hormones are going crazy. Your body is trying to heal from a huge event while it provides the needed nutrition for your baby. By the way, you're doing great with nursing and pumping, but understand that if it doesn't work out or you need to supplement with formula, it's okay. I was a mess when the doctors told me I needed to give my baby extra formula because she wasn't getting enough from me. But, once I relaxed and realized she was fed and happy, we were all able to settle in and just enjoy." Grandma sipped her tea. "Oh lordy, I got off track. You have every right to feel whatever you're feeling. Maybe it would help to talk about it?"

Jay was silent for several moments, watching Bella now sleeping in the crook of her arm. "I'm just scared."

Grandma was quiet, just waiting on Jay to gather her thoughts.

"Scared of Kendrick not getting better. Or getting better and realizing he doesn't want to be saddled with a single mother and her baby. Scared we'll find out the baby isn't his, and he won't be able to deal with it after all." Jay drew in a shaky breath. "He's not contacted me once since he went to rehab."

Grandma grabbed her cane and hefted herself from her easy-chair. Shuffling to Jay's seat on the couch, she sat down and wrapped her arms around the girl.

"Jay, Kendrick may not be my flesh and blood, but I've gotten to know him over the years. All of those boys, that entire family, they are all special, unique. But none of them have ever held a candle to Kendrick. That boy, from the time he was small has been larger than life. He loves a good time, a good laugh, but sometimes he lets all of that hide what he's really feeling. His jokes and barbs and comments are genuine, but they are also his shield. Kendrick is one of those who comes across invincible, but he's actually more fragile than the rest of them." Grandma paused to position herself on the couch and lay her cane down. "That boy built up such a wall around him, he wasn't able to recognize or admit he was in trouble. Most people didn't see it because he was still the happy-go-lucky jokester he'd always been, working hard, playing hard, putting his family first. But from the moment that girl killed herself until he snorted those pills, he's been silently screaming for help. No one noticed it, or no one wanted to admit it. *You* noticed. *You* admitted it even though it almost killed you. *You* saved his life."

Jay was quiet for a while, taking in all Grandma had said.

"Now, I know I'm an old lady so I get a free pass to ramble and never really answer a question. But that's not what I'm doing here. I said all of that so you'd believe me when I say Kendrick loves you. I see it, they all see it. He loved you before you saved him. I watched that boy go through girls like underwear, but everything changed with you. His swagger changed. He went from a cocky bastard who flew through women faster than I can change the TV channels to a man whose very presence exuded he had something special. Your heart, your spunk, your ability to challenge him, he fell in love with all of those things. So there is no way he's giving up on you and Bella. The two of you are likely his main reason for getting clean; he wants to be home with you both so badly. Yes, he wants to get better for himself and his family, but I would place money the two of you are his main reasons. As far as that baby not being his, phooey. Once that boy sets his mind to something, there's no dissuading him. Will it cause some bumps here and there if the baby's biological father wants to be involved? Sure. But Kendrick considers you and Bella to be his, so he will work around it. As for you being a 'single mother', this old lady thinks that won't be the case for much longer if that boy has anything to say about it."

Jay stood to place Bella in her bassinet. Grabbing Grandma's cup, she brought it to the woman. "What about the fact he hasn't called or contacted me? I feel like I'm going crazy waiting for some sort of contact from him."

"Well, you know Jeremiah talked to Dr. Parks the day Kendrick left. He'll be limited on the phone calls he can make, but Dr. Parks had said this first week would be the worst and Kendrick would likely not feel up to calling or speaking to anyone." Grandma reminded Jay.

"I know, I know. It's killing me thinking about what he might be going through right now. And it hurts to think he may need to call his parents or cousins before he would call me. How selfish does that sound? I just hurt knowing he's hurting and going through this alone." Jay's tears fell.

"Hey now, he's not alone. He's got a team of people trained to get him through this. Dr. Parks said the physical detox would take a week or two from start to finish. The emotional healing would take longer, but the doctor said Kendrick was already a couple steps ahead since he'd been doing therapy before the pills got out of control. Plus, Zoey is going to be doing that yoga and neurokinesis with him. All of that incorporated with the fact he's got his entire family, you, and Bella supporting him, loving him, and waiting on him to come home? He's going to beat this and be back better than ever." Grandma patted Jay's hand before kissing her cheek.

"Now, since Bella has eaten, pooped, and is taking a nap, I think I'll follow her lead. But I better find my fiber powder if I want to stay as regular as that little thing is." Grandma chuckled as she tottered off to the kitchen.

Jay sat in the bay window, Bella in the bassinet beside her, watching Torey Hope go about its day. Before long, her eyes were droopy and she curled up on the window seat to sleep. *Sleep when the baby sleeps was the best advice ever.*

She woke later to voices.

"I think you're right, she needs to hear from him. I don't want to make him have to decide between calling us, the guys, or her. Let's talk to Dr. Parks and get the phone call set up to come in when we can all be there to take it. We can all talk, then give them some time to talk privately. Dr. Parks updated us today, that's why I came over, I wanted to share with Jay, but he's expecting Kendrick will be ready for phone calls in the next day or two."

Jay cracked an eye to find Audrey cuddling Bella on the couch. Feeling peace that she'd talk to Kendrick soon and her baby was safe, Jay let the new mom exhaustion take over again.

23

He was in hell. The fiery depths of hell had opened and swallowed him into the very pit.

He couldn't sleep, but longed to sleep. Every hour, every minute, every second was wrapped around the thought of making it all go away, he just wanted to take away the pain and darkness.

His clothes were soaked in sweat from hot flashes and night sweats.

Why the hell couldn't he stop yawning; he'd never yawned so much in his entire life.

No one entering his room was safe from his biting anger and excessive irritability. It seemed to him that everything made him angry. If the sun was shining, he was pissed. If rain was falling, he was pissed. Hell, he was pissed just for being pissed.

He couldn't eat, and his stomach gnawed at itself as he rode waves of nausea every moment of the day. Between both ends of his body, he wasn't sure there was one more ounce left to purge.

His head was pounding, his body ached, his heart hurt, hell, even his teeth felt like they were burning into his gums.

He was hot, he was cold. His skin hurt, his eyes burned, his nose stung, even breathing was too much at one point. He wanted to just curl into a ball, shut out the world, and make it all go away.

A couple pills would lessen the pain, take away some of the hell.

No, he had to get clean for Jay and Bella.

But, if he could get his hands on some pills, he could work at getting clean in a less traumatic way.

No! Damn it. If he could just stop thinking about the pills, maybe he could focus on something else. But every time he closed his eyes, the image of pills danced in his head. He imagined the warm euphoria washing over his body if he was able to take just a couple pills. He wanted to get better, but almost dying while doing it wasn't going to be beneficial for anyone involved.

Dr. Parks assured him he wasn't in danger of dying, even though he felt like he was going to. The doctor had talked to him about the options available. He could have taken the slower ease-down option of detoxing, but it would have taken longer. Dr. Parks had consulted with the team at the rehab facility to determine Kendrick was physically stable enough for the quicker detox process. It was what Dr. Parks and Kendrick had decided on, and Kendrick knew in the long run he'd be glad for it, but the days of fiery hell were almost more than he could manage.

A picture of Jay and Bella kept him going. Sawyer had snapped a photo of the two of them and sent it to Dr. Parks since Kendrick's phone had been locked away for the time being. Dr. Parks had allowed the picture to be printed and hung in his room.

That beautiful pixie and precious baby girl were his two main reasons for living the hell of detox. Yes, he knew he owed it to his family and himself as well, but Jay and Bella were what he pictured each and every moment as he shivered through the pain those first several days. Every time a pill came to mind, he pictured Bella and Jay. When he woke from nightmarish dreams with dark thoughts swirling in his head, strangling his heart and choking his lungs, he clung to Bella and Jay.

"How are you feeling today, Kendrick?" Dr. Parks smiled at him from across his desk.

"Well, I haven't bitten anyone's head off. I'm able to sit upright in a chair without wanting to vomit, light doesn't hurt every cell in my body, and my teeth have stopped throbbing, so overall I'd say I'm on my way to being back among the living." Kendrick chuckled a bit.

His body still ached. He still thought about those little pills. But the aching and craving were less now. His head was clearer, he felt less irritable, and he'd slept through most of the night for the first time since arriving at rehab.

"Good, good. You look much better." Dr. Parks made notes as he spoke.

"Yeah, it's amazing what a nice hot shower can do for you. I even ate a little breakfast this morning. I feel like I'm coming off a long bout with the worst flu of my life." *Not to mention feeling like I'm waking from the scariest, darkest, most horror-filled dream I've ever had.*

"It's a killer while you're living it, but you're on the other side of the physical detox now. Each day the physical symptoms should get better."

When Dr. Parks stopped speaking, Kendrick heard the words he hadn't said.

"So, the physical part sucked but is almost over. But you're telling me the emotional part, the mental part is going to suck and last longer?" Kendrick took a deep breath, steeling himself for the challenge that faced him. *Great, so the nightmare isn't over.*

"I'm telling you I'm confident you're ready to take on this next step. You'll be here another week or so. You'll attend group sessions, individual sessions, and I'd like to get some family and Jay in here if possible. Then we'll discharge you into outpatient care. You'll see me three times a week. I think the yoga and neurokinesis with Zoey will be great for both your pain and your mental well-being. There will be days when you feel on top of the world, able to tackle and defeat anything in your path. Then there will be days when the tiniest obstacle or issue will send you spiraling. That's when the support of family, the yoga or meditation, and having a group to turn to will be important. You're going to feel more tired than usual as you heal from this. Don't push yourself, but also don't give into the desire to sleep life away. As long as Zoey can help you get that neck and shoulder a little more pain-free, you can start playing basketball or boxing or swimming with your cousins. Speaking of the pain, how is it?" Dr. Parks raised his brows in question.

"You know, Doc, it's sort of funny. And I don't mean haha funny, I mean fucked up funny. When I was messed up with those pills, I would have sworn the pain in my neck and shoulder was the worst it had ever been and *that* was why I *needed* those pills so badly. But, now that the pills are out of my system and I'm thinking clearly for the first time since before the wreck, I realize the pain wasn't all that bad. I mean, yes, they still hurt, but I was using them as an excuse to keep popping those pills and hiding from the fact I was in trouble. I've been doing little bits of yoga from what I can remember Zoey teaching me in one of her classes, and one of the staff members gave me a CD with meditation sessions on it. It's nice to just zone out with those."

"That's good, Kendrick. I have to tell you like I told your parents, I'm feeling quite positive about your recovery. You'll never *not* be an addict..."

Those words stung at Kendrick's heart, but he listened as the doctor continued.

"What I mean by that is you'll be recovered and living a happy, healthy life, but you'll never be able to *just take a pill* like others. You'll have to be in constant communication with your family and friends and medical professionals if any medications are needed for some reason down the road. Most successful recovering addicts who had a problem with pills find themselves refusing to take even a Tylenol; they'd rather talk it out, work it out physically, or breathe it out than take a pill and possibly lose control to the vicious cycle. That part will be up to you."

"Gee, Doc, you make the future sound so very bright and inviting." Kendrick couldn't keep the sarcasm from his voice.

Dr. Parks laughed. "It's not said to bring you down. I say it because I have complete confidence in your total recovery. I've seen people worse off than you, with less support and determination than you, become successful recovering addicts. So my point to all of this is you're ahead of the game. Family support, stable job, Jay and the baby, physical and mental exercises in place, and the fact you'd already been working through the anger and depression of Sarah's suicide before the pills got out of control...all of that puts you one or two steps ahead."

Dr. Parks made a few more notes. "So, we'll start with a group session later today. Individual stuff will be with me in the mornings. And we'll set up some family sessions within the next few days. Our individual sessions will deal with getting rid of the anger and guilt from Sarah's death and the loss of the baby. I know you were doing better with that before the wreck, but I think you maybe just covered up with Jay and the baby rather than really coming to terms with it. And the guilt from ten years ago was subconsciously compounded by the guilt you likely felt in letting Jay and the baby take the place of Sarah and your first child. But, no worries, I'm pretty good at what I do, so I'll get you through it one day at a time."

The doctor smiled at him. "Now, are you ready for your big surprise?"

"Surprise? I didn't know I was getting a surprise. But, yeah, I'm ready for it. Unless it's one of those *big surprises* that suck, if it's going to suck I don't want it." Kendrick shifted uncomfortably in his chair. The anxiety of the unknown was a new feeling for him. In the past he was all for new and unknown and surprises and fun, now he felt himself a little more anxious, cautious, unsure.

"How about a phone call home?" Dr. Parks suggested.

"No shit? Really?" Kendrick felt his eyes grow wide as he smiled. But just as quickly, the smile faded. "Damn, how do I decide who to call first? Maybe I should wait until tomorrow and have them all get together in one place so I can talk to them all?"

"Already one step ahead of you, Kendrick. I've been in touch with your family. They will all be anxiously awaiting your video call tonight at 7:00 p.m. We'll set it up here in this office so you'll have some privacy. Usually the facility limits the calls to fifteen minutes, but since you were already my patient before being admitted, I've talked them into allowing a thirty minute call."

"Thanks, Doc. Best news I've heard since emerging from my own personal hell. But, damn, now I've got all day to wait."

"Well, you have lunch, the group session, time for yoga, and dinner to keep you busy. Why don't you go get some meditation time in before lunch?" The doctor smiled as Kendrick nearly bounded from the office.

"Shit, why am I so nervous? I've talked to these people every day for most of my life. I have no reason to fear them or worry, but I feel like I'm about to puke over making this call." Kendrick's hands were sweaty, his heart was pounding, and he felt sick to his stomach, but it had nothing to do with the detox.

"This is the first time you've talked to most of them without all the shields and walls. You're still the jokester, the clown, the fun guy, but it's time to show them the fragile, sensitive, more at-risk side of yourself. It's okay to feel however you're feeling. They are probably just as anxious as you are." Dr. Parks patted him on the shoulder.

Setting up the video call, Dr. Parks instructed Kendrick to push the button when he was ready to make the connection.

"I'll be across the hall doing some paperwork. Let me know if you need me. I'll leave the door open so I can see you, just wave if you need my attention." Dr. Parks nodded

Kendrick sat staring at the screen for several moments. He wanted more than anything to connect with his family, to hear Jay's voice, to see Bella's beautiful face. But he was scared. Scared their eyes would hold pity or judgment.

"Damn it, man, grow some balls." He shook his head in disgust and punched the connect button a little harder than he probably needed to.

Within moments, his screen lit up and he saw the whole fam-damn-ly appear in the frame. They were at his parents' house, he saw the kitchen in the background.

Taking just a moment to look at each and every one of them, he took a deep breath and fought down the lump in his throat.

It seemed everyone on the other end was taking a moment to gather themselves as well.

Finally, thankfully, someone spoke.

"Hi, Kendrick. I'm glad you're not dead. Taking drugs was stupid. You're supposed to just say no to drugs." Uncle Nicky, adept at getting straight to the point as usual.

"Yeah, thanks Uncle Nicky. I was acting stupid there for a while, but I'm doing better now." Kendrick chuckled.

The family chit-chatted for a few moments, different members shouting out comments and questions at random.

Eventually, the older members said their love and good-byes, leaving the screen to the younger generation.

"So, how are you feeling?" Zach asked.

"Overall, physically, much better. I'm anxious about the mental and emotional stuff, but Dr. Parks says I already have a good head start on that part. He has confidence in me, and I trust him, so I think it will be okay."

"That's good. It's really good to see you looking so much better. I don't think I'd realized how bad things had gotten, but you look really, really good now." Decker nodded at him. "Oh, and just so you know, we've implemented random drug screenings at The Center+. We lost one employee with the first screening, but I think the random aspect will help to keep the issues at bay."

Kendrick could only guess that the one employee had been Billy. The man hadn't forced him to take those pills, but Kendrick sure couldn't muster a lot of sympathy knowing Billy was no longer at The Center+.

"Listen...," Kendrick squeezed the bridge of his nose

before taking a deep breath and plowing on, "I want to apologize to all of you. The way I acted, the things I said, the stuff I did, it was wrong and I'm sorry. I want to say it wasn't me, but that would be a cop out. It *was* me. Yeah, I was under the influence, but it was still me making those decisions, and I'm sorry for breaking your trust in me. And thank you for sticking by my side. I don't deserve it, but knowing I've got you all supporting me makes this a bit easier to face."

"Kendrick, don't ever say you don't deserve our support. You're family. You fucked up. But that doesn't mean we'll leave you to deal with this on your own. Besides, if we don't support you through this, who's going to kick your ass when it needs it?" Sawyer smiled at him.

At the sound of the baby's cry, Kendrick's heart clenched.

Looking straight into Jay's eyes, he whispered, "Can I see her?"

Jay smiled and lifted the baby girl up so her beautiful face filled the screen. Dark hair, long lashes, tiny pink mouth. She was dressed in the outfit Kendrick had liked the most from their registry. At that moment, all else ceased to exist. Jay and Bella were the only things he saw. He was vaguely aware of goodbyes being said and the screen emptying as the others left the room, but he could do nothing but stare at his beautiful girls.

"Hey, Pixie." His voice caught as he fought the tears in his eyes.

On a deep, shuddering breath, Jay smiled, "Hey."

Bella made a squeaky baby noise, and they both laughed through their tears.

"Hey there, Bella Marie. How's my baby? Daddy loves you so very much." Kendrick's voice was rough and raw as he spoke the words.

As if she recognized his voice, Bella peeped one eye open before squirming in Jay's arms and letting out a miffed cry.

Audrey popped onto the screen. "Here, let me feed her while you two talk. I've got a bottle ready." She left with the baby, making little cooing sounds at her granddaughter the whole way to the kitchen.

"Looks like Miss Bella has everyone wrapped around her little finger, huh?" Kendrick smiled, watching Jay's eyes.

"Yeah, she really does. Everyone is so good with her. They've all been incredibly helpful. Even Asher has come over and offered to watch her for little bits at a time. I think he's pretty scared of her, but he wants to help." Jay kept the chatter neutral.

"How are *you*, Pixie?" Kendrick wanted to gather her in his arms, feel the heat of her skin, the taste of her skin. Seeing but not touching was killing him.

"I'm good. Bella sleeps pretty well, nurses like a champ and takes a bottle for others, she's gaining weight. Overall everything is good." Jay's smile was tight.

"That's great, I'm so glad Bella is doing well. But I asked about *you*, Pixie. How are *you*?" Kendrick pressed at her.

"Don't do this here, not now. I love you and miss you and

want you back home. Can't that be enough for now?" Jay spoke through gritted teeth.

"I love you and miss you too. There's nothing I want more than to be back home. But if something is bothering you, I want to hear it." Kendrick didn't want to fight.

"Kendrick?" Dr. Parks' voice sounded from the doorway. "Time is up. Let's hold off on Jay's feelings until our session tomorrow. It will be a good starting point."

Kendrick backed down, and Jay's shoulders slumped in relief.

"I love you, Pixie. Everything I'm doing in here is to get me back home to you and Bella. But I've gotta know, do I still have a home with you and Bella?" Kendrick felt the nausea building in his gut. If Jay didn't want him in her and Bella's life, he wasn't sure if he could handle this recovery.

"You'll always have a place with us if you want it, Kendrick. I just need more than one phone call to feel like things are all better." Jay kissed her fingers and touched them to the screen. "I love you, Kendrick. I'll see you tomorrow. Sleep well. And get yourself ready, late night diaper and feedings at 2:00 a.m. are a total bitch." She smiled softly at him before disconnecting the call.

Blowing out a breath, Kendrick turned to the doctor. "Well, that went well, but I feel like it could have gone better."

Dr. Parks smiled knowingly. "You and I can talk about it a

little before Jay comes for her session with us tomorrow. For now, get some sleep."

"So you felt a little let down after talking to Jay last night. Tell me more about that." Dr. Parks spoke quietly.

"I don't know. I mean, it was great seeing her and my family, and seeing Bella was the best. But I guess I wasn't ready for the coolness from Jay. I think I knew she'd be mad, but I was hoping...I don't know. I guess I was just hoping for more...enthusiasm? I know it's not fair of me to expect that from her, I just feel like she was distant." Kendrick attempted to explain his jumbled feelings.

"Kendrick, Jay responded very much like I expected her to. She watched both of her parents choose drugs and alcohol over her until their deaths. You pushed her and the baby to the side, albeit for a very short time, in favor of drugs. She loves you, and she wants you in her and Bella's life, but I'd have to assume she's wary of letting you back in and losing you to the addiction again or even to the depression that was building before the accident. You need to give her some time. She likely feels bad saying how she's feeling in light of you working so hard to get better, but you've got to let her have her fears and feelings and let her know you're committed to her and Bella and to staying clean."

"That makes sense. Maybe she needs to let go of some anger, punch me, scream, cry. I don't want to push her to do that, but if that's what she needs, I'll be here for her. How do I prove to her that I'm not going to let the addiction and depression take over again? Hell, I don't even know if I believe it myself when I say it."

"You've got to show her. Each day that you aren't high, each day you use your supports and techniques instead of turning to substances, you'll show her you're serious. It won't all happen overnight. She watched her mom go through a couple rounds of rehab with no success from what you've told me. I'm sure part of her wants to believe you've kicked this, but her only experience with addiction screams otherwise."

Dr. Parks looked at his watch. Smiling slightly at Kendrick, he shrugged. "I'll deny it if you tell anyone this, but I may have set up the appointment a bit early so you and Jay could have some time together before we sit and talk. I hope you're okay with that."

"Hell yeah, I'm okay with that, Doc. Wait, you don't mean *time together* like a conjugal visit do you? Gotta tell ya, as much as I'd like to make that happen, I'm afraid performance anxiety in a rehab facility is a real thing."

Throwing his head back, laughing, Dr. Parks spoke jovially, "No, not a conjugal visit. I just thought you'd enjoy the extra time."

As if on cue, a knock sounded at the office door.

Jay stood in the doorway, looking beautiful as always, but there was a tension in her face. In her arms she held...*Bella*.

Jerking his head toward the doctor, Kendrick looked questioningly at him. He wasn't supposed to get visitors, Jay was only allowed here because of the session.

"What? I couldn't take a nursing baby away from her mother, so Bella sort of had to come." Dr. Parks winked and left the room.

Thirty minutes later, Dr. Parks came back to the office to find Jay curled up at Kendrick's side, Bella sleeping on his chest, and Kendrick asleep with a smile on his face.

The clicking of the door woke both Kendrick and Jay, baby Bella stayed comfortably asleep on her daddy's chest.

"If that's not a picture of love, strength, and family, I don't know what is." Dr. Parks smiled at the couple. "Are you two ready to get started?"

Jay looked at Kendrick uncertainly. "I love you. Please don't be angry at anything I say today."

"Pixie, I've got to prove to you I'm trustworthy. It won't happen today or tomorrow, but I'll work at it every day of my life. You go ahead and say anything you need to say in here today. I'm strong enough to beat the pills; I'm strong enough to take your anger." He leaned in and kissed her softly. "I love you, too."

"Okay, Jay, last night you were frustrated when Kendrick pushed you to say how you're doing. Let's start with that." Dr. Parks began.

Taking a deep breath, watching her daughter sleep in Kendrick's arms, Jay spoke, "I feel bad for not trusting you, and I feel guilty for not being completely happy. But, if I'm being honest, I'm scared and angry. Scared you'll pick the pills over us again. Angry that you picked them over us in the first place. Scared the next time I find you face down, it won't be passed out, it will be dead. Angry that you were stupid enough to snort pills and risk taking yourself away from us." She paused before taking a deep breath. "Scared that the only daddy Bella will ever know will turn out to be an addict like my own parents. Angry that you've been away, getting clean, while I've been walking the floor at 3:00 a.m. trying to soothe a crying baby."

She closed her eyes as she finished. Kendrick's pained expression turned to her.

"That's good, Jay. Does it feel better to say all of that?" Dr. Parks asked.

"Yeah, it actually does. It's like I was hiding it before, but now that's it out there, I don't feel so guilty about my feelings." She smiled slightly.

Handing the baby to her, Kendrick knelt in front of her. Taking her free hand, he whispered fervently, "Jaymison, I'm so very sorry. I made terrible mistakes. I let the pills cloud my judgment, and I scared you with my actions. If you'll let me, I'll live every day for the rest of my life proving to you that I can be the man you fell in love with and a good father to Bella." He stopped, afraid to offer her an out, scared if he gave her the option of leaving him she'd take it.

"Kendrick, you are so deep in my heart, I'm not sure I could ever leave you or your family. You are still the man I fell in love with, you just got a bit off track. And whether you're Bella's biological father or not, she will never know a time when she wasn't loved by her daddy. I want to work this out; I truly believe we can. I just need you to know it won't always be easy. I need more than empty words and promises; I need to see those promises in action." She shifted on the seat, "I have some non-negotiables. We will keep seeing Dr. Parks, together. You will take a drug test at the drop of a hat if I ask for one. I will keep every single prescription and OTC medicine under lock and key. Neither of us will so much as take a Motrin without the other knowing about it and approving it. And we will talk to each other and our families constantly, sharing at all times if things get rough."

Kendrick smiled at his beautiful, spunky pixie. He knew she would hold him to each and every item she'd just listed, and possibly more, and he was more than okay with living by those rules.

"I can live with those." He kissed her nose.

"How do I know I can trust him? Trust this to work?" Jay looked questioningly to Dr. Parks, but the man looked pointedly at Kendrick.

"Jay, I can't say I'll never screw up. I can't promise perfect. There's no guarantee I won't relapse. But there's also no guarantee about anything in life. We could give up on all of this because we're scared of it not working. Or we can cling to each other and find ourselves blissfully happy twenty-five years from now because we gave it another chance." Kendrick's heart beat hard in his chest, waiting on Jay's response.

"Yeah, okay. It may not be easy, but a wise man who sometimes makes bad choices once told me, 'Bring it.' So, yeah, *bring it*. Let's do this." Jay smiled at Kendrick, rolling her eyes when he held out a hand for a fist pump.

At the end of the session, Kendrick wiped tears away as he kissed Bella's head one last time. "Bye-bye, Baby Bella. Daddy loves you. I'll be home soon. I promise."

Leaning in to kiss Jay, he deepened what started as a soft kiss, tracing his tongue along her lips, nipping a bit before breaking away. "You and I have a lot of time to make up for. Once you've got the all clear and I bust out of here, we're calling Sawyer and Luke for a weekend of babysitting so we can lock ourselves in our room and not come out until neither of us can walk right." He punctuated his little speech with a final kiss to her mouth while Jay snorted, and Dr. Parks attempted to hide a chuckle. "Don't laugh, Pixie, that's a promise."

24

Kendrick was counting down the days until he could sleep in his own bed. He'd been granted extra phone call privileges which allowed him to speak to his cousins, his parents, and Jay a few times a week.

Three days before heading home *for good*, he wouldn't even let himself think about ever having to be back in rehab; he dialed Jay's number from the desk phone in his room.

Confusion, worry, and anger danced in his spotty vision when a man's voice answered, "Jay's phone, she's busy right now, may I take a message?"

Swallowing down his gut reaction to bark, "Who the fuck is this?" Kendrick gritted his teeth and took a quick cleansing breath.

"This is her boyfriend, Kendrick, may I ask who this is?"

He felt proud he'd been able to keep both a quiver and a growl from his voice.

After a moment's silence, the man spoke. "Kendrick. This is Tony."

Tony's steely voice held no friendliness. Never mind the fact the two of them had been intimate on more than one occasion, it was immediately clear to Kendrick that Tony was *not* happy with him.

"Tony, good to hear from you. Are you back in town for good or just to visit? How's the friend and family in Chicago?" Kendrick knew he sounded pathetic, but he wasn't sure just how much Jay had told Tony, so he erred on the side of caution.

"Just visiting. Aunt and Uncle are no better and no worse. Friend is now my husband." Tony snorted much like the better conversations they'd had in the past, "Yeah, guess I'm a lot more gay than bi." He paused. "So I came to visit, pick up a few things I'd left with friends, thought I'd look my Jay up and see how she was doing. Imagine my surprise when I find out she's had a *baby*, is living with *you*, there's a possibility the baby is *mine*, and you're in fucking *rehab* for drugs." He let the sentence hang.

"I'm clean now, Tony. I never meant to hurt her." Kendrick's voice sounded pleading and tight.

"How many people actually set out to purposefully hurt another person, Kendrick? Of course you didn't *mean* to hurt her. But you did. Now she's on her own, with a fatherless baby, and a bleak future." Tony snapped.

"Whoa, hold up. She's *not* on her own. She has me and my entire family to support her. Bella isn't fatherless. I don't care if you or someone else is the father, I will be in that baby's life for as long as Jay will allow it. And her future is not bleak. She has a place at The Café. I have a stable job; she can do anything she wants with her life. If I have my way, she'll be home with Bella and the rest of our babies as *my wife* as soon as possible." Kendrick paused, taking a deep breath to calm the anger and volume of his voice.

"We had the paternity test run today. Should hear back in a day or two. I'll be staying with her until we get the results. Either way, father or not, I'm offering to take Jay and Bella with me to Chicago. My husband and I have a fabulous place just outside the city. He works from home, and my interior design has really picked up. Jay and Bella would want for nothing. She can do the hair stylist thing, tend bar, take up a new hobby, or sit on the couch and watch Sesame Street every damn day for all I care. But she'll be safe and happy with me, away from you."

Feeling as if he'd been punched in the gut, Kendrick doubled over, fighting against the nausea and panic threatening to take over.

Closing his eyes, breathing deeply, he tried to center himself.

"Does Jay know about this plan?" If she chose to leave

with Tony, he'd have no choice but to let her go. Unless Bella was really his. Then he'd fight her tooth and nail.

"I haven't told her yet. We spent most of today talking and playing with Bella. She asked me to move her back into her place from Katie's house. Tonight will be the first night she's here on her own, but I'll be here for the next couple nights." He stopped momentarily. "Listen, Kendrick, I'm not trying to hurt you. I know Jay loves you, and if she chooses you, then so be it. But that girl was my best friend for quite a while; we got each other through some rough times. I love her in my own way. I want her safe and happy. If that means getting away from you and Torey Hope, she'll always have a place with me."

"Why would she need to be away from me or my family? We love her and Bella with our entire hearts." Kendrick asked defensively.

"You wrecked her, forced her to live through a nightmare, left her on her own with a brand new baby. She may decide it's just too much." Tony didn't sound like he completely believed what he was saying.

"Cut the dramatic act, Tony. Jay is a big girl. Even without me or my family, she could raise Bella with one hand tied behind her back. She can make her own choices, but I don't think running with you to Chicago is going to be one of them."

Kendrick was quiet for a moment. "What will you do if the baby is yours?" He didn't want to know, but he had to.

Taking a deep breath, Tony sighed. "If Bella is mine, I'll try even harder to convince Jay to move to Chicago. If she won't, then I'll be making a lot of trips to Torey Hope to see my baby girl."

Kendrick was silent, fears assaulting his heart.

"Can you tell Jay I called and I love her, please?" Kendrick's voice was barely a whisper.

"Yeah, I'll tell her." Tony's voice had softened a bit. "Kendrick, I hate what you did to her, but even through all of the hell you put her through, I've never seen her look happier, brighter, more in love."

"I love her more than life itself, man."

"Yeah, I know." Tony paused again. "Hey, Kendrick?"

"Yeah?"

"Bella looks just like her daddy."

And with that, the man hung up.

Now what the hell was that supposed to mean? Was Tony rubbing it in Kendrick's face that Bella wasn't his? Fuck. He needed to get home, needed to hold Jay and Bella. He needed to know if Tony was going to take them away.

"OH YES, *just like that. So good. Harder, harder.*"

"*Mmm, Jay, you feel so good. Ride me baby.*"

"*Tony!*"

"*Yeah, Jay, I'm right here baby. You and me and Bella, we're a family.*"

Kendrick sat bolt upright in bed. Wiping sweat from his eyes, he took giant gulps of air. *Just a dream. Fucking nightmare more like it. But not real.*

He looked around his room. He was going home the next day. Home. To Jay and Bella? Or to an empty place with just his memories of them?

He called Decker.

"Man, if Jay doesn't want me at her place or she decides to go to Chicago with Tony, can I move back in the house with you guys?" Kendrick ran a hand down his face, sighing heavily.

"Kendrick? You okay? Why would Jay not want you at her place? She was excited to get settled back in there in time for your homecoming. And why would she leave with Tony?"

He heard Decker shuffle the blankets and sit up, "Wait, is Bella Tony's? Is that why you think Jay may leave?"

"I don't know if she's Tony's, but Tony wants Jay to move to Chicago to live with him and his husband. I know it's a long shot of Bella actually being mine, but she's already mine in my heart, and I don't know what I'd do if Jay left for Chicago."

Kendrick flopped back down on his bed, absentmindedly glancing at the clock. 2:00 *a.m.?* "Fuck, Decker, I'm sorry. I woke from a bad dream and didn't even think about the time."

"Don't worry about it. Do you want Katie and me to be

over there tomorrow when you get home? We can have the whole crew there."

"Yeah, man, that would be great. It can either be a celebration homecoming or a going away party for Jay and Bella." Kendrick snorted before the tears caught in his throat. "Deck, what am I going to do if I lose them?"

"Don't worry about that now. You need to get some sleep so you're in good shape to come home. We'll be there to meet you tomorrow, the whole crew, and we'll figure out what's going on then. Try to get some sleep and not worry." Decker paused and Kendrick heard Katie mumble something near the phone. "Katie says to let you know Jay is very much in love with you, not with Tony, and she'd be crazy to leave Torey Hope and our family." Decker lowered his voice, "Of course, I think she said all of that in her sleep, so she likely won't remember it in the morning. But she's right. If Jay was going to leave, she would have done it when the pills first started. She's waited for you, supported you, gone to therapy with you. She's not going anywhere."

Too choked up to speak, Kendrick disconnected the call. He stared up at the dark ceiling, lit only by a sliver of light from the hallway, and tried to prepare himself for the next day.

He'd be out of rehab.

He still had a long way to go.

If Bella was Tony's, they'd deal with it. It wasn't like he'd lose Jay's love to Tony.

If Bella wasn't Tony's he still had to accept there was a very slim chance she was his own child. Would Jay want to find that guy?

No matter what, no questions asked, he loved that baby girl like she was his very own. She'd either get a daddy out of him, or an unbelievably attached 'uncle' if she was really Tony's.

Kendrick, she looks just like her daddy.

She had dark hair. Tony and Kendrick both had dark hair. Her eyes weren't a specific color just yet. He never thought babies looked like real people. Just who did Tony think Bella looked like?

Flopping over on the bed, careful not to jar his shoulder, Kendrick sighed, "I should have bought <u>Go the F**k to Sleep</u> for myself in rehab. I think I need it."

He STRETCHED his legs out as he stood from the car. His mom and dad had picked him up from rehab. The drive could have been awkward, but his parents made it as easy as possible.

"Kendrick, I'm sorry we didn't see the issues you were having all those years ago or over these past few years. And I'm sorry we either didn't see the problems you were having with the pills, or we turned a blind eye to them." Audrey stated these things matter-of-factly. "In all honesty, I'm ashamed to admit I think I turned a blind eye to them more than most because it made me feel that my messed up past maybe caused you to be more likely than most to mess up too. And I'm sorry I didn't trust Jay when she first came to us."

"Mom, we all screw up. You and I just do it bigger and better than most, right?" Kendrick smiled at his mom. "And we can work the other things out with Dr. Parks. You've apologized to Jay and me both. It's okay to move past it."

He looked around and saw various vehicles parked in front of Jay's place. The unknown black car was likely Tony's.

With a hug from his mom and dad, he waved goodbye to them and walked through the door.

Every cousin was there. Tony stood silently in the background, holding Bella. With his knees threatening to buckle under him, Kendrick made a beeline for Jay. Gathering her in his arms, he kissed her thoroughly. Holding her face in his hands, he whispered roughly, "I will never leave you alone again."

Jay smiled through tears, "Welcome home, Kendrick."

Katie and Zoey wiped away tears of joy, as the guys just smiled.

Tony cleared his throat. Walking toward Kendrick with Bella in his arms, he smiled. "I'll be back to visit, and I'll be the best damn godfather I can be. Take care of my girls, treat them right, or you can answer to me." Tony leaned in to kiss Bella's head, "Bye-bye, Bella."

Pulling Kendrick into a hug, he clapped him on the back. "Be good to each other. Give me a call if you ever need a third..." All eyes in the room bugged out. "...pair of hands when it comes to diapers or potty training or teaching her to ride a bike. I'll be here in a heartbeat."

Laughter bubbled over then.

"Jay, sweetie, thank you for being my friend and being there for me. We were good together, but nothing I did ever made your eyes shine the way they do for this guy here. Take care of you." He kissed Jay's cheek.

With a quick wave, he walked to his car and drove off.

"Shhh, they'll hear us." Jay giggled as Kendrick tossed her on the bed.

He walked to the door, threw it open and stuck his head into the hall. "Sawyer? Luke?"

"Yeah?"

"You're aware I'm planning on having lots of loud sex with Jay for the next several hours, right?"

"Yep, that's why we're taking Bella for a drive over to Grandma Cindy's house until evening."

"Good plan, boys. Enjoy." Kendrick started to close the door, but hesitated. Walking into the hallway to where Sawyer was packing up the diaper bag, he added a couple diapers, another outfit and blanket, and two extra packs of breast milk.

"Just in case. You never know." Leaning down to nuzzle Bella's downy soft head, he whispered, "Have fun with your mannies, Bella Marie. I'm going to ravish your pretty momma now."

"Kendrick! Don't talk dirty to the baby!" Jay hollered from the bedroom.

"Go on, go have fun. We've got the baby all taken care of." Sawyer shooed him back to the bedroom while Luke loaded Bella into the car seat.

Before they were even out the door, Kendrick had pounced on Jay. "Mmmm, post pregnancy sex...is it as good as pregnancy sex? Let's find out." He wagged his brows at her. "Best part is I don't have to worry about poking the baby's eye out."

Jay laughed and smacked at him. "That was never a danger, and you know it."

"Oh, I think you underestimate the reach of this big boy." He hefted himself in his hand.

Jay rolled her eyes.

By the time Sawyer and Luke returned with Bella, Kendrick and Jay had worn themselves out.

"Damn, you two look like porn stars who just finished a marathon recording session. Go shower and sleep. We'll stay through the first late night feeding."

Kendrick gratefully steered Jay toward the bathroom, a

hot shower and sleep would be the perfect ending to a perfect day. Looking over his shoulder at Sawyer and Luke, Kendrick couldn't help but smile as the two men fussed over Bella. That baby girl was going to be the most loved and protected child on the planet.

After a scorching hot shower, Kendrick gathered Jay in his arms as they settled into bed. *Their* bed.

"So, was Tony upset?" Kendrick hadn't been able to get a good read on the man before he drove off.

"Mmmm, it's hard to say. I think he was shocked and petrified at first, but then the idea grew on him. I think he sort of liked the idea of playing house, helping to raise Bella. And I know he would have been there for us every step of the way. But, in the long run, I think he was relieved to just get godfather duty. This way, he can spoil, play, and pamper her, but have no real responsibility or obligations."

He reveled in having Jay cuddled against his chest. No pill could ever bring him the euphoric feeling of having this woman by his side.

"What about you? If we open that envelope and it says you aren't the father, do you still want to take on the responsibility and obligation of raising Bella for the next eighteen years?" Jay's eyes looked up at him expectantly.

"Hell no."

When she gasped, he chuckled, "I plan on raising Bella *and* the rest of our kids for the next eighteen plus years."

"And if you *are* the father. Will it change anything?" Jay

furrowed her brow.

"Not at all. Either way, I'm marrying her mother the first chance I get and making both of my girls Jordans." He kissed her neck, her ear, her mouth. "Now, no more talking. Let's sleep before the little beast needs the boob or her butt wiped."

"Kendrick?"

"Yeah, Pixie?"

"I love you. Thank you for showing me what it truly means to be a family, to stand by someone, and to love unconditionally." She kissed his chin.

He shook his head. "No, Pixie, I should be thanking you."

"For what?"

"For showing me it's okay to be vulnerable, to make mistakes, and for saving me. I love you."

"Wow, we're pretty good for each other, huh?" Jay smiled at him.

"Well, take away the unplanned pregnancy, unknown father, unwed mother, prescription pill addiction, suicide and depression, yeah, I'd say we've really got it going on." He laughed at her snort of laughter before kissing her. "Joking aside, you are my heart, my soul, my forever."

She sighed, "At the risk of sounding completely cheesy, you complete me. You really do."

"Are we doing cheesy movie lines now? Well then, Jaymison Marie, you had me at 'Wanna have a threesome?'"

Their laughter slowly faded, and they slept with thoughts of the future dancing brightly through their dreams.

EPILOGUE

*T*he wedding took place in a crowded courthouse. It wasn't crowded because of others using the space, it was just hard to fit that many family members into the small room.

"I think this is quite possibly the largest courthouse wedding I've ever seen." The justice laughed.

"You know this family, Judge. Go big or go home." Kendrick laughed.

Jay handed Bella to Katie before turning to take Kendrick's hands.

"I understand you both have written something. Jaymison, you may begin." The jovial old man nodded at her.

"Kendrick, I wasn't looking for love. More like I was running from anything resembling love. But you somehow snared me, without even meaning to, and showed me a world of love and family I never knew existed. Today, I vow to love, honor, and cherish you. But I also vow to support you through the good and the bad, kick your ass if it becomes necessary, and continue the love of family you've shown to me." She slid a simple band on his finger to cover the tattoo ring Kyle had inked not long ago. Even when his ring was off, *Jay* would be there.

"Jaymison, you found me at what I thought was my lowest point. You gave me a reason to fight through the blackness. Little did I know the depths of darkness that awaited me. Your love, your courage, and your heart saved me. Today I vow to love, honor, and cherish you. But I also vow to support you, protect you, and let you kick my ass whenever necessary. Thank you for being my heart." He slid the band over the *K* on her finger.

Taking Bella into his arms, he kissed her head. "Bella, today I vow to be your daddy forever. I will love you, cherish you, teach you, and protect you. You've been mine since the moment I first heard of your existence, and no slip of paper will ever change that. Bella Marie Jordan, I love you forever."

The little envelope containing the results of his paternity test sat snuggly in the safety deposit box at the bank. Kendrick had stared at the envelope for over an hour while rocking Bella one evening.

"Jay, I don't want to open it. She's mine no matter what this slip of paper says. Nothing will change that. Let's lock it away in case we ever need it for medical issues, but I don't need to have a test to prove to me this baby girl is mine."

The other man who *could* have been the father was found dead from an overdose in Florida. The eerily similar paths Kendrick and this man took were not lost on Kendrick. The difference? Love and support from family and friends, a determined woman, and a beautiful baby. Without those things, Kendrick's path could have been much different.

And so the envelope sat, unopened, while Kendrick, Jay, and Bella happily became a family of three.

When Jay tossed the bouquet, laughter abounded as it broke into two pieces. Katie catching one piece and Luke grabbing the other before it landed on the judge's head.

Decker and Sawyer could only smirk at each other. Twins did everything together, right? Maybe a double wedding?

"I WANTED to thank you all for being here for me today, it means a lot." Kendrick stood at the edge of the park with his family surrounding him.

"I recently heard a song by Pink called *Beam Me Up*. It's a very touching song about the loss of a loved one, especially a child. There are days when I'd give anything to talk to my son just for a moment. I was lucky enough to see him in a dream once. He's a beautiful boy, and I wish he would have had the chance to live in our family." Kendrick cleared his throat, fighting the tears as Jay took his hand.

"I wanted to release butterflies today in memory of my son, Ricky. And in memory of all the other babies taken from this world. Like butterflies that are gone too soon, these babies' lives were cut short, but they live on in the beauty surrounding us." With a single tear running down his face, Kendrick opened his own small box of butterflies as the rest of the family opened theirs.

The family stood quietly for several moments watching the butterflies flutter away.

"I love you, Ricky," Kendrick whispered as he pulled Jay to his side and cuddled Bella to his chest.

FROM THE AUTHOR

I started writing my first book (For Nicky) in October 2013; I had no clue if I could do it, and even less clue about what to do when I finished it. About halfway through that book, I realized that the mean, terrible sister, Audrey, had a story to tell; I started Because of Beckett as soon as I finished For Nicky.

I had no intention of continuing the Torey Hope Series. However, readers had fallen in love with the stories and they asked for more. I created a heartwarming Christmas novella to lead into the third full-length novel, Loving Josie.

One day, in the shower (where else do great ideas come from?), I realized that the younger generation of Torey Hope had some stories to tell. I ran the idea by readers, and they loved the prospect of continuing the Torey Hope Series. So, voila, Torey Hope: *The Later Years* was born!

The first three books in *The Later Years* can be found on my Nook author page (bit.ly/ADEllisNook). The titles are Decker, Sawyer, and Zach.

One of these days, I'll let the other characters and stories out of my head and create some new books and series; until then, I continue to fall in love with the hearts of my Torey Hope characters in each and every story.

THANK YOU FOR READING! I hope you enjoyed; please take a moment to leave a review. If you're reading on a file/device that doesn't take you to a review option, you may click here to leave a review on Nook (bit.ly/ADEllisNook)

A.D. Ellis

Notes

I found these websites helpful in researching addiction and recovery. I hope, if you're dealing with an addiction, you're able to find assistance to begin your recovery.

http://www.addictionsandrecovery.org/opiates-narcotics-recovery.htm

http://luxury.rehabs.com/drug-detox/opiate/

http://www.futuresofpalmbeach.com/drug-detox/coping-with-withdrawal-symptoms/

http://www.healthline.com/health/opiate-withdrawal#Overview1

https://www.addiction.com/3517/change-in-addiction-recovery/

https://www.addiction.com/3277/death-addiction-stages-grief-addiction-recovery/

http://www.webmd.com/pain-management/features/painkiller-addiction-warning-signs

http://www.webmd.com/pain-management/features/pain-medication-addiction

This page will help to explain the therapy Zoey is trained in and how it can help those with pain like Kendrick deals with. A big thanks to my friend Megg for giving me details about this therapy.

http://neurokinetictherapy.com/

BOOKS KENDRICK GOT FOR BABY BELLA

Love You Forever http://amzn.to/1n5ecYe

On the Night You Were Born http://amzn.to/1RZDhiS

The Monster at the End of this Book http://amzn.to/1RZDpik

Go the F**k to Sleep http://amzn.to/1RZDRx9

In searching for funny books Kendrick may have registered for, I came across a whole page of them. Here are some hilarious titles you may want to read for yourself or purchase for friends.

Funny books about babies and children: http://amzn.to/1RZDCSK

ABOUT THE AUTHOR

A.D. Ellis is an Indiana girl, born and raised. She spends much of her time in central Indiana teaching alternative education in the inner city of Indianapolis, being a mom to two amazing school-aged children, and wondering how she and her husband of almost two decades have managed to not drive each other insane. A lot of her time is also devoted to phone call avoidance and her hatred of cooking.

She loves chocolate, wine, pizza, and naps along with reading and writing romance. These loves don't leave much time for housework, much to the chagrin of her husband. Who would pick cleaning the house over a nap or a good book? She uses any extra time to increase her fluency in sarcasm.

ACKNOWLEDGMENTS

This is always one of the hardest parts of finishing a book, but quite possibly the most important part. It's so hard because I fear I'll miss someone who has helped me out, supported me, been a listening ear, or offered advice and encouragement. If I miss listing your name here, please know it wasn't on purpose, and I love you dearly!

I wouldn't have been able to complete this book without input from many readers who have dealt with addiction/suicide/recovery. If you answered any of my many questions, THANK YOU for making this story what it is. To C and C, thank you for being willing to share such a deeply personal part of your life with me. I appreciate your openness and honesty more than you can imagine. And I'm amazed at your ability to overcome the obstacles in your life.

To my editor, Stephanne, thank you from the bottom of

my heart for your sharp eyes and constant professionalism. You were a gift to me over 10 years ago, and you continue to be a blessing.

To my dear beta readers. Your input, feedback, and encouragement has proven invaluable to me! I truly trust you all and value your opinions more than you'll probably ever understand. Thank you to my newest betas as well. When I needed fresh new eyes who had never read any of these characters you were there for me and helped me so much!

To my street team/pimpers. Those of you who list me in contests and comments and shout outs all the time, you're amazing and I love you for always working to get my name out there! If I start naming people here, I'll be sure to miss some; just know if you've ever shared my name or my books, it means the world to me and I appreciate you more than you'll ever know!

To my READERS!! Without you, there would have never been a third book, let alone an eighth book! Thank you for loving Torey Hope and the characters as much as I do. Knowing you are looking forward to another book is a lot of what keeps me writing some days. As long as these stories are in my head, I'll keep sharing them with you.

To the BLOGGERS who read and review and share my books!! You are beyond a shadow of a doubt some of the most dedicated and selfless people I've ever known! Thank you so much for being such a support to those of us who have stories to tell. I love BLOGGERS!

To my girls at The Indie Erogenous Zone. You are beyond fellow authors, you're my support, my heart, my friends. There have been days I wanted to give up, but I had you to turn to; days when a bad review breaks my heart, but I talk it out with you. I truly consider you all my close friends and I wouldn't want to be facing this crazy journey without you! IEZ4Life! T&F girls!

To my Juice Box ladies! Thank you so much for welcoming me into your crew and sharing your knowledge, experience, advice, and fun with me! Having some real-life authors/friends I can collaborate with is a great feeling. Dance parties, lunches, movies, videos, wine, painting, pizza...the list goes on and on! Thank you for letting me be a Juice Boxer!

To my fellow authors. Those of you who read my work, share your work with me, cross-promote with me, and offer advice and support, THANK YOU! You make this a little easier and even more enjoyable.

To my family and friends. I know most of you don't understand my obsession with getting these stories out of my head and on paper, but you're proud of me either way. Some of you get to read my books, some of you get to see cover ideas, some of you have to watch me lose myself in a story, some of you have to hear me vent about the hard parts of all of this; all of you love me and support me and for that, I am truly lucky and grateful.

Connect with A.D. Ellis

Check my Nook page for updates bit.ly/ADEllisNook or find me on Facebook http://www.facebook.com/adellisauthor

If you want to get updates about releases, interviews, sales, giveaways, and more please sign up for my newsletter bit.ly/EllisNewsletter

You can also find me on Twitter http://www.twitter.com/ADEllisAuthor

Find me on Spotify if you'd like to listen to the playlist for this book (mainly just the songs I listened to while writing— THERE ARE SOME AMAZING SONGS ON KENDRICK'S PLAYLIST THAT GO ALONG WITH HIS STORY PERFECTLY!) or any of my other books. Just search for A.D. Ellis.

Excerpts from other Torey Hope Novels

(These books are the beginning of the Torey Hope books. The parents and grandparents in Decker, Sawyer, Zach, and Kendrick are the main characters in these earlier books.)

A *Torey Hope Novel Series* starts with **For Nicky**. Meet and fall in love with Nate and Nicky Morgan, twin brothers. Find **For Nicky** here: http://getbook.at/NickyAmzn

"Hey, Audrey, what's up? Come in." Audrey smiles, which

seems a little fake, and comes on in. She's dressed to the nines as usual. Heels, tight skirt, tighter shirt, hair styled much bigger than you'd think is possible. I can smell her perfume and hairspray as she walks past me. Who dresses like this for a normal day? Audrey does, obviously. She looks me up and down. "Are you going somewhere, Beth?"

I tell her I have a date. She looks pissed for a moment, then gives me a smile that doesn't even begin to reach her eyes, and says, "Oh, that's nice. Who's the poor shmuck?"

Obviously, she's baiting me, but I don't think quickly enough and I just reply, "Nathaniel Morgan."

Audrey rolls her eyes. "Beth, sweetie, I'm going to try to say this in the nicest/sisterly love type of way. But, Nathan Morgan is way out of your league. You are dressed in a flannel shirt, you might as well wear a sign that says 'frumpy' on the front and 'won't ever get laid' on the back. Nate is an animal in bed, I should know. He needs sex. I doubt you're giving it to him yet. If you ever decide to try sex again, it will probably be as bad as it was with Austin. Not because Nate isn't good, because the good Lord knows that man is G.O.O.D in bed, but there's no way your 'basically a virgin' body can live up to what he's used to. Hell, the boy wore ME out and I have as much experience as he does, if not more. I'm not sure why he's hung around this long. Maybe he sees you as a challenge. Yeah, maybe he's decided to string you along long enough to get in your pants, but, Beth, he's not going to stick around. Nate needs hot sex, a variety of girls, no strings. I don't want you to get hurt when he fucks you and leaves you. Oh, God, Beth, seriously, stop with the teary puppy-dog eyes. I'm just telling you the truth." ~Libby {Beth} Decker in **For Nicky**

~

The sequel to For Nicky, **Because of Beckett** (this is Audrey's story and as much as you hate her in For Nicky, you will find yourself liking her in Because of Beckett and you will fall in love with Jeremiah Jordan!) Find **Because of Beckett** here: http://getbook.at/BeckettAmzn

The one girl he should stay as far away from as possible, the one girl who had made him feel more alive in one evening than he had in several years, the one girl who threatened his well-designed single-dad, good role model position in life was Audrey Decker. Instead of letting her off the hook and planning the party himself, he had practically begged her to stick with it and all but promised her there would be no problems. That was all well and good, he was truly glad she was going to take the party, except for one small problem, he hadn't been able to get her out of his mind; he couldn't stop thinking of those gorgeous blue eyes or her beautiful hair or luscious curves. His heart jumped into his throat when he saw her walking toward the shelter house; his breath hitched in his chest when her hand touched his knee; he wanted to hold her hand and start right back where they had left off the other night. But, they'd agreed that this was a business deal only, so he wouldn't complicate it. They'd get through the party and move on. They were living in the same town; they'd surely see each other. Jeremiah was determined to keep things cool between them so the party would be a success and they could be friendly toward each other in social settings.

And then, he watched her eyes light up as she knelt down and opened her arms to Beckett. He was gone; hook, line, sinker. Audrey didn't strike him as the type to be particularly caring towards anyone, let alone a child with special needs. But, there she was, on her knees, hugging his son... How was it, the woman he had just promised he wouldn't pursue, was on the ground hugging his child like his real mother never had? Jeremiah's gut clenched at the thought. He wanted this woman in his life. But, she'd made it clear that she wasn't interested and Jeremiah wondered if he had lost his chance to indicate any interest. So, he decided he'd have to settle for having her in his life as a friend. ~Jeremiah Jordan in **Because of Beckett**

The families celebrate the holidays in **Christmas in Torey Hope, A Novella**. Love and family and friendship abounds and readers get to learn of the older couples' love stories. Find **Christmas in Torey Hope** here: http://getbook.at/ChristmasAmzn

"Libby-girl, you never cease to amaze me. That was amazing." He kissed her and they proceeded to clean up and redress. "Now, we better get back to the house before everyone knows what I've been doing to you." Nate winked.

Libby's cheeks blushed but she said, "Nate, I'm pretty sure this is exactly what your mom had in mind when she sent us away for a bit."

"Well then, I'll have to sincerely thank my momma!" Nate kissed her lips as they headed back out the door, locking it soundly behind them.

~

"Uh, Mom, I'm all for reminiscing and I know you and Dad love each other, but could we please keep it G-rated. For the love of all that is good, please don't make me listen to sex stories involving you two." Jeremiah shuddered but smiled good-naturedly at his mother.

"What? We all had to see you and Audrey and Nate and Libby come in here glowing after your little 45 minute romp; I think a little steamy romance story about your dad and I would serve you right." Judy laughed at her son's expression. "Don't worry, I'll keep it clean." The whole group laughed at Jeremiah's visible relief.

Before the story could get started, Nate cleared his throat and said, "Mom, Dad, let's keep in mind that I've walked in on the two of you in some compromising positions that are now burned into my delicate mind; please don't add anymore trauma to my already scarred psyche." Everyone laughed at Nate's statement. "You all think I'm joking but I'm really not. You don't know the images that still float through my mind." Nate teased his parents and pulled Libby against him as they settled onto one of the couches.

Loving Josie is a story of second chance love for two lost souls. This is a standalone novel in A Torey Hope Novel Series, so you can read it without reading the first books. Find **Loving Josie** here: http://getbook.at/JosieAmzn

"What the hell are you thinking, Josie Decker?" This from Audrey. She continued, "I just left my house after calling in my reinforcements here. Did you know Kyle's over at my house talking to Jeremiah? He's all dressed up, pierced up, tatted up, bleached up, and styled up. Do you know why? He's got a date. Oh, but that's right, you already knew he had a date, didn't you?!"

When I didn't respond, because I wasn't sure if this was a rhetorical question or not, she powered on. "It was bad enough

when you bought a house with the man. But now you're going to 'pretend date' him?! This isn't a good thing, Josie. If he weren't so fucked up, I would be cheering you on. And, honestly, I think dating you would be truly good for him. But, he's so damn stubborn, I worry he'll never let go of the notion that he can't love you the way you deserve and, in the end, you're going to end up being hurt." ~Josie Decker in **Loving Josie**

~

Turning me around he tipped my chin up, "We need to talk, Jo. Some things have changed. No more practice dating. No more stopping kisses and pretending they shouldn't happen. I want to see more than my ink on you; I want to see me on you." With that final comment he brought his mouth down on mine. This kiss was different than all of the others had been. This kiss was all Kyle, he was holding nothing back. ~Josie Decker in **Loving Josie**

~

Decker, Torey Hope: The Later Years (this is the first book in the new series) http://getbook.at/DeckerAmzn

"Hello, this is Decker Morgan at The Center+. I'm calling for Ms. Katherine Turner in regards to her recent resume and job application." Decker held the phone away from his ear as he heard an earsplitting blare coming through the line.

"Oh my God! I'm so sorry! Hold on please Mr. Morgan! This is Katherine Turner....hang on just a second! Where's the damn broom?!" A cacophony came through the phone and Decker was tempted to hang up; if this was the way Ms. Turner conducted herself on the phone she was obviously not the one for the job.

"Shut up, damn it! Just shut up!" Her words were barely distinguishable over the shrill alarm-like noise. "There! I'm so sorry, Mr. Morgan. Mr. Morgan? Sir? Are you there? Please accept my apologies. I was helping my grandma bake cookies. I didn't realize that Grandma had accidentally turned the oven up to 500 and the timer to thirty-one minutes rather than thirteen minutes. Needless to say, our little cookies are now burnt offerings. On the bright side, we know her smoke detectors work." Katherine Turner spoke in an airy, breathless way that had Decker picturing her in a smoky kitchen, hair askew, with a broomstick to turn off the offending smoke detector.

"Well, Ms. Turner, you're the first applicant I've called who has provided so much entertainment in such a short amount of time. I trust that there's no danger to you or your grandmother?" Decker really couldn't explain why he felt the need to continue with this phone interview; the girl obviously wasn't management material, but he wanted to hear her answers to his questions because she had him feeling something he hadn't felt in a long time. Intrigued.

Forty-five minutes later, Decker hung up from the most enjoyable phone interview he'd ever conducted. Katherine Turner was not the typical uptight management applicant that he'd been speaking to; this woman was genuine, whip-smart, well-spoken, and on the same path as him. It amazed him just how much they had in common both personally and professionally. Before ending the call with her, Decker had done something he'd never planned on doing; he offered her the job over the phone, sight unseen, no further interview. She had accepted, and he was pumped to meet her in person the next day and get the paperwork filled out so she could get to work right away.

Looking at the clock, he realized that it was late enough he could call it a day. There was really nothing else he needed to do right then. He texted his brother to see if Sawyer wanted to play some basketball before they headed home. As it turned out, Sawyer's meeting with the potential martial arts instructor had run over so he wasn't available; Zach, Kendrick, and Decker played a little game before their dads and uncle showed up. Nate Morgan, Jeremiah Jordan, and Kyle Martin had been playing ball together for years and gave the younger men a run for their money. In the end, all six men were sweaty but laughing. Decker paused as he left The Center+ on his way home. Yeah, it was good to be back.

~

"Unknown caller" flashed on his phone screen as he worked on some paperwork for Katherine Turner. Absentmindedly he picked up the phone, "Decker Morgan."

"Hello, Mr. Morgan. I'm really sorry to call you at home in the evening, but you gave me your number and said I could call if I had any questions. I have to apologize, I think the whole cookie burning had me flustered today; I don't normally accept a job sight-unseen and without meeting my boss in person. I still plan on coming in tomorrow, but I was hoping to discuss the position with you a little more now that the smoke has cleared from both my head and my grandma's kitchen. That is, if you have a moment to speak to me." He admired her straightforwardness and knew she was just as knocked off-kilter as he was after their whirlwind phone interview earlier that day.

"I have time, Ms. Turner. Please, ask anything you'd like." Decker waved to Sawyer as his brother popped his head in the office to say hello. Plopping down on the couch, Decker stretched his 6'2" frame out and got comfortable.

"Well, I've been doing some research on The Center+, but I'd like to hear your description of it. Please." Katherine had a smile in her voice as she added the please to her request.

"The Center+ has been a part of my family's life since long before I was born. My Uncle Nicky attended school there and my Grandma Cindy worked there as an administrative *assistant for several years. Uncle Nicky had finished schooling, but he attended several recreational programs even after high school and he met the new librarian, Libby Decker who later married my dad. Not long after, my Uncle Nicky met my Aunt Carly while they were both working there. When my brother and cousins and I were younger, we spent almost every spare second at The Center+, although it was just The Center in those days. We enjoyed all of the programs available and took full advantage of the recreational sports. We used to always talk about growing up, going to college, and coming back to Torey Hope to expand the programs; make The Center+ bigger and better than ever. That brings us to today; we are adding two new wings, several new programs, revamping and improving the sports program, and enlarging the arts program by leaps and bounds. My family owns The Center+ now, so we have the ability to grow the business as we've always dreamed." Decker paused in his description; on the other end of the phone Katherine was touched at the sense of pride the man had in his family's business.*

Several minutes later, Katherine had asked as many questions as she could come up with and their conversation turned to more personal information. Decker learned that she had also recently graduated and returned to Torey Hope, her childhood home. She and her mother lived across town and her elderly grandmother lived with them. She had always planned to leave Torey Hope for college and thought she would move to the big city, but when her mom divorced and her grandmother moved in she took inventory of her life and her plans for her future and realized that Torey Hope was her heart, and she didn't want to leave.

Decker found himself lulled by the melodic lilt of her voice and nodded in agreement with her that finding a business management job in a small town was a definite challenge. He smiled when she shared her excitement over the potentially perfect job opportunity he had presented her with.

Through their conversation, Decker felt a definite connection to this girl; she shared his vision for success, she was a hard worker, she was self-motivated, she was a people person, she knew how to get a job done. She was perfect. Damn, the first girl he'd ever felt truly drawn to was going to be his assistant manager which meant that the connection he felt to her couldn't go anywhere. One of his hard and fast rules was that business and pleasure never mixed. Never.

"Well, Mr. Morgan, thanks for answering my questions. I feel a little bit more at ease over my spur-of-the-moment acceptance of this job. I just want to say one thing, please remember how perfect I am for the job when you meet me again tomorrow." Katherine had a smile in her voice as she spoke. "Goodnight, Mr. Morgan."

Meet her again? What the hell did that mean?

~

Sawyer, age 16

Shirts discarded and arms entangled around torsos, the young men rolled around the bed as if wrestling. Hidden, she watched from the doorway in fascination, not disgust or horror. Her mind struggled to make sense of something her heart had already accepted. As the boys' lips met in a sensual kiss, she brought her hand up to cover her surprise. She knew, instinctively, the act happening in front of her was what Sawyer had been missing, seeking, craving.

Knowing she should look away, afford them privacy, she couldn't unglue her eyes from the awkwardly arousing scene transpiring before her. Hands roamed, cupping ass cheeks; hips and tongues thrust in simultaneous dances. Red basketball shorts and tight gray boxer briefs slid down firm, muscular legs followed quickly by black shorts and black briefs moving down a second pair of toned legs. She'd seen the male anatomy in Health class, but the young men on the bed were aroused from their sensuous exploration and she felt her eyes widening in impressed awe at the size of their... male anatomy. Sawyer, the dark haired one, reached a hand down and grasped the other boy; the act was reciprocated and a delightful display began to play out before her. Mouths, teeth, and tongues clashed as hips thrust and fists pumped;

rough breaths, sexually charged, resonated in the otherwise silent room.

She knew she should have left, should have allowed him this intimate moment, but it was too late; an ill-timed sneeze, obstructed by a quick pinch to the nose, but not thwarted completely, literally blew her cover.

Walking arm-in-arm, they headed back toward his house. "So, Josh, huh? Do you want him to be, like, your boyfriend?" Katie nudged Sawyer's hip in teasingly playful way.

"I like Josh, but I think I like him because he's the first guy I've kissed. I like his body next to mine; I like to have my hands on him; I like to kiss him. Do I like *him*? I don't know. I don't think he's any closer to admitting or accepting his sexuality than I am, so I don't see us becoming a couple and publicly outing ourselves. If anything, we'll spend time behind *closed* doors and try to figure things out for ourselves, individually." Katie blushed at the mention of *closed* doors.

"Hey, bud, that door was practically wide open. I probably should have just walked away, but you two were astonishingly beautiful in your sexy little coupling, and I couldn't help myself. You should thank your lucky stars it was me and not your mom or dad or brother!" Katie wagged a finger sternly in front of his face.

Sawyer blanched yet again at the thought of his parents or twin brother, Decker, finding him in a compromising position with another man. He knew in his heart that his parents and brother would accept him no matter what, but he didn't want to bring undue stress or drama into their lives; for now, he'd keep it secret, but he'd tell them once he was a little more comfortable with it himself.

But, the thing with keeping secrets and not being truthful with those who love you is that it gets harder and harder with each day. As the years passed, Sawyer realized he'd missed several prime opportunities to be upfront with his parents and Decker.

I'm gay.

His brother, Decker, had taken the news fairly well. He'd needed a solo walk through the woods to gather his thoughts; Sawyer suspected his always-in-control, serious, black and white brother also needed to come to grips with the fact that he'd never suspected his brother's sexual preference was different than his own. How ironic that the one person Sawyer was the closest to in the whole world was the one person who was the most clueless.

Sawyer had held his breath practically the whole time Decker had been walking through the woods. A deluge of rain poured down as the dark sky broke open, yet Sawyer still sat alone at the campfire. His head had started playing tricks on him. *You disgust him...he can't stand the thought of having a gay brother...you've lost him...he's not coming back.* But Sawyer held out hope that Decker was just doing his usual thinking things through.

He had breathed a sigh of relief when Decker emerged, soaking wet, from the woods. Walking towards him with purpose, his twin had stopped in front of him and spoke the most heartwarming, sincere words Sawyer had ever heard from him.

"You're my brother, always have been, always will be. I wish you could have told me sooner, but nothing has changed between us. I'll be there in any and every way that I can." Decker grabbed Sawyer and pulled him into a deep embrace, communicating his love and acceptance through his touch.

Telling his cousins, Zach and Kendrick, had been less emotional, and a lot more entertaining. Sawyer had to laugh at the questions his admission had stirred up.

"I'm gay."

Two words that held such power. Would they laugh? Would they walk away in disgust? Would they be angry?

Zach smiled and nodded. "I think I've known that for a long time, man, but thanks for telling me."

"Wait, you knew? Why didn't you ever say something? Why did you joke with me about girls?"

"I don't know, I guess I figured you'd tell me when you were ready. I didn't want to bring it up if I was wrong and it offended you. I think I joked about girls thinking it would give you the opportunity to bring it up if you wanted to." Zach stood and walked to his cousin, reaching a hand down, he pulled the other man up into a hug. "Nothing changes, I've got your back, man."

Kendrick sat with his hand rubbing his chin. Would he be the one who couldn't accept it?

Eyes twinkling and a shit-eatin' grin on his face, he finally spoke. "What's it like to suck cock?"

~

Zach, Torey Hope: *The Later Years* (http://getbook.at/ZachAmzn)

The big truck backed slowly out of the driveway and headed toward the next town over.

"Are you going to tell me where we're going?" Zoey asked.

"Now, what would be the fun in that?" Zach smiled at her pout. "We'll be there in about thirty minutes. I think you can wait until then."

The entire half-hour drive was filled with laughter and chit-chat. Zach realized that nothing had changed between them. It was like they were four years prior, she had always been his best friend, and she still was. The only difference was he'd gone from someday wanting to kiss her, when the time was right, to being able to hold her and kiss her anytime he wanted. But, other than that small tidbit, she was still his favorite forever girl. His heart warmed.

"So, speaking of sleeping arrangements. I planned on doing whatever you thought would be best. We can get completely separate rooms, one room with two beds, or just one bed. It's your decision, but either way I don't want anything going too far tonight. Your birthday is so close, then after that we can start talking about the next steps." Zach knew she was disappointed, so he reached over and lifted her chin so she was looking in his eyes.

"Zoey Belle, the first time I make love to you isn't going to be in a hotel room. It isn't going to be an afterthought or mistake. I'm not going to back down on that. I love you, I've always loved you, I will always love you. But, I'm determined that if we've waited this long, we can wait until you're 100% legal and do it right." He leaned in and kissed her before entwining his fingers with hers. "But that doesn't mean that I'd be against holding you close while we sleep tonight."

"Okay, Zach. I know where you're coming from, and I know you're right. It doesn't diminish how much I want you, how badly I want to feel what it's like to be with you that way, but I'll settle for whatever we can get. Let's get one room, one bed. You can hold me all night long." She leaned into his body and breathed deeply.

"Pretty girl, I'll hold you all night long, and for the rest of our lives. That's a promise."

They arrived at the zoo.

Zoey looked at him confused. "Zach, I think the zoo is only open at night on certain dates. It doesn't look like it's open this evening." She looked like she felt bad for him.

"You're right, the *zoo* isn't open tonight, but the butterfly garden is. And, if the lady I talked to on the phone is right, we should see some butterflies hatching this evening."

"Zach, this is so neat. I've lived close to this exhibit since it opened five years ago, but I've never taken the time to come over to see it. Thank you. You know what a sucker I am for butterflies and flowers." She smiled sweetly at him and kissed him lightly.

They walked the short distance to the entrance. Once Zach had paid their entry fee and the price for both of them to feed the butterflies, they walked into a tropical oasis filled with lush plants and flowers and over 100 species of butterflies.

For the next two hours, Zoey was in heaven. Zach couldn't have cared less for the plants and insects, but watching his girl enjoy the evening was his own little spot in paradise.

"We *have* to come back here sometime. I think the grandmas and moms would enjoy this too. I can't believe there are so many different types of butterflies. I wish I could grow some of these plants, but I am definitely planting a butterfly bush so the backyard will be full of them this summer." Zoey babbled on as she gazed at the beautiful vegetation, and giggled when the light tickle of butterfly wings danced along her skin.

All too soon, the clock struck closing time.

"Come on, pretty girl, we need to let the butterflies get their sleep." He had let her wander the gardens freely, but grasped her hand in his and pulled her close to his side as they walked out the door.

Stopping in the protected area between the inner and outer doors, they let an employee check them over to be sure they weren't carrying any stowaways with them.

"Oops, you've got one trying to make an escape here on your shoulder. If you'll just hold still a moment, I'll get him off and back into his home." The employee made a move to gently remove the butterfly.

The insect fluttered from Zoey's shoulder to her hand.

"Oh, Zach, look how pretty it is. It's the biggest one I've seen. He's gorgeous." The awe in her voice filled the small area.

As if pushed by a whisper of breeze, the butterfly zigged and zagged around Zoey's strawberry-blonde hair before lighting on her nose.

Trying her best to stay still so as not to startle the gentle creature, a breathy giggle escaped her.

Zach's heart filled, his breath caught in his chest. He would keep the image of her giggling with a butterfly on her nose in his heart for the rest of his life. Never once had he doubted the girl standing in front of him was his soulmate, and watching her smile as if the winged insect was the most precious thing in the world cemented her place in his heart and soul.

Once the tagalong had been safely returned to his garden home, they walked out into the evening. Arriving at his truck, Zach quickly gathered her in his arms and pressed her back against the shadowed driver's side away from onlookers. Running a gentle hand across her cheek, he swallowed audibly when her sparkling emerald eyes lifted to meet his own.

"Zach?" She whispered, her chest rising and falling quickly.

"You are the most beautiful, special, amazing woman I've ever known. I don't know how or why watching you in there affected me so strongly, but it did." He stopped speaking and slowly lowered his mouth to hers.

This kiss was different. This kiss was a promise of something more to come, and Zoey felt the heat sear through her body. When she thought her heart would explode, he stumbled backwards breathing heavily.

"Zoey..." With fire in his eyes, he reached for her again, but simply pulled her into his chest. Allowing their breathing to return to normal, they stood in the shadows of the evening.

"We need to go somewhere, anywhere, but not to the hotel just yet. Let's get some supper or dessert at least. I can't be in a hotel with you right now." He adjusted himself as he spoke and his eyes twinkled at his girl's flushed cheeks and swollen lips.

"I think there's nothing I want more than to find a hotel right this moment." She quipped.

"Hey, sassy pants, don't tempt me. There's nothing more I want right now either, but that's not what this weekend is about. We both need to cool down before we climb in bed." He tapped her nose and kissed her gently. "Come on, let's get out of here."

As they drove away, Zoey sighed and watched the butterfly garden fade in the distance.

"Well, tonight was special from the moment we arrived, but that kiss just put the evening into my Top Five best dates ever." She looked at him and smiled.

"Only in the top five? Which dates were better? And since I've not taken you on many dates, you better not tell me about dates with other guys." Zach teased her.

"Well, for now, it fills the number one spot. But we've got a whole weekend ahead of us, so we'll see if it can hold onto its ranking." She teased him back.

"Wow, the pressure is on." He chuckled as he opened her door and slowly let her body slide down his as he huskily whispered, "I look forward to the challenge of filling all of your slots." He threw his head back and laughed at the look on her face.

"Oh my gosh, you just sounded so much like Kendrick!" She laughed and threw her arms around his neck.

Her voice whispered in his ear and the heat instantly returned, "You can fill any and every slot you'd like."

He growled into her mouth as he kissed her.

"Pretty girl, you're making things very hard with your teasing." He let his heat press against her belly.

"Hard is just the way I like it." She tried to say it seriously, but dropping sexual innuendos was so foreign to her she couldn't help but to crack up laughing.

Walking into the little coffee shop, they worked hard to control their laughter.

Had either of them seen the lone figure who watched them from a corner booth, their laughter would have died instantly. His angry heated eyes watched silently. Hatred and lust filled him. He had plans for the girl, and her dickhead boyfriend wasn't in those plans.

If you'd like to read any or all of the books from which I've shared excerpts, please find them on Nook page bit.ly/ADEllisNook

RECIPES

Snickerdoodles (Jay learned how to make these from her grandma)

1 ½ cups sugar

½ cup butter, softened

1 tsp vanilla

2 eggs

2 ¾ cups flour

1 tsp cream of tartar

½ tsp baking soda

½ tsp salt

2 TBSP sugar

2 tsp cinnamon

1) Preheat oven to 400 F

2) Combine 1 ½ cups sugar, butter, vanilla, eggs. Mix well.

3) Stir in flour, cream of tartar, baking soda, salt. Blend well. Shape dough into balls. Combine the 2 TBSP sugar and 2 tsp cinnamon. Roll dough in sugar/cinnamon mixture. Place 2 inches apart on ungreased baking sheet. Bake 8-10 minutes or until set. Immediately remove from cookie sheet to cool.

www.ingramcontent.com/pod-product-compliance
Lightning Source LLC
Chambersburg PA
CBHW051332250626
47155CB00007B/2564